I AM CALLED
RANJIT

Bev Clarke

CREATESPACE

COPYRIGHT 2012

All rights reserved.

No part of this book may be used or reproduced by any means, graphic, electronic or mechanical.

This is a work of fiction. All characters names and incidents are products of the author's imagination and are used fictitiously.

ALSO BY THIS AUTHOR

BORN IN THE BRIAR PATCH

BORN IN THE BRIAR PATCH 2
(BENEATH THE FLOWERING FLAMBOYANTS)

THE SECOND HEARTBEAT

JUST ONE HANDFUL OF SNOW

BLACK PEARLS

THIS IS DEDICATED TO ALL THOSE WHO HELPED TO
MAKE THIS BOOK POSSIBLE

SPECIAL THANKS TO HEATHER FOR HER INPUT.

A GRACIOUS 'THANK YOU' ALSO TO BRUCE WALLACE
FOR HIS INPUT AND FOR PATIENTLY ANSWERING MY
MANY QUESTIONS. ALSO FOR THE BEAUTIFUL COVER
WHICH SCREAMS INDIA.

FOR THEIR UNSWERVING ASSISTANCE, THANKS ALSO TO
WOLFGANG, RANDY AND LORRAINE.

I am called Ranjit

1

"I am called Ranjit," he replied when we asked him his name.

That was the first time we had ever seen him. He was sitting comfortably on a bench not far away from the entrance to our hotel driveway; a filthy street urchin dressed in a T shirt the colour no longer recognisable and a mop of black curls which danced around his shoulders. He was about eight or nine years old and when he stood up, we realised he had only one leg, because he had placed his crutch out of sight behind the back of the bench. He smiled with us showing two rows of perfectly white teeth and we smiled back, but ours were not smiles of encouragement for one had to be on guard against the beggars who were usually a nuisance and were found everywhere in the city. They all wanted a rupee or something unintelligible. To open one's purse could be a suicide mission, because like sniffer dogs they seemed to be able to pick up the scent of that rupee from a mile away would suddenly appear from every corner with outstretched palms. Once they caught sight of it, all hell would break loose. We would immediately be surrounded by people who smelled like sour milk, mildew or had a musty odour, so we would tuck our handbags securely under our arms and make a quick getaway. But this young boy Ranjit seemed different. He didn't beg for anything; all he wanted to do was to talk to us, and realising we had nothing to fear, we allowed him to hobble along beside us, all the while chatting away in limited

English. We asked him if he knew the restaurant which the hotel concierge had recommended and he beckoned us to follow him. We did so, vowing to stay along the well-lit streets in case he was not as innocent as he seemed. He was as polite as he was dirty and we wondered about his discomfort, noticing that the padding of the crutch under his arm had long been worn away, but he seemed to get along without a problem. He accompanied us to the restaurant where we said goodbye thinking that was the last we would see of him.

The restaurant was packed to capacity with well-to-do locals and ex pats who had been relocated to the city to work in some of the profitable Bombay businesses. Among the customers were also other airline crews from all over the world. We recognised them because of the in-flight stories which we could overhear, or rather eaves-dropped on, and sometimes we would break into fits of laughter just at the appropriate moment and they knew we were listening to their conversations, which they seemed to embellish for our benefit.

Contrary to popular western belief, we were allowed to have wine and alcoholic beverages with our dinner. Dishes of hot, rich Indian curries, vindaloos, tandoori chicken, prawns, fish, mutton biryanis, naan and paratha were set down before us. The aromas that trickled past our noses stimulated our appetites and made our mouths water. It was way too much food for our western stomachs, but we were willing to give it a try because everything was not only delicious, but absolutely mouth watering. Finally to wash it all down we chose a mango lassi, Indian beer, or rich Indian tea from Kerala.

With heavy stomachs, we left the restaurant for the slow walk back to the hotel, but we wouldn't be alone for Ranjit was sitting on the pavement with a friend waiting for us to come out. I thought of all that delicious food we had not consumed and I knew they were hungry, so two of us returned to the restaurant and ordered two box dinners. Hopefully they would enjoy it as much as we did.

"Hungry?" I asked them.

They both nodded. Ranjit's friend who didn't seem to have any visible impediment took the boxes and we walked together. On reaching the bench at the end of our hotel driveway, they sat and hungrily consumed the dinners. His friend slapped his full belly and laughed.

"Tomorrow?" asked Ranjit.

He insisted he would wait for us the following evening, but we did not commit ourselves. From that night on, it was always the same procedure. He would walk with us to our restaurant of choice and we would come out with a doggie bag, because we knew he would be waiting to make sure we made it safely back to our hotel, and in addition he would get his dinner. We wanted to do something for him. After all he behaved like our protector, especially when the flower sellers threw jasmine garlands around our necks and then demanded to be paid. What could we do for him? Should we bring him a new crutch? That would be difficult, because for that he needed to be measured, and since none of us was in the medical field, we did not want to make his plight any worse than it already was. Besides we knew he would probably never get the chance to use it, for some bully would take it away and sell it for a handsome price. We decided to bring him clothing due to the fact that he was always so filthy.

Every evening he would surprise us with another English word or sentence and we knew he was doing this so he could communicate with us. But where was he picking up those English words?

That was twenty five years ago.

**

November 2008

We stared out the window as the aircraft banked to the left over the Arabian Sea, and the lights and the beauty that is Bombay by night came into view. The Queen's necklace, so called because of the shimmering lights which hug the curve of the coastline of the Arabian Sea, brought back long forgotten memories. Tonight she looked resplendent. Every jewel sparkled. We were once again close to setting foot in that mysterious land with which we had a love-hate relationship. We loved Bombay for its treasures, its hustle and bustle and most of all, its friendly people; but we hated the poverty, the homelessness, the many beggars, the cripples and the street children, their little bodies horribly distorted just to make a few rupees. The stench, the heat and the odours clinging to our skins and hair, would almost bring us to the point of suffocation.

To me Bombay is like a wart. It doesn't belong on the skin, but seeing and feeling it on a daily basis, it becomes a part of you. I had gotten used to her, just as I had gotten used to the red splotches of spittle on the sidewalks which I tried to avoid. One could always tell the source of those red stains on the street, by the colour of the peoples' teeth, because those who chewed paan, the betel nut and tobacco mixture, all had teeth and gums which were dyed a deep red colour.

However, the hospitality of the people, especially the store owners and shopkeepers is unparalleled, even though sometimes what you are told isn't necessarily the complete truth. Of course whenever one spends money, one expects to be treated with courtesy and politeness and in Bombay, this is not taken for granted. There's always a cool drink or a cup of tea waiting for the potential customer.

**

It seemed like eons since we had first set foot in that land of great fascination. Land of the gods and goddesses! Shiva, Krishna, Vishnu, Lakshmi and Ganesh! It was twenty five years ago to be precise, and tonight as the aircraft door opened and the humidity wrapped itself around us, and the odours assaulted our nostrils, we knew we were once again in that land of mystery.

My friend Billie McPherson and I looked at each other and smiled. The unspoken question lingered on our lips.

'What the hell are we doing back in Bombay?'

Billie could cry at the drop of a hat, but she had an adventurous soul. Go to a theatre comedy together and she will find something to cry about while other patrons are howling with gut-wrenching laughter. When I decided to make the return trip to India, Billie was the first person to flash across my mind. We had previously been based together in Bombay as stewardesses and had invaded the streets of the city on our off days searching for bargains and back then everything in India was a bargain. We do not know if this has changed, but we will soon find out. We loved those shopping expeditions which took us to the Portuguese colonies of Goa and Diu in search of whatever we could find; and if there was something which we discovered in a back alley, regardless of the sanitary conditions, we would jump on it. The city of Cochin which lay to the southwest had been highly recommended because of its antiques and spices, but unfortunately we never did make it there. This time it is high on our list of places to discover in India.

We now live in different parts of Canada, but we still keep in touch and when I am in need of a good laugh, I will always call on Billie.

It is two o'clock in the morning and we are again on the tarmac in Bombay or Mumbai as it is now called, and we wait patiently to disembark the aircraft. A feud has started between the heat and the air conditioning, and vapour pours from the air vents bringing with it the smells of the city; Curry, urine and sweat. It's a fierce battle, but the heat is quickly winning as it creeps into the aircraft through the open doors. We long to escape and once inside the terminal, which hadn't changed much, we marched along like little wooden soldiers behind the procession into passport control and waited in line. The wait was long and I shifted from one leg to the other while my weary body cried out for rest. Finally it was my turn to face the Indian officials, and I handed my passport over to the immigration officer. Our eyes met for a brief moment.

"Madam, it says here you were born in nineteen fifty seven," he said perusing my document. "Are you sure this is your passport?"

"Of course it's my passport," I replied feeling a little flustered.

"You look very young for someone born in nineteen fifty seven," he said with jerking head movements and a smile which was partially hidden behind his handle-bar moustache.

He was obviously displaying a sense of humour which at first I didn't realise. I smiled and thanked him for the compliment. He found the visa in my passport. Bang! Bang! He stamped one of the pages and looking past me, called out to Billie.

"Next please," he said his eyes glued to her blonde locks.

She cheerfully struck up a conversation with him and I heard him ask in halting English and rolling movements of the head, the words I hadn't heard for over twenty five years.

"Is this your first visit to India Madam?"

"Heavens no," she replied. "I spent a year here back in the eighties."

"Welcome back to India and have a pleasant stay Madam," he said handing her back her passport and still devouring her with his eyes.

We moved on to the customs area, where the world now seemed to be moving in slow motion. No one hurried. I had the impression that the hands of the clock were now moving backward. Pencil-thin women with sad eyes, dressed in brightly coloured saris sauntered around in a comatose-like state with brooms and dustpans. Crouching down, they would gather up bits and pieces of rubbish that lay on the floor, occasionally stopping to observe the passengers patiently awaiting their luggage. What could they be thinking? Could it be that they envied those who could travel back and forth and they couldn't? They manoeuvred their little brooms around mountains of clothing and the regurgitated insides of suitcases which were strewn across the floor, while customs officials slowly emptied bags and suitcases, occasionally stopping to chat with each other while the tired and patient passengers waited. Boxes were hammered open and heated exchanges were going on between the officials and some of the Indian passengers who still had the energy and temperament to put up a fight.

The smell of urine hung in the air like a cloud waiting to burst into rain. Caustic, strong and pungent! It was a lengthy wait for our luggage and when it finally arrived along with four or five porters, each one vying to grab them, we politely declined the assistance much to their annoyance. Then with great trepidation, we approached the custom's officer hoping that he wouldn't open our cases, for I pictured my undergarments displayed across the counter much to his delight, and my freshly laundered clothing scattered across the floor, and there was nothing I could do about it.

For the Indian traveller, customs inspection is truly an exercise in patience, for the officers meticulously peer into every crevice and corner of his luggage, stopping occasionally to chat with each other or just stare at the goings on around them. Goods are then either confiscated or heavy duties are imposed. Do these things happen only to those who aren't willing to grease their palms, or is it normal procedure? We didn't know and hoped we wouldn't find out, for our bottle of gin was secretly hidden away between my clothing. We both lifted our bags onto the wooden table and Billie went to work again with her charm. It worked! It was obvious he wanted the world to know he was not a menial worker for the nail on his pinkie finger was very long. I couldn't help but stare at it and let my imagination run wild. I pictured him cleaning his ear or perhaps picking his teeth. He was friendly and after a few questions regarding the contents of our luggage, he waved us through. Thank heavens he didn't risk breaking that nail by opening and digging through our luggage. Off we went, passing through a secondary screening on our way out. This we gathered was just in case he had missed some hidden and forbidden substance, which no doubt would've gained us free board and lodging in one of her Majesty's prisons in the guts of the city. As the sliding glass doors opened, the heat slapped us across our faces, and we were immediately surrounded by beggars, some of them children no more than two or three years old.

"Rupee Madam," they said with outstretched dirty palms.

Luckily there was a driver waiting for us and we set off in a fast trot behind him and slid into a waiting van which would take us to our hotel. We looked around as the driver sped along the highway. Nothing much had changed. As a matter of fact, something had changed, for there appeared to be more homeless people making the sidewalks their home. We pointed out buildings and structures which we remembered. They all looked old and dilapidated in the dark of night. Perhaps in the daylight hours they wouldn't have such a ram shackled look. The familiar black and yellow taxis hovered at intersections waiting to grab a fare from that last straggler heading home from a club or a restaurant, and apparently there seemed to be many stragglers, because the fleet was out in full force.

We knew we were close to our destination when the lights of Nariman Point came into view and our driver swung into the hotel. We were once again on familiar territory. Two handsome doormen dressed in white livery opened the doors simultaneously and welcomed us to the hotel. Standing in line at the reception desk, I again marvelled at the beauty of the younger Indian men and women. The women I considered to be the most beautiful I had ever seen; skins as smooth as satin and long flowing black hair accompanied by their easy smiles. How did they allow themselves to get so out of shape once they reached a certain age? Their svelte bodies having lost all elasticity, would be replaced by bulging midriffs jutting out between the tops and bottoms of their saris, and heavy arms not caused by the amount of gold which covered the wrists to the elbows and jingled with the slightest movement, but by lack of exercise, for most of these women could afford household help for every little chore.

Although we were tired, excitement took over and the

adrenaline flowed through our veins. We decided to relive a little of our past. Billie suggested sitting in the hotel restaurant across from the entrance, and do what we done so many years before; drink Indian beer until the sun crept up from its hiding place. The restaurant was crowded, no doubt with airline crew members enjoying themselves much the same as we had done back then. We ordered some snacks and two bottles of beer, and watched as the glycerine magically trickled down the middle of the potent beverage. It was like Déjà vu! We laughed and talked until the first rays of the sun magically appeared over the Arabian Sea and then we knew it was time to go to bed, and to wake up later to face the cruel, unmerciful midday heat of the city.

My longing is great. I want to see her again. She is now called Mumbai, but to me she would always be the city of Bombay. I also hope I get the chance to see Ranjit again. He was a young boy back then, living on the sidewalks, barely existing and incapacitated by the harsh realities of life in a tumultuous city.

**

I got out of bed and pulled the curtains aside. It was just after twelve and I looked down at the throngs of people and the goings-on on Marine Drive. Saris of all colours billowed like hot air balloons in the wind. Saffron, crimson, red, gold and blue! It was a beautiful sight. Office workers were having their lunch by the shore and the vendors pushing their carts loaded with nuts, fruit, coconut water, coconut jelly, ice cream and samosas were calling out to their would-be clients. A crow in a nearby Gulhomar tree, spotting a tasty morsel, quickly flew down to the pavement. Instinctively it looked left and then right, then stepped gingerly into the middle of the street avoiding the heavy traffic and triumphantly flew away with its prize.

"Aren't you tired?" asked Billie opening her eyes and staring at me. "I can't believe I let you talk me into this."

"You know you love Bombay," I said. "You were elated when I asked you to join me."

"At the time it seemed like a good idea, but now that I'm here, all I can think of are the beggars and the heat. How do you know that Ranjit is still around? This is a life of hardship for the poor in Bombay and having only one leg certainly doesn't help. Why after so many years have you decided to look for him anyway?" she asked for the very first time.

"That's what age does to you. Sometimes I think I would've been a better person if I had channelled my energy in a different direction."

"Mother Theresa," she said laughing out loud.

"I've got an idea. Why don't we go out during the cooler morning hours and reacquaint ourselves with the city, then in the afternoon we can each do whatever we like. A bit of shopping in the morning and some sightseeing in the afternoon! Maybe I can try to find Ranjit during the morning hours when it is a bit cooler."

"Have you forgotten? They sleep most of the day and come out only in the early evening. I would like to lie out by the pool. You know how much I love those rays," she said with a smile.

"He can't be sleeping during the day. He's probably about thirty five years old. They wouldn't keep him in the orphanage at that age. And you should take it easy in that Indian sun," I told her.

"After all, this is not the sun in Canada, this is unmerciful Bombay heat."

"Gotta watch out for those rays," she said laughing again.

"How time has flown by," I said staring again at the goings-on below.

Day one in Bombay and it was just past midday, and still we hadn't decided what we would do or where we would go. I threw a handful of sweets and a bottle of water into my purse because I had made it a point never to eat from the many stalls which lined the sidewalks. We decided it would be better to have lunch in the hotel before we set out. We returned to the same restaurant where we had dined earlier and were quickly seated by a very beautiful, young Indian waitress. A quick meal and thirty minutes later we were on our way to the best shopping there is in the world on Colaba Causeway. That's where we had done most of our shopping back then. It was either there or on Fifth Avenue, so named because one could find anything and everything and the quality was good eighty per cent of the time. Obviously it was not as good as the renowned Fifth Avenue, but it was pretty close. With the meter still running, our taxi driver pulled to the curb and bought a packet of paan from a roadside stall, which he immediately stuck in the corner of his cheek and then drove away. We smiled as we noticed the bulge in his face, but our happiness was short lived, when from the bottom of his digestive tract, he expelled the loudest belch we had ever heard. Billy and I looked at each other, as he merged into the midday traffic, totally oblivious to the fact that we found his lack of manners offensive.

"Could've been something worse," Billie said fanning the air around her face.

As the taxi manoeuvred through the streets, we noticed the progress that had been made. Many more high-rise buildings dotted the landscape, but what struck us most of all, were the wall to wall people on the sidewalks. It was heavily populated twenty five years ago, but nothing compared with what we were now observing. Every lamp post carried a poster with the face of a gorgeous Bollywood starlet, and they were indeed gorgeous. Beggars seemed to have multiplied tenfold and rushed to the car windows whenever we approached a traffic light. The heat made it impossible to keep the windows closed, so we would quickly roll them up whenever we approached a red light. Sometimes a shout from the taxi driver made them retreat, perhaps those new to the game, but most of the time, they simply ignored him and pressed their mutilated faces and hands against the windows.

The Jacaranda trees, in their last flowering stage, threw a blanket of purple onto the streets and along the sidewalks. This beauty lasted only for a short time, because it all turned to muck when trod upon by the thousands of feet which criss-crossed the city. Happily, the flamboyant trees with their red flame like flowers, now replaced the spent jacaranda blooms. It is ironic that in a city ravaged by poverty and disease, so much natural beauty abounds. After losing our way a few times in search of Fifth Avenue, the taxi driver finally understood where we wanted to go. We knew we were close to our beloved shopping area when we saw the drink factory at the top of the street, but as we drew near, to our surprise we realised that our shopping area was no more. In its place stood an imposing high rise apartment building, adorned with beautiful gardens and an attending doorman to keep the unwanted out and there were many of those with outstretched palms, waiting for the well-to-do resident to emerge from one of the condominiums. Perhaps a Bollywood actor or actress or a computer genius relocated from Bangalore. The place where we once haggled for goods was only a memory.

"It's called progress," said Billie looking back at the tower as the taxi turned the next corner with the driver tapping gently on his meter. "How many of those people are probably now unemployed or begging on the streets?"

"Such a shame," I replied. "That was a nice shady spot under that big, beautiful Banyan tree."

"Well it ain't there no more," she said laughing.

"Stop please," I suddenly shouted to the driver.

He stepped on the brakes and turned around to face me. Billie was also staring at me, and I was looking out the window at the man with black and white curls bouncing around his head. He had only one leg.

"Stop when you get closer to that man," I said to him.

"That man madam?" asked the somewhat surprised driver, for the man with the salt and pepper hair and the limp was a horrible mess.

"Ask him if his name is Ranjit," I said.

He stared at me through the rear view mirror and then slowly drove alongside the man. They exchanged a few words and the man came closer and peered into the taxi. His front teeth were missing and his weathered face told us all about his life; one of hardship and need.

"Is his name Ranjit?" I asked anxiously.

"No madam."

"Are you sure?" I asked staring at the driver who was my only means of communication with the man.

"Very sure madam."

"Alright then," I said ushering him on.

The driver kept staring at us through the rear view mirror. Two lunatics! Strange persons these tourists! He drove past Crawford market and onto Colaba Causeway, where we decided to get out. He said he would wait for us but we declined the offer.

"Madam, you looking for Ranjit?" he asked.

"Yes," I replied quickly closing the door.

"If you want, I take you where you can find him," he said moving his head from side to side.

"Thank you. I will think about it," I replied.

"Madam, I park very close to your hotel. I am called Jalal. Ask for me. I take you to find Ranjit. No problem at all Madam."

"Thank you," I muttered.

As if he had just been the recipient of a mouthful of sour milk, displeasure slowly crept across his face, and in a farewell gesture, he hawked and spat a red glob onto the street. Then he slowly drove away, eyeing us all the while through the side mirror of the vehicle.

"I hope you're not thinking of going anywhere with him," said Billie.

"Of course not! I find him rather uncouth. Besides there are probably one thousand men right here in this city named Ranjit.

"We've still got to be careful," said Billie staring into a show window.

At every corner there was someone trying to sell us something or beggars telling us how hungry they were. We would take refuge inside a store when we saw them approaching because we knew they wouldn't dare follow us. However when we left the store, they would be waiting for us around the next corner. We had just left a leather store when we heard raised voices. Yes, amid the din of Mumbai, one could still hear raised voices. A shop owner, a seller of costume jewellery was shouting and pushing a little girl away from his door. A little beggar! She was persistent, and he lost his temper and slapped her across the face. The blood rushed to my face and I could somehow feel the sharp sting of his fingers. Without a moment's hesitation, I rushed over and looked at her little cheek. The imprint of his short stubby fingers lay etched across her jaw line. The child did not whimper.

"She's just a child," I shouted. "How could you treat her this way?"

The shop owner glared at me not knowing what to say, and the little waif, realising that someone was now defending her, let out a blood-curdling scream. Only when I opened my purse and gave her some sweets along with my bottle of water, did she stop wailing. She stared at me, removed the paper from one of the sweets and stuck it in her mouth. All eyes were on the child, but no-one came to her assistance.

"Shame on you," shouted Billie at the store owner. "Why don't you pick on someone your size?"

He continued to stare at the stupid tourists and without a word, turned around and disappeared inside the store. Then from nowhere a woman with a baby at her breast and a bindi dot or third eye on her forehead, approached the child and took her hand. It was her mother. She never even glanced at the child's tear-stained face; instead she came to us with an outstretched hand. This was enough to bring our shopping to an abrupt halt.

"I've had enough,' said Billie with tears in her eyes. "Let's get out of here."

We climbed into the nearest taxi thanking the Gods that we had not been born in that part of the world. Did the child understand love and kindness? Did she know when it was the appropriate time to appeal to the Western conscience? We could never understand such cruelty and we pitied the child. Unfortunately in a few years,

I am called Ranjit

she will most likely be in the same position as her mother. Some unscrupulous man will give her five rupees, impregnate her and the vicious cycle will start all over again. Doomed to a life of hardship at the bottom rung of the ladder!

2

The only thing on our minds as we crossed the hotel threshold was a nice long refreshing drink because the heat had left us drained, and that meant a cool beer. The waiter came and we placed our order and satisfied that our thirst had been quenched, we sauntered around the lobby inspecting the shops with their array of beautiful leather goods, ivory figurines, gold and all that the city had to offer. We recalled that there were shops on the fifth floor, and climbed into the elevator to do a little more window shopping. Of course the prices were much higher than those on Colaba Causeway, Crawford Market and Fifth Avenue, but it didn't hurt to look. At each door we were greeted with smiles, enticing us to come in. Then I saw a face which I thought I recognised.

"Lila?" I asked.

"Yes," she said with a questioning look.

"You don't remember me?"

"It's so good to see you again," the petite woman said.

"You're still here," I said hugging her. "Do you remember Billie?"

"Of course I remember Billie. How are you?" she asked turning to Billie.

"Life couldn't be better," replied Billie with her trademark laugh.

"You remembered my name," the petite woman said her voice full of surprise.

"How is the fashion business these days?" asked Billie.

I am called Ranjit

"Business is very good. Not as good as when you were here, but it is good."

"Great stuff," said Billie going through the clothes rack outside the store.

"I forgot your name," Lila whispered to me.

"It's Christine," I said pretending to be annoyed.

"Yes, that's right. How could I have forgotten?" she asked hugging me again. "I saw your friend Sabia last week. She was here with her husband Vijay Mahajan. Come into the store and let's talk. What would you like? Tea? A cold drink?"

"No thank you," I said to the beverage, eager to hear about the friends I had not seen for many years. "Did she really marry Vijay? Where do they live?"

Before she could reply, another store owner stood in the doorway and greeted her. I remembered Lila with black curly hair and smooth dark skin; a very petite young woman whose ready smile had endeared her to us all. The lady who stood before us was still petite, but her hair was now silver with golden highlights. Their conversation over, her friend said goodbye and we were left to carry on before she had interrupted us.

"Where can I find Sabia?" I asked.

"Who is Sabia?" asked Billie.

"Christine's friend from Italy! She's married to Vijay Mahajan," Lila said.

"Oh yes. I remember her," said Billie. "That's the beautiful no-nonsense Italian woman!"

"I've lost contact with them both. I didn't know they had gotten married," I said.

"Yes and they have a son Dean. He's about twenty or twenty one."

"What about you? How is David?" I asked feeling proud that I had remembered about that part of her life.

"David?" she asked with a look of surprise. "He returned to Scotland over fifteen years ago. There is so much to tell. What are you doing later? Why don't we meet for dinner?"

"Good idea," I said.

She gave me a card with a telephone number and wrote the name and address of the restaurant on the backside.

"So what do you think of Bombay now?" she asked handing another card to Billie.

"Whew!" said Billie. "We've been here less than twenty four hours. What a difference!"

"Lots of changes huh," she said with a smile. "We can talk later. Let's meet at seven at the restaurant."

"Good. That will give us some time to rest before we hit the road again," I said.

We said goodbye to her and walked to the elevator. Once inside, we read the card.

Lila Chandra
Chandra Fabrics
Store 14, 5th Floor
Nariman Point, Bombay

"I can't believe she is still there in the same store," Billie said.

"After all those years! I wonder what really happened between her and her Scottish boyfriend. When we left Bombay, they were inseparable."

"Didn't she say he's back in Scotland?"

"What a shame? She's such a lovely person."

"Isn't Vijay that handsome young man who was head over heels in love with you? Yes," she said answering her own question. "He was the same hunk who sat beside you on the flight from London to Bombay?"

"That's him alright."

"Tell me, wasn't Sabia also your friend?"

"Yes. I introduced them to each other. He was becoming too serious and I couldn't entertain the thought of living in this city. They seemed to like each other, just as friends," I said as the thought of their marriage swirled around inside my head.

"Looks as if they did more than like each other," said Billie laughing. "See what you've missed? You could've had a good life here."

"Oh yes I could've! Like I said, back then it was unthinkable and now that I am here, I know that I was right. I just can't get used to the squalor, and most of all, the children on the street bother me too much. I just can't look into their pitiful little faces."

"That's the worst part," Billie replied.

The hotel lobby looked deserted. The guests were probably out shopping, sleeping or relaxing beside the pool.

"I'll get some sleep before we go out on the town," I said.

"And I'll lie in the sun for a couple of hours," Billie replied.

I returned to my room and looked out the window at the crowds on the street, and wondered how they coped with such unbearable heat on a daily basis. I was exhausted and my body cried out for sleep so I willingly submitted my soul and body to the bed which looked absolutely inviting.

**

"I've been invited to dinner," said Billie as she later returned to the room. "I told him we already had an invitation and he asked if he could come along."

"Him?" I asked.

"Yes, he's Australian and he's here on business."

"I hope Lila won't mind," I said feeling a little annoyed at her presumptuousness.

"We're paying for ourselves, aren't we? You'll like him. He's a lot of fun. I spent the whole afternoon laughing."

"And does he have a name?"

"Hugh Baines."

"Is he a Qantas pilot?" I asked since many airline crews called the hotel home.

"No, he's actually here on business."

As we stepped out of the taxi, the smell of jasmine and sandalwood lingered in the air, and the flower sellers were out in full force pressing their garlands on the unsuspecting tourists. With a fast trot, we escaped and entered the restaurant, where we found Lila sitting at a table with a Caucasian gentleman. So engrossed were they in conversation that they didn't see us enter. Finally he looked our way.

"We meet again," the man said on seeing Billie.

"This is my friend Brian. Where did you meet?" Lila asked as the waiter patiently waited while the conversation went on.

"We met by the pool this afternoon," said Billie.

"When I went to meet Hugh, he was by the pool chatting up this lovely lady. Where is he anyway? He said he would meet us here," said Brian.

The waiter shifted from one leg to the other, but there was a smile on his face. I assume a well-looked-after Ranjit would've looked just like the young man at the same age. We ordered our drinks and as the waiter was about to leave, another Caucasian gentleman, Billie's friend, walked in and headed for our table. More introductions were made and we all settled in for an evening of good Indian cuisine. I could tell by their accents that they were both of Australian descent, and also by their constant use of the word 'mate.'

"I understand that this is a reunion," said Hugh.

"It's been such a long time since we've seen each other," I replied.

"So how did you meet Lila?" Brian asked.

"We discovered her store when we were based here. Our home away from home was the same hotel where we are now staying. After we met her, we would often pop into her store because we knew we would always find something fashionable to wear around the city, and when we were thirsty there would be a nice refreshing drink waiting for us."

"So after twenty five years, how do you find Bombay?" he asked nudging Lila.

"Crowded," I said as they all burst out laughing.

"Are you trying to say it wasn't this crowded back then?" Hugh asked.

"It was crowded, but not to the extent it is today," said Billie. "A flea wouldn't find a resting place in this city."

"So what really brings you ladies back to this city?" Brian asked.

"Christine asked me if I wanted to do something adventurous and I said yes, not knowing that Bombay was on her agenda," Billie replied.

"You always loved it," I said teasing her.

"I understand you're also looking for someone," said Hugh.

"Yes. I met a little boy whom I befriended and I am hoping I can find him again."

"What little boy?" asked Lila.

"One of the street children; he was around eight years old."

"That must've been some kind of a connection that after all those years you've come back hoping to find him," said Brian.

"Christine's a very kind person," said Lila. "I remember when she would bring clothing and food for the children on the street."

"But that was over twenty five years ago. Do you think you will still find him?" Brian asked as the waiter brought our dinner to the table.

"I don't know, but at least I can say that I've tried."

"What happens when you do find him?" asked Hugh.

"I hadn't thought about that."

"Well you've still got time, but be careful," he replied.

"Yes, be careful. Bombay isn't what it used to be," said Lila.

3

After an evening of fun and good Indian cuisine, Brian invited us back to his flat. Driving through the belly of the city and then seeing his home, was like walking straight from hell directly into paradise. It was the ex-pat hideout of Malabar Hill. A security doorman was there to see that everything was kept orderly and to greet each resident, preferably by name.

One could easily think one was in a fashionable condominium complex in Toronto or some other western city. There was no carpeting to gather up the odours of the city; instead beautiful mahogany hard wood flooring wormed its way through the modern flat with its floor to ceiling glass windows, and we immediately settled into his plush furniture. He set the bottles on the bar and Lila assisted him with the drinks. It was obvious that their relationship was more than just a passing fancy, but I longed to be alone with her to find out more about Vijay and Sabia, even though I hadn't really thought much about them over the past years. Lila seemed to have all the answers, but I had to wait for the right moment. The conversation circled around me and feeling like a fifth wheel, which I was, I stepped onto the balcony to see the view. I stood there and admired that part of Bombay where the unwelcome were usually forced back to their homes on the sidewalks. Cars flew by ferrying their passengers back and forth and for a city which was one of the noisiest at any time, day or night, this area of Bombay was unusually quiet.

"What are you looking at?" asked Lila creeping up behind me.

"It's beautiful, isn't it?"

"Yes, by night it's a beautiful city."

"Tell me more about Vijay and Sabia," I said quickly.

"Come by the store tomorrow and I will give you his telephone number. Sabia no longer lives in Bombay. She moved to Daman about six years ago."

"There is nothing to do up there."

"She doesn't like it, but her choices are limited. Anyway I think it is slowly growing on her," she said as an afterthought.

"Why on earth would she move behind God's back in the first place? It's nice there, but for a weekend or a holiday during the monsoon season."

"There were many complications. Her son Dean got hooked on drugs and they thought that getting him out of the city would take him away from all the temptations, but he found his way back to Bombay. And I understand that their marriage was finished a long time ago. I don't know why they haven't divorced each other," Lila said. "It's very stressful for him, and his mother makes it even worse. She was making Sabia's life a living hell, so he put distance between them. I'm sorry, I shouldn't be gossiping about your friends."

"I don't consider it gossip. You are just filling me in. Do you see them often?"

"I see quite a bit of Vijay because his business supplies me with the material for my store."

"I had forgotten about that part of his life."

"He is now one of the biggest textile industrialists in India, and a very nice man," she added.

"I know that he is. And where is their son?"

"If we had driven around the city earlier, I'm sure we would've seen him. A very handsome young man with so much promise! It's unbelievable what drugs have done to this city."

"How did he reach that point?" I asked struggling to understand the situation.

"I really shouldn't be saying this, but Sabia was partly to blame. She hung around with the party crowd, leaving her son and husband alone. I know it must be difficult for a western woman to fit into the lifestyle here in Bombay, but that's the decision she made. In addition her mother in law didn't think she was a good mother and told her so."

"What about Vijay's brother?"

"Oh Ravi and his wife Rahela moved back to London. She hated it here."

"But isn't she also Indian?"

"That doesn't matter. Not all Indians love India. If I had the chance, I too would leave this city."

"You never liked it here. What exactly happened to David?"

"He said he would go home and get things straightened out, and then I was supposed to follow. His calls became less and less and then his letters stopped altogether. We spent ten long years together before he returned to Edinburgh."

"Maybe with Brian it will happen," I said hoping she would open up about their relationship.

"Brian is a very nice man, and he loves it here in Bombay. We have been together for the past six years, but I have stopped putting my trust in men."

"Do you think you will marry?"

"He hasn't asked me."

"Yet," I said.

"Who knows?" she said with a giggle.

We could hear the laughter emanating from inside and went in to re-join Billie and the two gentlemen.

"Caught up on all the news?" asked Brian.

"We need a couple years for that," she said pouring a drink and settling in next to him on the couch.

I was amazed at the amount of alcohol which she consumed. Having a bit of wine with dinner was one thing, but when I saw her down one scotch after the other, I could not help but wonder about her. It was unusual to see a Hindu woman drinking alcohol. Yes she was westernised, but she went to toe to with the two men and their consumption. Was it because of the social stigma of being unmarried past the age of twenty five? I did not know her real age but by rough calculations, I estimated her to be around forty years old.

"There's an ex-pat party here on Friday night. Why don't all of you come?" asked Brian.

"That would be wonderful," said Hugh. "However I must call it a night. Tomorrow promises to be another hot and humid day in Mumbai."

"Yes we should be going too," said Billie. "I intend to lie by the pool and just raise my hand to get my drink when the waiter comes around."

We all chuckled at the remark and since we were staying in the same hotel as Hugh, we decided to share the taxi ride.

"Come by and see me tomorrow," said Lila. "I will have the telephone number for you."

"By the way Christine," said Brian, "I have a friend who may be able to help you in your search for the boy. I can take you around to see her on Thursday. It's better that way."

"That's great. I hope Lila won't mind."

"She won't mind. She understands these things, don't you mate?" he asked draping his arm around her shoulders.

He was very kind, but I had no desire to attend an ex-pat party. I remember those parties of years gone by where the foreigners all sat around finding only negative things to say about the host country, forgetting that they had made the decision to move to India. One habit I detested was the way they would always compare their home countries to India. She has her faults, but she also has many wonderful positive influences.

On the way to the hotel, Hugh kept pointing out things which he thought would interest us. I couldn't help but stare at the sidewalks where body after body was stretched out diagonally, and among them the rats were playing and checking for a midnight snack.

"It's amazing that's there's not a lot of rabies and airborne diseases in this city," Billie said.

"It boggles the mind that these people who will probably be running the lunch carriers to the office buildings tomorrow, sleep among the vermin on the streets," Hugh replied.

"We are lucky," I said remembering a friend's bout with a rat on the twenty seventh floor of our hotel twenty five years earlier.

Hugh paid the taxi driver and invited us to the bar for a drink. I declined the offer, knowing full well that it was Billie's company he really wanted. Opening the door slowly, I carefully inspected the room, then rolled a couple of towels and pushed them against the bottom of the door. The mere mention of rats made my hair stand on end.

I awoke on Wednesday morning to the sound of the footsteps moving up and down the hallway. Then there was a knock on the door. The cleaners were there. We had forgotten to put out the 'Do not disturb' sign. They apologised profusely and went on with their duties. I opened the curtains and peered out. Mumbai had been long awake and we had overslept. Billie lay on her back, her mouth wide open.

"It's time for the pool," I shouted.

"What's the time?" she asked in a panic stricken voice.

"It's just after ten."

She jumped up and headed towards the bathroom, her night shirt barely covering her body. While she baked her body to a crisp by the pool, I would visit Lila and catch up on the gossip.

"You must be tired," I said as Lila greeted me.

"It was a long night and I'm not used to it anymore. I've got the telephone numbers for Sabia and Vijay. I put them out so that I wouldn't forget to give them to you. I'm sure they will really be glad to hear from you."

We chatted and drank tea until it was just after one. Then it was time for her lunch and she invited me to go along with her, but I had no desire to infringe on her time, so I decided to take a taxi to explore the city. I put the photo of Ranjit in my purse just in case someone along the way would recognise his face. On the way out, I stopped to talk to the concierge and showed him the photo. He shook his head and said I should ask the doormen. I chose the older man who studied the photo carefully then said he had known the child, but that was a long time ago. My heart almost leaped from body. There was the possibility that I would see Ranjit again.

"I will get you a taxi Madam," he said as we stepped outside.

It felt as if the devil had thrown open the doors to hell and let his fury out. I scrambled into the taxi which was just as hot, while the doorman spoke to the driver in a black turban. Not an uncommon sight in the city. They were probably both from the Punjab region. The doorman raised his hand to the driver and the taxi started to move away.

"Where is he taking me?" I asked.

"He will take you to see the boy Madam," the doorman said with a smile.

"He's no longer a boy. He must be around thirty five by now."

"I understand," he said smiling. "I explained it to him very carefully Madam."

The breeze from the Arabian Sea seemed to soften the harshness of the heat, and I stared at the well-dressed couples joking with each other seemingly unaware of the humidity. The cell-phone users were not all back in Canada. They were out in full force in Bombay. Those who weren't texting were busy conversing as they stepped in and out of the traffic or shunning the beggars on the sidewalk. It was a city brimming with the latest technology. Brian said there was a joke going around that even the beggars were using mobile phones to inform each other of potential clients.

Billboards all over the city advertised the up and coming Bollywood stars and starlets. Beautiful young women clung to their heroes, some in the throes of passion, others with tears running down their cheeks, perhaps over a lost love. It was a billion dollar industry and we learnt that every beautiful woman and every handsome man from all over the Indian subcontinent were pouring into the city, hoping to grab that shining moment in front of the camera and to improve the lives of the family members left behind. Unfortunately many of them returned to the countryside empty handed and disappointed. The competition was just too great.

Just when I started to fully enjoy the breeze, the driver said I should close the window. At the traffic light we were immediately surrounded by street people. Peering through my sunglasses, I must say they were indeed a pitiful lot, and just as the traffic light turned green, the car ahead of us moved away followed by a loud ruckus. One of the beggars lay moaning and groaning in the street while other vehicles careened around him. The driver did not stop.

"What's going on?" I asked.

"He say he was hit by the car ahead of us," my driver said with very little emotion.

"Then why didn't the driver stop?"

"The car did not touch him Madam."

"It didn't?" I asked in disbelief.

"No I see that. He want money. They do that all the time. If you go back now, you see him going to the other cars begging."

"Good Lord!"

"Lots of tricks Madam," he said looking at me in the rear view mirror.

After that, he didn't say too much and the game of lower the window and raise the window continued until we passed through a grove of trees. The refreshing breeze kissed my face and I relaxed for the first time since we set out and began to enjoy the scenery. Such serenity! Then I heard a voice calling out to me. A voice which seemed to come from a distance.

"Is this where I will find Ranjit?" I asked as the car came to a stop.

"Yes, go along the bridge and step into the village below. I will wait for you here."

There was no one on the bridge at that hour of the day and so I followed his instructions and descended into the village. A group of dirty children ran up to me. Instead of asking for rupees, they were asking for dollars.

"I am looking for Ranjit. Do you know where he lives?" I asked.

They stared at me with wide open eyes, not understanding anything I said.

"Dollar," the oldest of them said.

I kept on walking and soon the whole village was behind me. A one-eyed man was in the forefront of the crowd, his one eye seemingly overgrown to compensate for its overuse. The blind, the legless, the armless all wanted something from me. Their wailing noises filled my head and I was unable to think. Alone and petrified, I wondered why I thought I could do this single handedly.

"Does anyone know Ranjit?" I shouted.

Only wailing and unintelligible sounds emanated from their lips! Before me, all I could see was a sea of outstretched palms moving towards me in slow motion. I started to run and they followed. I stumbled. Nothing came from my lips even though I tried to scream. A hand reached out to me and when I looked up, there he was. Just like before, Ranjit appeared from nowhere. He hadn't grown very much, and like an ocean, his black curls cascaded down his back and played like waves around his shoulders. I would've recognised that smile anywhere in this world. He no longer had a limp and didn't walk with a crutch.

"I am very happy to see you Madam," he said

"What happened to your leg?" I asked.

"Madam! Madam!" a voice called out. "We are there Madam."

It was my taxi driver. I opened my eyes and realised that I had fallen asleep and had been dreaming. Ranjit weighed heavily on my mind, and I was disappointed, because the dream had been so vivid. I had seen him but he was still a child. What did it mean? Hadn't he grown into manhood? Did the powers that be take him away before his life grew into one of agony and suffering?

"You alright Madam? Want me to go with you?" the driver asked noticing my anxiety.

"Yes I'm alright and yes, would you go with me?"

He parked the taxi and we walked into the place we thought Ranjit called home. It was horrifying. The stench, the flies and the unsanitary conditions made me feel nauseated. Opaque bubbles of sewage bobbed along the insect-infested gutters attached precariously to bits of floating garbage. How was it possible that human beings could survive under such primitive conditions?

"Not a nice place Madam," the driver said.

"I see that. Would you ask them for Ranjit?" I begged him as the crowds started to appear from the little hovels and gather around us.

I handed him Ranjit's photo, and there was much interaction between them and the hovel dwellers. Some of them pointed in one direction, still others in the opposite direction and in my heart I knew Ranjit was not there, because he too would've joined the throngs. It was futile and we quickly made our way back to the taxi.

"If you want, I can ask around for you Madam," he said.

"If you find him, please tell the doorman at the hotel and I will get the message."

I couldn't dispel the odour from my nostrils and as disappointed as I was, I knew I shouldn't give up. If he were here in the city, I knew I would find him.

My thoughts were interrupted when I noticed a group of young women in beautiful saris standing and chatting in front of a well-kept high rise building. They laughed and teased each other. How different and fulfilling their lives were! An over-loaded hand cart operated by a very thin and gaunt man shoved his load through the traffic, as impatient drivers honked their horns trying to bully him out of the way. The turban he wore was the only protection against the heat and I watched as the sweat poured from his shoulders all the way down his back. His sinewy legs were stronger than they looked, for he manoeuvred the cart with the skill and precision of a racing car driver, but his was a hard life.

Neatly-dressed school children in their uniforms walked in groups laughing and talking, unaware of the hardships life had presented to men like the hand cart operator. A bus full to capacity made a stop and three more people found room and climbed in. The conductor, who was busy on his cell phone, had his arm wrapped tightly around a pole as the bus lurched and zigzagged through the traffic. Fully aware of his precarious situation, he continued his conversation with great ease. It was loud and it was noisy and I was happy when the taxi driver turned into the driveway of my hotel. I knew he had done his best to help me so I gave him a handsome tip for which he seemed grateful. At the same time another taxi drove up and the driver came towards me. It was the same man who had taken us through the city a couple of days earlier.

"Madam I can take you to find the man," he said.

"I have already found him," I replied.

Without another word, he got back into his taxi and drove away. Learning of my disappointment, the doorman said he had thought of another area and would speak to the taxi driver. Another tip was given for which he showed great appreciation.

4

Billie was obviously still sunning by the hotel pool, so I took the opportunity to call Sabia. It took a while before anyone answered the telephone.

"Miss Priddy is resting," said a female voice with an Indian accent.

"It is very important. My name is Christine and I must speak to her immediately."

I could hear her threats as she came to the telephone. Strangely enough, she seemed to have also taken up the Indian way of speaking.

"Hello?" she said with apprehension in her voice.

"Hello Sabia Tosi. This is Christine. Remember me?"

"Christine?" she asked as the wheels in her head started to spin.

"Christine Bonnett," I said.

"Christine Bonnett! My Lord! Christine I am so happy you called. Why didn't you write? Where are you? Are you in India?"

"Which question should I answer first?" I asked laughing.

"We've got to see each other. I've got so much to tell you," she said, the excitement in her voice ringing in my ears.

"I'm in Bombay," I said quickly before she had a chance to say anything else."

"Why didn't you call yesterday? Darling Vijay drove up from Bombay only last night. You could've come up with him."

"Does that mean you will come to Bombay?"

"Yes," she said. "No it is better for you to come here to Daman to get away from the heat."

"I would really like to see you," I said.

"Darling Vijay is not here at the moment, but I know it's not a problem to get you here."

She was rattling away much too quickly, then suddenly said she would take my telephone number and promised to call later that evening or sometime the next day. Vijay had apparently flown to Jaipur and wouldn't be back until the following afternoon. I was surprised by her constant use of the words 'Darling Vijay' since I had heard from Lila that their marriage had been over quite a long time ago.

I hadn't really thought much about Vijay or Sabia for that matter since I had left Bombay. I had gone on with my life and my travels, but tonight I find my thoughts fully focused on Vijay Mahajan. I remember how kind and generous he was and how much fun we had had together. I remember the dinners and our visits to the many clubs in the city. While the rest of my co-workers were boarding buses to go sight-seeing, he would take me to places like Elephanta Island, where he explained all there was to know Shiva. He took me to The Gateway of India, The Kanher Caves, The Hanging Gardens, some of the Hindu Temples, and he explained all about the Dabbawalas, the men who run from homes to office buildings collection and delivering lunches. He showed me The Tower of Silence where the Parsis laid out the bodies of their deceased relatives; The Dhobi Gat, which is the biggest outdoor laundry I had ever seen and most of all I loved Chor Bazaar and Crawford markets, where antiques could be found for a fraction of the price at the high-end shops.

Back then his business was getting off the ground and he was doing well for a self made business man, but the prosperity which he attained, I assume, had only been achieved with great determination and struggles.

When I returned to Bombay after a two week holiday in Cuba, and a two week holiday at home, I called him to say I was back in town.

"Where were you?" he asked. "I really missed you. I called the hotel a couple of times, but they said your name wasn't listed. Can we get together tonight for dinner?"

I accepted the invitation and said I would meet him downstairs. He seemed a little disappointed, and I assumed it was because I said I would meet him in the lobby. I couldn't help but notice how handsome he looked when I went down to meet him. His rich butterscotch complexion contrasted with his white clothing always gave him a dashing appearance, and that night was no exception. He was wearing a white cotton shirt and a pair of black slacks and in spite of our small setback he seemed genuinely pleased to see me. We drove to a very small Indian restaurant at the edge of a forested area with only six tables. The air was heavy with the fragrance of jasmine and sandalwood. We sat across from each other and I couldn't take my eyes away from his face. He seemed like the most handsome man I had ever seen. His sculptured lips looked luscious and inviting and his dimples appeared each time he laughed, which he often did.

"Where were you? Somewhere on a beach?" he asked.

"A girlfriend and I went to Cuba for two weeks. Why do you ask?"

"Because you've got a tan," he said pushing my watch strap

further down my wrist.

I laughed and he reached across the table and held my hand, which was nothing unusual, but that night it caused my heartbeat to accelerate, making me very nervous. I started to laugh.

"What's so funny?" he asked.

"Nothing," I replied, glad that he couldn't hear my heart racing.

"Tell me what's so funny," he said squeezing my fingers.

I was attracted to him. That I knew, but not the way he wanted or expected. However something seemed to have taken over my body that night and I couldn't help myself. I couldn't take my eyes off him. My thoughts began to run wild. We had known each other for almost eight months and there had never been any intimacy between us. Ours had been a fun relationship, but that night something had changed. After a delicious dinner and lots of white wine, we returned to my hotel around midnight.

"May I come up?" he asked.

Instead of the usual, 'it's really late,' or 'I'm really tired,' I was actually inviting him to my room.

"Of course," I heard myself say.

We climbed into the elevator which was full to capacity, with local people and hotel guests. No one spoke. All eyes were focused on the floor indicators and suddenly someone called out to me. Luckily we were getting off on the next floor. It was one of my colleagues whom I didn't know very well, so I didn't introduce him to her. We entered the room and I placed my purse on the bed, turned on the radio and walked over to the window. I was looking down on the throngs of people still out on the street at that hour of the night, when I suddenly felt his arms around me.

"What's so interesting down there?" he asked.

"I like to look at the crowds."

He spun me around and those lips kissed mine. My heart began to race and my knees grew weak. I could smell his cologne, the same cologne which he always wore. For eight months we had remained just good friends; not that he didn't want more, but where would it all lead was the question which was constantly on my mind. I could never live in India, so it just didn't make sense starting a relationship that would end in heartbreak. That night my emotions over ruled my head. I kissed him back. Long and passionate! Just when I thought we would fall into each other's arms, he raised himself on one elbow and smiled at me, dimples and all.

"I guess I should be going," he said.

"Why?" I asked totally confused by his reaction. "Is something wrong?"

"Don't tease me," he replied.

I brought his face down to mine and gave him a big wet kiss.

"Uhhhm!" he moaned as he responded. "I'm surprised that you are so responsive tonight. What made you change your mind?"

"I missed you," I replied.

"Oh Christine, that's so good to hear," he said hugging me tightly.

He stared into my face, smiling, all the while slowly unbuttoning my blouse.

"Why are you allowing me to do this?" he whispered in my ear.

"I don't know. Perhaps too much wine," I said.

"Never! We have had much more wine on several occasions. Many times, and you always said no to me."

"Maybe you paid the waiter to put something in my wine."

"Why didn't I think of that before?" he said laughing.

He was gentle, paying attention to every little detail. His kissing and touching almost drove me to the edge of madness.

"You really wanted me, didn't you?" he whispered when it was all over.

"Yes," I replied, my hands covering my eyes.

"That was beautiful. I really never expected that to ever happen," he said running his fingers gently along my face.

Desire rose within us again and the second time was more earth-shattering than the first, and we fell into each other's arms, totally exhausted! When I awoke the following morning, he was gone. I recalled what had gone on the night before. I had allowed Vijay Mahajan to seduce me. Why? It really didn't matter because he had awakened my body from its dormant state. I turned over in bed and noticed the note he had left on the mirror.

"I loved last night. It was worth waiting for. See you later." Vijay.

I hugged myself and could still smell his lingering cologne on the pillow. I knew that I loved him, but until this moment, I didn't know I had fallen in love with him. His face, I had deeply etched into my memory. I read the note over and over again as I gazed out the window recalling everything that had transpired the previous evening. The phone startled me and I picked it up on the very first ring.

"I couldn't wait until tonight. You don't know what you have done to me Christine. I find it really hard to concentrate today. All that flows through my mind was the wonderful time we had together last night. You will never know how long I waited for something like that to happen."

"I enjoyed it too," I found myself saying.

"What should we do later? Would you like to go out?"

"What about your place?" I asked. "You've never invited me to see your home."

"I can't. I live with my mother."

My God, he is a mother's boy, I thought.

"I'm looking for another flat, so in the meantime I am staying with ....

Damn! Damn! Someone was knocking and interrupting my beautiful thoughts. Had Billie forgotten her keys? No, it was house cleaning. I was actually thinking and dreaming of Vijay Mahajan; a man I had not seen for many, many years. He was now married to my friend Sabia, although Lila had said it was not a good marriage. Just the thought of his being in a bad marriage made me want to see him even more. Would he look the same? Would seeing him cause my blood to boil? What would his reaction be when he sees me? I had disappeared from his life without saying goodbye.

I climbed onto the window ledge and sat down. Looking at the orange in my hand, I thought it better to wash it before I started to peel it. A rule we adhered to during the time we spent in the city. Brush your teeth with mineral water. Keep your mouth closed when under the shower and most of all keep your toothbrushes and creams safely out of sight. As I unscrewed the cover on my bottle of water, my mind started to wander again. I thought of Ranjit! Suppose I did find him! What would I do? Give him a couple rupees? He probably had no address. I couldn't help him from the distant shores of Canada. It was the same question Brian Langley had asked and a question worth considering. I'm sure there was a way I could find to help lighten his load. After all he had not asked to be born into such a life of misery.

The untouched orange still lay on the ledge beside me. Thinking of Vijay Mahajan it seemed, had wiped away my appetite, and so I turned my attention again to the crowds below. The coastline along Nariman Road seemed like a meeting point for the locals, as they would come and go throughout the day. I watched as the vendors walked to the water's edge to do their business and return to their carts or stalls to serve the waiting customers. That was another of my rules. Under no circumstances, would I eat street food for there was no running water or taps in sight.

The hinges on the door creaked and Billie walked in, looking extremely healthy. She looked as though she were painted in gold.

"Where were you?" she asked. "I came back here looking for you but you were gone."

"After I left Lila, I took a taxi ride around the city. I didn't feel like coming back to the room."

"Still looking for Ranjit?" she asked.

"Yes and I thought I had found him," I replied recalling my earlier disappointment.

"What happened?" she asked with wide eyes.

"We went to the area where I thought I would find him, but no one seemed to know him."

"You should be careful. As one friend to another, this isn't the Bombay we left behind many years ago. They have learnt all the tricks of the trade."

"The taxi driver was with me."

"That crooked man?" she shouted.

"No, it was someone the doorman recommended. He actually went into the area with me. Dear Lord! You wouldn't believe how those people live."

"I can very well imagine. Why don't you wait for Brian? He said he would take us both around the city tomorrow. Just be a little patient."

"What's on for this evening?" I asked.

"I haven't any plans. Perhaps Hugh will call later and we can go out together."

"What kind of business is he in anyway?"

"Something to do with technology! Computers or something like that."

"We would've been two rich women if we had played our cards right," I said.

"Who would I have married?" Billie asked laughing.

"Do you remember the wealthy sheik who thought he could buy you? Remember the message you sent him? The answer is yes if there is a house in it for each of my friends and for me, my weight in gold. Little did we know that he was really serious about his purchase."

"Good Lord! That seems like a lifetime ago. Did we or didn't we have a great life?" she asked.

"We certainly did and now at our tender ages, we are alone in this miserable world," I said with a smile.

"I'm not miserable. I am actually enjoying my life," she replied.

"Don't you wish you had gotten married, had a couple children and a rich husband?"

"Hell no," she said as we both burst out laughing.

"I guess we are doing pretty well. How many other people can pack up on the spur of the moment, fly off to India and stay in five star accommodation?"

"Not many I guess."

That evening we ate at the hotel restaurant across from the hotel entrance, and when we returned to the room, there were two messages waiting for us. The first was from Brian Langley who said he would pick us up around nine o'clock the following morning, and the second was from Sabia who said someone would

"Brian, you've brought the ladies with you," she said with the warmest of smiles.

"Yes. This is Christine who is looking for the young boy; I guess he's no longer a boy and this is Billie. They both have spent a bit of time in Bombay, but that was quite a while ago."

"You must have left when I was arriving," she said. "So what do you think of the city now?"

"Not a lot has changed," Billie replied, "especially for the poor."

"Come in," she said. "The children are always happy to see new faces. It seems to make their day. Yes I agree with you, the poor will remain poor until the end of their days, but I am trying to change as much as I can for the children. It may be just a drop in the bucket, but every little bit helps."

"So where are they?" I asked surveying the room.

"Most of them are at school, and those who aren't, are playing in the back garden. Come on I will show you."

When she opened the door and they caught sight of us, a cheer went up like the chant at a baseball game. The children came running to meet us in spite of the fact that the caretaker tried to keep them calm. The smiles on their little faces brought tears to Billie's eyes. I think the assault on the child on Colaba Causeway had come to mind.

"They are such little angels. Just so unfortunate to be born in the wrong place," Janice said with a sigh.

"So how are you able to look after them?" I asked.

"We prey on our friends like Brian here, into giving us a little of their salary. And when one gets to know the wealthy of this city, a little begging never hurts."

"Can you depend on their generosity?" asked Billie.

"So far we have succeeded. The Government gives us a monthly

I am called Ranjit

be at our hotel on Friday afternoon around four thirty, to us to the train station where we would be met by her driv Daman. We returned their calls and got into our beds. Tomo could be a long day.

At nine o'clock the following morning, as promised, Br Langley was standing in the lobby making a call on his cell pho He looked every bit the tourist in his black shorts and a cott shirt. He hurried us into a waiting car which was illegally park and we drove off. At that hour of the morning, the streets were sti jammed with traffic and wall to wall people lined the sidewalk Such madness! Where did they all come from? Where were the going? We were on our way to meet his friend; an Australian lady who had been running an orphanage in Bombay for the last twenty years.

"She was here on holiday and her heart just about broke when she saw the plight of the street children. She had also met and married an Indian gentleman who moved to Australia but it didn't work out. So after her divorce, she sold her home and returned to Bombay to help the children," he replied after my many questions about her.

"Her name is Janice Weatherall. Her family and friends thinl that she is crazy, but she is committed to helping the unfortunate You will like her easy going ways."

After what seemed like hours, the car eventually came to a sto and we stepped out over an open gutter. He rang the bell and lady dressed in a bright red sari came to the gate. Probably fif two to fifty four years old and she wore her blonde hair in a kn at the top of her head. She was about five foot six inches and ha medium build. Her dark eyes sparkled when she saw us.

stipend and because of that, is often our only stumbling block to getting things done. Sometimes I must dance to their music, because I need their help, but more often than not, I never seem to finish the dance. We haven't the money to bribe the officials, so bureaucracy stands in the way, but we must be patient. Our goal must always be in the forefront of our minds. We are here for the children. Brian, tell them what it is like to live in this city."

"You've got it much more difficult than I have, because for such tedious things I usually find someone who knows someone and who is willing to help me."

"He means he bribes them. Let me show you around," she suddenly said.

"We followed her up a rickety staircase and entered the first room. Bunk beds lined the walls and books were placed neatly at the feet of the beds. The walls were painted green and above each bunk, the children had written their names.

Drashti, Alisha, Chamali

Enakshi, Manisha, Lila

Gurpreet, Fida, Esha

And on the wall beside each bunk bed, the list went on and on.

"How many children sleep here?" I asked.

"On this floor there are about twenty and the on the upper floor, there are thirty."

Three bathrooms were on the end of each floor. They were clean but were badly in need of a little sprucing up. Water in the tropics I noticed played havoc with pipe fittings and also with the colour on the walls. At the rear of the ground floor was a dining room. It looked more like a mess hall where the children ate in two shifts. Janice led the way to the kitchen where there were four burners on a big stove, each with a big iron pot on it. Stacks of metal bowls were placed in cupboards without doors over the stove. In a little room off the kitchen, were two washing machines, gifts she said, that were from generous donors. We passed through an open door and were in the open again, where many little dresses were blowing in the wind.

"This is where we dry the clothes," she said.

"But there is only girls' clothing here. Are there no boys?"

"Yes I have two little boys here," she said guiding us to a small room behind the dining room, where there was one bed and above it were the words Gopal and Hasit. At the back of the room, boxes were piled high almost to the ceiling.

"Storage," she said. "There are more girls because the parents consider females children a liability and they are very easily discarded. These are the lucky ones."

"What do you mean by the lucky ones?"

"These girls have been fortunate enough to be brought to the orphanages. The others have perhaps been destroyed at birth or left on the streets to die."

"Dear Lord!" I whispered as I noticed the tears running down Billie's face.

"So tell me about this Ranjit," she suddenly said as if she had been talking too much. "What is his last name?"

"I don't know," I said as it suddenly dawned on me that I didn't know his surname.

I showed her the photograph which I had brought along. She stared at it and then turned away. I noticed that she seemed a little forgetful. Dealing with so many children without much help, seemed to have made her a little absent minded, but her heart was in the right place.

"Give me a moment," she said as she went to the back door and spoke to someone.

"I thought so," she said returning to us.

"Do you know him?" asked Brian.

"Yes, this was our little Ranjit. He wasn't little. He was quite tall when he came to stay here."

My heart missed a thousand beats. We were on the right track and I noticed the tears start to well up in Billie's eyes. Finally there seemed to be a breakthrough.

"So what are you planning to do when you find him?" she asked.

"I was hoping you could help me with that."

"Ranjit must be around thirty five by now," she said pulling a bundle of files with the years written on the outside from inside a drawer. "There is so much work trying to keep this all in order."

"May I help?" I asked.

"You won't know what to look for. It's better if I do it alone. Keeps things the way I want them."

"What was his last name?" I asked.

"Gowdi! Yes Ranjit Gowdi. I missed him when he left because he was quite helpful with the younger children," she said as she continued to search the files.

"Where did he go?"

"They moved him to a Government run orphanage. Sometimes he would come by to say hello but I haven't seen him for at least ten years."

Now I felt like crying. We had come so close and he had slipped through our fingers.

"Let me make a few calls," she finally said. "Maybe I can track him down."

"Thank you," I said. "We'll come back to see you sometime next week. We are driving up to Daman tomorrow and won't be back until Wednesday or Thursday."

It was twelve forty five when we said goodbye. She hugged and kissed Brian and walked us out to the street.

"She's an angel," said Billie. "Imagine giving up a good middle class life to work with the street children in India."

"She has friends in high places, so she will succeed," said Brian.

"Does she now?" asked Billie.

"I should have said, a friend in a high place," he said smiling.

We read between the lines, and no one asked him what he meant.

5

"I've made a reservation for lunch at Breach Candy," said Brian. "Have you been there before?"

"Yes, but that was a long time ago. We were very excited back then at the prospect of lunching at an old colonial club," I said.

"And how did you find it?"

"I really don't remember too much about it, but I do recall it was still festering with what they called old colonial charm."

"Still is," he replied.

Walking into the club, we found it still did reek of colonialism, but the British had long left and were now replaced by affluent Indians. In the good old days, as they say, it was a club which only the British could frequent; however nothing much had changed. The waiters still wore white gloves and white jackets while ceiling fans whirred noisily overhead and the menu still seemed like one from bygone days. In one corner sat an old man, whom we presumed to be British. He wore a white linen suit and his straw hat was perched on the spindle of a chair back. Since there were only a few guests in the club, the waiter conversed with him and reaching over with a white gloved hand, would either fill his water glass or replenish his cup of tea. It was obvious he was in a talkative mood. Our stares compelled our waiter to tell us about him.

"That's Mr. Berkeley. He has lived in India for most of his life."

"Does he live here in Bombay?" Billie asked.

"Oh yes he does. This is his weekly ritual. He comes in every Thursday at twelve thirty and has been doing that for as long as I have been here, and that is about fifteen years. He has ordered the same thing every week; a bowl of Mulligatawny soup, a cup of tea and a glass of water. At Christmastime, he has the same soup and adds plum pudding for dessert. Then he walks to his home taking the route along the shoreline."

Our conversation was interrupted when our waiter was called away, and we watched an Indian family at poolside. Well-to-do we guessed! The children jumped in and out of the water while their doting parents looked on.

"How are you getting to Daman?" Brian suddenly asked as if it was something he had forgotten.

"We are taking the six o'clock train," I replied still staring at the family by the poolside.

"You should get there early because it is very crowded at that hour, added to the fact that it is also Friday afternoon."

"Sabia is sending a driver to get us and he will also show us to our compartment on the train."

The old man with whom the waiter was conversing rose from his seat, put his hat on and with the aid of his cane walked in our direction. He nodded as he reached our table and we did the same. Then he turned to me and smiled.

"You must be from the West Indies. I've lived on and off in Jamaica for three years. That was around the time when we were exporting sugar to the Mother country. Do you like cricket?" he suddenly asked.

"Yes I do," I replied surprised at the question.

We thought it impolite to have him stand and invited him to sit with us and then introduced ourselves.

"Not for too long. Daisy is patiently waiting for me to come home. Maxwell Charles Berkeley the third," he said in a rather pompous tone while extending his hand.

"Is Daisy your wife?" Billie asked.

"Heavens no! She is my cat. My faithful companion," he said with a laugh reminiscent with that of a cigarette smoker.

We noticed his suit was frayed around the cuffs and worn on the elbows, but was perfectly pressed with seams along the arms.

"Yes my dear," he said turning to me again, "I remember the three men who made cricket what it is today. Weekes, Worrell and what's the other chap's name?"

"Walcott."

"You do like cricket!" he exclaimed. "Those boys from the West Indies were the best. They thrashed England in nineteen fifty and I don't think they ever got over it. I was a young chap back then working as a barrister in the West Indies. Ah the West Indies! Such intoxication!"

We were not sure what he meant by the statement. Was he forever in a drunken stupor or did he find the lifestyle in the West Indies intoxicating? And was he happy that the West Indians had thrashed the British? It was difficult to determine what he really meant.

"And where do you call home young lady?" he asked turning to Billie.

"I'm from Canada," she said smiling at him.

"Do I detect a Scottish accent?"

"I guess you do. My parents were from Scotland."

"Unfortunately I have never had the privilege to travel there. I arrived in this country as a boy and except for the three years of travelling and working in Jamaica, I have lived here. And you sir," his focus now on Brian, "do I detect an Australian accent, and have I have seen you in this establishment before?"

"You heard correctly and yes I have been here before."

"Tell me my good man, what is an Australian doing here in India?"

"I live and work here. Is there something we can offer you?" Brian asked as our late lunch arrived.

"Since you ask, gin with quinine would be delightful," he replied.

"Is there anything else you would like?" asked Brian.

"That is most kind of you, but if I have something here, then it would spoil my appetite for my dinner and Momar would be very cross. He has been with me since I was a young lad. Sometimes I think I'm his man servant and not the other way around. Peculiar fellow he is. For the last sixty years he has been laying his mat outside my front door and sleeping there, and when I awake in the morning, he has already finished his ablutions and has started my breakfast."

"Very dependable employee," said Brian.

"Indeed, indeed!" he said taking a sip of his drink.

"Mr Berkeley, you have lived here for a very long time," Brian said to him.

"That I have young man. That I have! Perhaps before you were born."

"So how does the Bombay of today compare with the Bombay of old?"

"Ah Bombay or Mumbai as they call her now," he said with a sigh. "No comparison, no comparison at all! She is now a shell of her former self; she has fallen into disrepair. If you had met her when I first met her, you would have fallen in love with her also. She was beautiful. Today she is inhabited by thugs, drug addicts, rogues, and natives no longer willing to work for an honest shilling. They prefer to beg."

We did not interrupt him, and Brian signalled to the waiter and a second gin and tonic was placed before him.

"Ah Bombay! She takes your breath away. She's a lady riddled with challenges and she will chew you up, spit you out, and the crows waiting in the treetops will devour what's left of your flesh and bones. The rich shun the poor, leaving them condemned to a life of eternal hell here in the gutters and on the pavements of the city. It reminds me so much of the mother country during the Dickens' years, but worse! Much, much worse! But Bombay is still my lady and I will always love her."

"Do you have children Mr. Berkeley?" Billie asked.

"Heavens no! I did not see the necessity of bringing more challenges into this world. I would've been a terrible father. Such a pity so many men call themselves fathers when they should've let it all down the toilet. Pardon my expression," he said glancing at Billie and I.

We laughed and he continued to regale us further with stories of the glory that was Bombay; then suddenly without warning, he was ready to go. We all scrambled to our feet to bid him farewell.

"It was such a pleasure conversing with you; something which is quite rare these days. Thank you very much for your kindness. I have already taken up too much of your time with the ramblings of an old man. I shall stroll along the shoreline on my journey home and enjoy what's left of this city."

"It was a real pleasure," said Brian shaking his hand.

The waiter assisted him and before he descended the steps, he turned and doffed his hat.

"Charming old man," said Billie.

"I think he's a charming, lonely, old man lacking mental stimulation," said Brian. "People like Mr. Berkeley haven't the means to return to England and so they remain here, their memories still stuck in the good old days. Take Lila's father for example, he put convention aside, married Lila's mother and remained in India, and was well loved by the Indian community. Unfortunately he died a couple years ago, but he was the dearest Brit one could ever have met."

"I didn't know her father was British," I said.

"He certainly was. She could move to England if she wanted, but I guess the stories her father told her about the treatment he received at the hands of his countrymen because he married an Indian lady, left a sour taste in her mouth."

"She never told us anything about that part of her life. She's so friendly to everyone. No one would ever suspect that she too is a casualty of the system," Billie said.

"It's like that anywhere where there has been colonisation. There was much suffering involved," I said.

"We are all three from the colonies. What a coincidence!" said Brian.

"It's no wonder Mr. Berkeley is not willing to leave. What would he do in England? Where would he find a man servant in London? I loved it when he said that Momar thinks he is the man servant and not the other way around," I said laughing. "I get the impression he is still living in the past."

"The memories linger," said Billie.

Brian paid the bill and we left Breach Candy and its memories behind.

"I'll get you a taxi because I have a couple errands to run," he said. "And if you happen to see Lila, tell her I'll speak with her later."

"Will we see you before we leave?" I asked.

"I don't think so. Tomorrow will be a busy day for me, but when you return from Daman, we will get together again."

I hugged him and thanked him for his kindness, and so did Billie. He waved to us and was soon out of sight. It was that time of the afternoon when Bombay was at its busiest. The hustle and the bustle made me shiver and like Mr. Berkeley, long for the Bombay I had known so many years ago.

6

We were packed and ready for our trip to Daman, and a call from Hugh Baines sent Billie scrambling for pen and paper. She was about to receive the number from his cellular telephone. We then hurried down to the lobby where we were approached by the driver who was there to collect us. When we arrived at the station, we were happy that he had decided to accompany us to the train. He explained that many of the people who worked in the city always returned home on Friday evenings to be with their families. He skirted us around the crowds and deposited us into our first class compartment. It must have been quite glorious for the imperialists to sit in cabins such as these back then, and be pampered by people whose only entry into the cabin was to serve their colonial masters. Today the glory is gone. Cobwebs dance in the breeze from the ventilators which had probably kept the colonials cool on this northern journey; the upholstered seats have been replaced by plastic and the cucumber sandwiches, scones and clotted cream are now a thing of the past. In their place, the fragrant aroma of samosas and pakoras fill the cabins.

My thoughts drifted to those passengers travelling in less comfortable accommodation. There were no fans to keep them cool and the cabins were no doubt overcrowded with everyone falling over everyone else. Sitting across from us was an Indian lady in a light green sari and next to her, a well dressed Indian gentleman who kept stealing glances at us. He was handsome! His eyes, two big pools of green set in an olive background, made us also steal glances at him. Flecks of grey dotted his temples and I detected the slightest hint of his cologne. It was obvious he was not your everyday Bombayite. What was he thinking about us? A couple of tourists headed into India's interior? We could tell he was summing us up by the furrow which formed on his brow when he looked in our direction. I was happy that we had dressed well for the journey for it would've been embarrassing to sit in front of him and have him scrutinise us in our flimsy cotton outfits which we had bought for only a couple of rupees. I had also pictured the svelte Sabia Tosi-Mahajan, well dressed and waiting to greet us. We couldn't disappoint her. And after all I was the picture of sophistication when I met Vijay and must impress upon him the kindness of the years during the time we hadn't seen each other.

To pass the time, Billie and I kept looking out the window, trying to identify the trees and flowering bushes on the way. Banyan, Laburnum, Peepal, Flamboyants, Pride of India, The African Tulip and the Bottle brush trees! The gist of the game was to see who could first name the tree that appeared outside the window. This seemed to further heighten the curiosity of our travelling passenger, who looked up from his laptop each time we called out a name. He grabbed the opportunity when we couldn't identify a tree to join in.

"They seem to be everywhere, but I have no idea what it is."

"That's a Neem tree," he said. "They are found all over India."

"Do they have any medicinal value?" asked Billie.

"The local people use them for a variety of illnesses. Its leaves are known to control diabetes. It is also used as an organic insecticide when mixed with water, and young people of adolescent age use it when they have pimples. I've also heard it is good for inflammation, a base for cosmetics and toothpaste and also for pain relief."

"Sounds like a wonder drug. Is all that really true?" I asked.

"I've never really tried it, but the possibility exists that it does cure some illnesses. I understand they are using it in cancer treatment, but it's also what you believe."

"That's true," said Billie.

He went back to his laptop, and we continued with our game. However he soon closed it and joined in the fun. There was a very slight trace of an Indian accent. Maybe he wasn't Indian after all. Perhaps he lived in a foreign country. Daylight was slowly drifting away and the trees started to form long shadows. Darkness was soon upon us, so we sat quietly for some minutes.

"Are you here for a bit of rest and relaxation?" he finally asked.

"Yes and no," said Billie. "We are actually going to visit friends in Daman."

We introduced ourselves and learned that he was a journalist and also a budding author, who had left India when he was twenty, lived in California for over fifteen years, but decided to return to India where he would use his knowledge for the betterment of his country and its people.

"Don't you miss California?" I asked.

"Sometimes I do. Life was easier in America."

"So what do you think now that you're back here?" I asked.

"When you weigh the situation in the two countries, they are both basically the same," he said. "In America they speak of equality and fairness, but the poor have no say and the rich, just like those here in India are somewhat vulgar with their wealth."

"So why did you choose to return here?" Billie asked.

"It is my home. I intend to open their eyes with my writings. It is unjustifiable that the rich do not share a little of their wealth with the poor. In America the rich take advantage of the poor, the illegal immigrants and the blacks. Here in India, we are all one nation but the situation is much the same as in the United States. Imagine having a poor uneducated woman working in your home for forty years. She has helped to raise your children, attended you when you were ill and she walks from her home in the slums to be there at seven each morning. Her employer most of the time knows her only by her first name and has no idea where she lives and what her living conditions are."

For the first time the female passenger beside him started to show interest in our conversation although she never did join in.

"This woman has worked like a slave for so many years and yet her situation in life has not improved."

"But why can't the government step in and help to make their lives better?" I asked.

"Have you ever heard of greed and corruption? Just imagine, for forty five rupees I will get one US dollar. That's what many of the people here receive as a daily wage. Think about it! One U.S. dollar! I know for a fact that many of the wealthy here have accounts in America totalling millions of dollars. How do they do it? By stepping on the backs of the poor and down trodden. Some of them treat their help worse than the imperialists did."

The passenger beside him shifted her position. She seemed uneasy and it was obvious that she understood English.

"The system here, I find to be very complicated. You compare it with the United States, but at least the government there tries to improve the lot of the not so fortunate," I said not fully sharing his point of view.

"Excuse me," he said fumbling in his pocket and pulling out his cellular telephone.

He played around with it for a couple minutes, and we knew he was texting. The conversation or rather the communication over, he stuck the phone back into his pocket.

"My wife," he said with a smile.

"Is she here in India?" asked Billie.

"Oh yes, we live in Bombay. I'm making this short journey for a couple of days. I just hate leaving her alone, so we check in with each other every hour or so."

"A gentleman I'm sure," said Billie.

He smiled and continued the conversation where we had left off.

"As you said before, the system seems complicated, but it is not. It is arranged in such a way, that those who are taken advantage of don't know it. If it's not the complicated way, it will be the complex bureaucratic way. Who are those most likely to be affected? The illiterate, the poor, and those who are afraid to speak for fear of retribution! In the United States, who do these people turn to? The religious leaders who prey upon them! Their hard earned money goes to make the preachers wealthy; those men who chastise them from the pulpits every Sunday telling them how to live their lives and encouraging them to give generously in exchange for a smooth pathway to heaven. Give generously and your path to the Promised Land will be an easier road. I have travelled far and wide, have had discussions on religion, and I cannot think of one poor soul who has returned from the beyond to tell how wonderful life is over there."

Billie smiled.

"Did I say something funny?" he asked.

"No," I said nudging her. "But tell me, why does China seem to be doing so much better than India? There are hardly any beggars on the streets and the economy in the big cities is on an upswing."

"Unlike China," he said, "the economic boom has not helped the poor of India. They aren't enough manufacturing jobs and the poor in the countryside have not moved forward. Those who flock to the cities, mostly farmers in search of a better life, end up doing only the menial labour that the city folks don't want to do. In China, there is a building boom and those who manage to reach the big cities can still earn a living to help their relatives back home in the countryside."

Billie kept nodding off.

"I think I'm boring you?" he said.

"No it is quite interesting but I didn't sleep well last night, and in addition we spent the whole day running around the city. So please excuse me if I nod off once in a while," she said laughing.

"My apologies," he said. "It is boring! These are subjects that strangers should never embark upon. We really shouldn't discuss them any further."

"Please go on. I find your ideas most refreshing especially when you speak of the United States. So what do you think of the president elect?" I asked noticing that Billie was again in dream land.

"No, you won't trap me. We are again treading on dangerous territory."

"You don't like him," I said.

"I'm sure he will be a great president, but it won't be easy for him," he replied.

"Why do you say that?"

"His ideas won't sit well with the white establishment. I know that only too well."

"So do you think he will just be a one term president?"

"That is a question I can't answer right now. We must wait and see how things develop. However I wish him well."

"We are almost in Daman. How much longer before you arrive at your destination?" I asked.

"I will be disembarking two stops after you. When I asked you at the beginning of our conversation if you were here on holiday, you said yes and no."

"I'm actually looking for someone," I replied.

A smile crossed his face and his eyes seemed to lessen in intensity.

"A lost love?" he asked smiling broadly.

"Nothing of the sort! Billie and I lived here some twenty five years ago, and I made friends with one of the street children. We left the country at short notice and I never got the chance to say goodbye. I have thought a lot about him over the years and finally decided to see if I could find him again."

The female passenger now looked from face to face as we spoke. She seemed to become more and more interested in our conversation, but still never said a word.

"I find you a very fascinating person," he said staring at me and making me feel rather uncomfortable. "I wish we could have spoken a little more. This story would fit nicely into a project which I am working on. You will be getting off very soon. I hope that someday we could meet again."

"In your journal, would you paint a positive picture of me or would you describe me as an interfering westerner; pushing myself and my beliefs where they are not wanted?"

"Christine," he said, "my picture of you would be most positive. If and when you find your friend, I would like to know about it."

We collected our luggage as the train pulled into the station. He handed us both his calling card with his telephone number and email address and walked us to the exit, where we said goodbye.

There's that very strange thing about India; someone you have never met before, and is searching for you, will walk right up to you and call you by name. They seem to have a sixth sense. We were not the only foreigners disembarking at that station, but our meet and greet walked right up to us. As we approached the exit, I turned around to see Anand Banerjee standing at the window and waving to us, while chatting on his cellular telephone. Perhaps he was telling his wife about the two strange Canadian women and all about our conversations.

7

Our first stop would be the hotel where reservations had been made for us. There we would deposit our luggage and then be taken to the Mahajan home to meet Vijay and Sabia. Riding through the little town, we couldn't help but notice how dark it was.

"No electricity," said the young man who had picked us up, "but soon it will come back. Problem with some wires!"

Before he could continue, the town was again awash with light and at the same time his cell phone rang. We didn't understand anything because he didn't speak in English.

"Miss Priddy," he said. "She wanted to know if I got you from the station."

It took ten minutes before we reached the hotel since the railway station was approximately three miles from the town centre. When I glanced at my watch, I saw that it was after nine and my mind was telling me that it would be the decent thing to do, to see them the following morning, since we had no idea about their sleeping habits. I ran the idea past Billie who spurted her words of wisdom.

"They made the decision. If it was inconvenient, I'm sure they would've told us. Besides it's Friday night and they will probably not go to bed too early. I am looking forward to something nice and refreshing," she said smacking her lips.

A quick stop at the hotel and we were on our way to meet Vijay and Sabia. The mass confusion that was Bombay was not present in this little town. I wondered how Sabia, coming from a city like Rome could fit into this little town with no fanfare. I wasn't aware I was thinking out aloud.

"Money is the cure for everything," said Billie. "You want to go shopping, you need money. You want to go on vacation ....

"You need money," I said laughing.

"I think our friend on the train found you most interesting," Billie suddenly said.

"Of course he did. He liked the fact that I was being kind to one of his countrymen."

"It's more than that," she said. "You should've seen the look in his eyes when you asked him how he intended portraying you in his journal."

"It's all in your mind," I said changing the subject. "Are you going to call Hugh later?"

"I don't think so. We are just friends and I don't want him to think I'm running after him."

"Now that's a situation I think is more than just a passing fancy," I said.

The driver stopped the car and opened the gate; two gates as a matter of fact, revealing a home which looked like the kind of upper middle class home one would find in the suburbs of Toronto. It was a one story home. A woman was standing on the porch. It was Sabia. She had been waiting patiently for us to arrive. In the wash of light she looked like the Sabia of old. But where was Vijay? Why wasn't he there to meet us? She said he would be there. The years had been kind to her. Her arms hung heavily with gold from the wrist to the elbow and long golden earrings dangled from her lobes. We hugged, we laughed and then we cried. Then I heard that voice which I hadn't heard for almost a quarter of a century

**

He was handsome, not quite as handsome as some of the other Indians I had seen on the streets of Bombay, but nevertheless, a very handsome man. There was a feint smell of cologne when he stood up to allow me to take my seat next to the window of the aircraft. He was tall with a medium build and his hair was neatly brushed to the back of his head; and long dark eyelashes adorned his large light-brown dreamy eyes.

My hand luggage safely stowed in the little compartment beside me, I took my seat and immediately opened a magazine. I knew his eyes were on me and he wanted to talk, but I pretended not to notice. I thought he was Indonesian but I was not sure. When the stewardess brought my glass of champagne I accidentally spilled some of it on my skirt. While I was wiping it away, he offered to hold my glass and found the opportune moment to introduce himself. I then learnt he was from India.

"Cheers," he said raising his glass. "Since we are going to be travelling partners for the journey, I should introduce myself. Jay Mahajan," he said stretching his hand towards me.

When he smiled, I noticed he had two beautiful dimples which made him even more handsome.

"Christine Bonnett," I said. "I've never met an Indian with the name Jay."

"It's really Vijay. My friends call me Jay. It's easier," he said with a very slight trace of an English accent.

"Do you live in London Vijay?"

"My home is actually in Bombay but I was in London on business. I am happy to be on my way back home."

"Was it the food?" I asked with a wide smile.

"A sense of humour," he said. "I've actually had quite good food in London. Things are changing for the better in the mother country. I think there are more Bombayites in London than there are in Bombay. So what do you do Christine and what takes you to Bombay?"

"I am an airline stewardess and I'm stationed there for twelve months."

"So Bombay is more or less your home and you fly around Asia from there?" he asked.

"Yes. We fly to Dubai, Singapore and Kuala Lumpur, spend two days in each city and then fly back to Bombay. Then we have three days at leisure to discover India."

"How much have you discovered so far?"

"Not as much as I would like, but there is still a lot of time," I said flipping the pages of the magazine.

"If you would take me up on my offer, I would like nothing better than to show you a bit of my city."

"Thank you. I will keep that in mind."

It was a flight filled with laughter, and I was not surprised that he handed me his calling card when the aircraft arrived at the gate. That was the day Vijay Mahajan entered my life.

When I was in the city, I knew there would never be a boring moment for he kept me busy, much to the envy of some of my colleagues who had met him. There were dinners, day outings, and he showed me the city in its entirety. I loved being with him and I know he felt the same way, but he was becoming much too serious and demanding of my time. That's when I decided to take Sabia Tosi along on a date with him.

**

"Christine!" he said hugging me, "you look wonderful! Did you have a pleasant train ride into Daman?"

"Thank you. We had a really fun ride on the way from Bombay, but somehow I expected it to be longer from the train station into the town."

"You are confusing Diu with Daman," he said. "To Diu it would be a much longer journey, but it's just a short ride to Daman."

"You look great," I said noticing his very trim figure and his skin which was still the colour of butterscotch.

"Thank you and so do you. Please help me," he said turning to Billie.

"It's Billie, Vijay darling," said Sabia.

"You do look different. Yes, I remember you. Billie! You were the sun worshipper," he said laughing and showing those delectable dimples which I had always loved.

"I still am," she said as he shook her hand.

"What's up with your husband Sabia?" Billie asked. "Don't I deserve a kiss too?"

"I'm sorry," he said smiling and kissing her on the cheek.

The young man who had driven us to the home appeared on the veranda and handed us each a cold towel for the hands and face, and after a short conversation with Vijay in their native tongue, he returned inside the home.

"How about dinner?" asked Sabia. "Darling Vijay has made a reservation for us at the Copper Bowl."

"I am hungry. Not only for something to eat but to hear all your news. It has been such a long time," I said looking from one face to the other.

"How many years has it been?" asked Sabia.

"Twenty five," I replied.

"I can't believe it. It seems like just yesterday," said Billie, her eyes devouring everything in sight.

"May I suggest that we head straight to the restaurant? It is getting late," Vijay said.

We walked out to the car and he sat at the wheel. Five minutes later we arrived at the restaurant and it was obvious that he was known there for the only thing left for the Maitre'd to do was to kneel at his feet. It was crowded and we were ushered to a corner table where another waiter stood, napkin neatly folded over the arm. He greeted Vijay with much respect and smiled at us. All eyes turned in our direction and I wondered why. Was it because of the wealthy Mahajan or was it because there were two people at the table who looked completely different from everyone else. We pretended not to notice as the waiter handed us cold scented towels, along with our menus. Vijay shooed the menus away as he spoke quickly to the waiter who didn't write anything down and nodded each time Vijay made a selection. I wondered if he would remember everything that was ordered.

"I have chosen menu items for you which you won't get in Bombay. I hope you don't mind," he finally said.

"Not at all," said Billie. "Are we allowed to drink alcohol here?"

"You may drink whatever you want, as long as you don't carry it over the state line," he said.

"Then I will have a nice cool beer," she said.

"I'll have the same," I said.

The waiter returned with a wine menu and a choice was made. Soon three large bottles of Indian beer, three frosty glasses and a bottle of Australian red wine were brought to the table. The wine was offered to Sabia which she sipped and approved. Then he poured the beer into the frosty glasses.

"Uhhh! That's a good beer," said Billie taking her first sip. "Just what the doctor ordered."

I noticed that Vijay was staring at me and studying my face. Did Sabia notice? I felt great relief when the appetizer platter was set down on the table. A distraction! Some of the food items I recognised and some I did not. Giant prawns, pakoras, pappadums and something called khandvi which Vijay, described as a type of grain mixed with yoghurt to form a paste, baked and then sliced. Delicious!

In spite of the respect the couple showed each other, I noticed the distance between. She called him 'Darling Vijay' and he referred to her as 'Priddy' or nothing at all. Everyone seemed to call her Priddy or Miss Priddy. She told us that when she first arrived in Daman, the household servants couldn't pronounce her name properly and so they started calling her Miss Priddy because they thought she was very beautiful. They had never seen anyone who looked like her with a Sicilian olive complexion, auburn hair and sea green eyes.

She was still pretty. A little older, but behind those beautiful green eyes, lurked a guarded secret. Her beautiful olive glow which I had admired had been replaced by a pasty white colour and her hair was dyed honey blonde. Vijay on the other hand looked almost the same as the first day I had met him, full of humour, a quick smile and still lean. Many Indian men around his age usually sported a paunch or had a haggard look; the only difference I could see were the streaks of grey around his temples. After we had gorged ourselves on the finest the Daman cuisine had to offer, it was time to say goodnight, especially since we were the last patrons in the restaurant. He drove us to our hotel showing us points of interest along the way and promised to collect us the following morning.

Safely tucked away in our hotel room, Billie made a remark about Sabia.

"Does she seem happy to you?"

"I don't know. She presents a secure front but behind it all, she seems troubled. I guess it has something to do with her son."

"What's the matter with him?"

"Didn't I tell you that he is drug addict? Apparently the family was hoping that he would follow in his father's footsteps but he is a drug addict living somewhere in Bombay. A lot of the blame fell on Sabia because she was hanging out with the Bollywood crowd and ex pats and did not devote enough time to him."

"Where did hear all this? You seem very well-informed," said Billie.

"Lila told me all about it that night on Brian Langley's balcony. In addition, her mother in law doesn't like her because Vijay married a foreigner instead of a pure Indian girl that she would have handpicked."

"Well Sabia is still hanging in there, so there must be something that keeps her there."

"It's now a way of life. Imagine having to give it all up after having help at your beck and call. She wouldn't find this in Sicily or Rome for that matter. I could've had it all," I said with a laugh.

"Damned right you could've," said Billie.

The words were scarcely out of her mouth, when I heard the sound which resembled the scraping of a car clutch. Billie had fallen asleep in the middle of our conversation. I hoped that I too could fall asleep amid all the commotion, and just as I was finally drifting off, a lonely cricket started to chirp, it chirped all night until the first light of morning when it crawled back into its home. Finally there was peace but we had to be up in about two hours.

8

The shrill ringing of the telephone woke us both from our slumber. I glanced at my watch. It was eight forty five and I reached over and picked it up. Hugh Baines was on the line and I passed it over to Billie and went to the window. There wasn't much going on down in the streets, so I opened the window to let the cross draft works its way through, before turning on the air conditioning, but closed it just as quickly as I had opened it. We were still in India and it was hot.

Billie was having a private conversation, and even with a closed bathroom door I could still hear her trademark cackle. The coolness of the water running over my body was a soothing sensation and I just stayed there as long as I could and allowed the jets to massage my back and shoulders. Billie was still on the phone when I opened the door but she was speaking with Sabia. Darling Vijay would be there in half an hour to get us.

"What about breakfast?" I asked.

"You can't be hungry after that dinner we had last night," she said staring at me.

"Not hungry, but rather thirsty. I would love a cup of tea or coffee. So what did lover boy want?" I asked.

"He just wanted to know when we would be returning to Bombay."

"How did he find us?"

"Through Sabia I guess."

We were almost ready when we received a call from the reception that Vijay was waiting for us. We hurried into the elevator and when the doors opened onto the hotel lobby, I saw him leaning against a column, his hands in his pockets. Only the grey around his temples told us that he too had crossed over that fifty year bridge. He smiled when he saw us, and my heart fluttered when he looked at me. He was still as handsome as he looked the previous evening.

"Did you sleep well?" he asked.

"I didn't, but Billie did," I said as I started to laugh.

"I certainly slept well," she said.

"And why didn't you?" he asked turning to face me which made me very nervous.

"Someone in my room was snoring and then a pesky cricket joined in."

He looked back at Billie and smiled.

"Well we've got a full day planned for you. Priddy says she just wanted to lie in the sun but I think we should see a bit of Daman. It's quite beautiful. I was born here and although I've moved to Bombay, I still love it. There are lots of childhood memories here."

"So what do you have planned for us?" I asked.

"I've got to leave on Monday morning, so this is really the only opportunity we will have to spend some time together, and from what I can remember, you're like me Christine. Not really a sun person."

When we arrived at the home, there was an elderly woman sitting on the veranda sipping something from a cup, most likely tea. As we walked in, she lifted her head and acknowledged our presence. She was drowning in gold. Her arms, her ears, her fingers!

"Good morning Mother," said Vijay.

She replied in Hindi so we had no idea what she said, but the conversation went on for about fifteen seconds.

"These are our friends. This is Christine," he said opening his arms in my direction.

"Screen?" she asked.

"No Mother. It's Christine."

She tried again but was still unable to pronounce my name. He then introduced Billie and she did much better with her name. He excused himself and went inside the house, leaving us with his mother. What we could see from the veranda was just too much for the senses to absorb all at once ... mahogany furniture, a floor to ceiling tapestry depicting a tiger hunt and a baccarat crystal chandelier which dangled invitingly in the centre of the room. It said, come and see me. See my beauty.

The young man who had fetched us from the train station walked onto the veranda with a tray. There were four cups, a pot and a tray with biscuits, and he proceeded to pour our tea.

"Where you ladies come from?" Vijay's mother asked in broken English.

"Canada," replied Billie

"You from Canada too Screen?" she asked staring at me.

"Yes."

"You married Screen? You have children?"

I said no to both questions and she seemed perplexed by my answers. I felt a little uncomfortable since she was showing way too much interest in me. This soon came to an end when Sabia walked out. She looked stunning. I felt like a poor relative in my cotton blouse and black linen pants. She was beautifully made up, and wore a pair of white silk slacks, a matching blouse, and a beautiful straw hat all topped off by a very large pair of sunglasses. What made me envious was that she hadn't gained an ounce since I had last seen her, but when one lives in the lap of luxury, this is to be expected. Her mother in law glanced at her, not with hatred but with a look which said, 'life for you my dear is wonderful.'

"Darling Vijay is making a phone call. He'll be out in a minute," she said.

Our conversation seemed to flow too quickly for the old woman, and she gazed from face to face, sometimes just staring at Sabia.

"You know my grandson Dean?" the older woman suddenly asked us, changing the topic of our conversation.

The question wiped the smile from Sabia's lips. We said we didn't know him and she asked her daughter in law to bring his photo. She obeyed and returned with the photo of a handsome young man, perhaps in his late teens. She ran her fingers over his face and said something in her native tongue which seemed to make Sabia uncomfortable.

"Good looking boy, my Dean," she said with sadness in her voice.

We knew enough about Dean to know that it was not necessary to ask any questions. His name just seemed to put a damper on the atmosphere. After a couple minutes, the old lady rose taking the photo with her and leaving her cup and saucer behind. She was quite a heavy woman and as she moved, the gold on her body rustled like dried leaves in a storm. Inside the home, she seemed to remember that we were there, and turned around and waved goodbye, this time her jewellery jingling and clanging.

"She seems troubled," said Billie.

"She's a witch," whispered Sabia. "I can't wait for her to return to Bombay. Then I will have my peace again."

"Why is she here?" Billie asked.

"She comes and goes as she pleases. It is her home. When she thinks it's time to torment me, she shows up here."

"And what does Vijay say about it?" I asked.

"He doesn't want to hurt her feelings, so sometimes he gives into her. Here he comes," she said quickly.

"Are we ready to go?" he asked Sabia.

"We were waiting on you," she said nonchalantly.

"I must apologise. There is something I completely forgot about. I tried to get out of it, but I couldn't. My cousin asked me two days ago to play on his cricket team and I promised that I would. Seems someone is ill. It starts at one. I would love to invite all of you, but since you know nothing about cricket and wouldn't be interested, I'll go alone. So here is my plan, we can still do something together now and later I will go off to my game."

"Must you Vijay darling?" Sabia asked.

"I know as much about cricket as you do," I suddenly said.

"And she does!" interjected Billie.

"Would you like to go the game with me?" he asked.

"Let's wait and see what the rest of the day brings," I replied.

We set out to see the sights, but since Billie and I were both hungry, they stopped so we could have something to eat. Breakfast consisted of a rich cup of Chai tea, made with all those wonderful Indian spices like cinnamon, cardamom and ginger. Not only was it tasty, but it was filling.

Although we had been there on two previous occasions, we found Daman to be still an absolutely fascinating little town. The night time hadn't done justice to it. Sandwiched in a coastal enclave on the Arabian Sea, its beaches were some of the most beautiful I had ever seen. After the heat and humidity of Bombay, it felt heavenly to have the cool breeze lick across our faces. Beautiful trees adorned the landscape and I recognised the magnificent Casuarinas which brought back memories from my childhood. I remember my Grandmother calling them the trees that sing to you. It was also a bird watcher's paradise for I saw flocks of parakeets flitting by, followed by egrets, crows, pigeons and bulbuls.

We stood on a jetty and watched the fishermen, setting out to fish and releasing their boats from their anchors. On another beach, we watched as the camel owners paraded their animals up and down the beach awaiting the next prospective customer. We visited the massive fort at a place called Moti Daman; the Gothic churches and then the local market where one could buy leather goods, or bamboo mats or baskets and believe it or not, Indian whiskies.

Next we drove to the centre of town which was lined with restaurants and antique shops which carried many valuable objects, some from the days of the imperialist rule. Victorian jewellery, fine bone china and lots of porcelain figurines, European dolls, silver and vintage clothing all enticing the tourist to enter. It was a shopper's paradise. The people of Daman obviously had no interest in such items or didn't know the value of them and so they sat on shelves and counters gathering dust. I was in my glory and so was Billie. Items which we bought for only a few rupees would be purchased in Canada for hundreds of dollars. I left the shop after spending a hefty sum of two hundred and thirty dollars and Billie two hundred and seventy five and Vijay, well we weren't sure of the amount of his bill, but he also bought two objects. Sabia who had no interest in artefacts was found next door in the sari store. She was busy trying one on when we entered and showed delight in her choice, but her husband said nothing.

"So Darling Vijay, what do you think?" she asked as the

storekeeper fussed over her.

"It's beautiful. Looks nice on you," he said.

Why did I get the impression he was not in the least bit interested in the sari or her for that matter? Words came from his lips to satisfy her. He turned and continued conversing with us, while she paid for the mountains of purchases. It was almost time for the cricket match, and since the sun worshippers wanted to lay by the backyard pool, and the invitation to watch the cricket match was again extended, I happily accepted.

It had been a long time since I had watched the game, but I was happy that I decided to go. He introduced me to his cousin and a few of the team members. For those new to the game, cricket can be a bit of a bore, but I happily cheered as Vijay's team went on to bat, and some of them were indeed good batsmen. He had changed into his white flannels and we sat together and watched the game. Luckily I had borrowed a broad-rimmed hat from Sabia, because there was no cover over the seats, and the few Indian women who were in attendance, all gathered under the shade of the trees chatting and laughing. His friends seemed surprised each time I made a call. LBW, caught behind the wicket, clean-bowled, caught in the gully or run out. I made the calls for six runs and for four runs, and I cheered along with the other team members, when the batsmen ran between the stumps trying to get as many runs as possible. When it was Vijay's turn to bat, he walked onto the field looking ever the part of the great cricketer, but was bowled by the third ball, and that was the end of his batting for the day. Maybe he was nervous because I was watching and his friends teased him mercilessly about his poor performance. Another team member took his place at the wicket, and he too was out of the game in less than five minutes.

"Caught," I shouted.

"You should be cheering for our side, not the other team," he said laughing.

"I'm just calling it as I see it."

"You really understand the game," he said.

"Of course! Don't forget that I come from the West Indies and we always did beat India," I said laughing.

"That's because your bowlers tried to put our best batsmen out of the game by injuring them," he said.

"We both know that was an unfortunate accident," I replied.

We were referring to an incident which had occurred during a test match between the West Indies and India, in India in 1961. The Indian captain was struck on the head by a bouncer from one of the West Indian fast bowlers. It almost cost the Indian captain his life. After that incident, cricketers were forced to wear helmets to shield their heads and the Indian captain never again played in a test match.

There was a short pause in the conversation and I sneaked a glance at him. White flannels, copper skin! He looked like a prince. And wealthy to boot! How could I have let him slip through my fingers? I couldn't think of a single female who would've done something as nonsensical as I had done.

"You knew I was interested in you Christine. Why did you bring Priddy along when we went out, just before you left India?" he suddenly asked.

"I don't know. We all did strange things when we were younger. Age seems to make one wiser," I replied thinking he was reading my mind.

"Are you saying that you regret not having a relationship with me?"

"You are making me feel rather uncomfortable. I introduced you to a wonderful lady whom you married, didn't I?"

"You never did tell me how you and Priddy became friends."

"We almost didn't," I said.

"What do you mean?"

"During my third month in Bombay, I received my new work schedule and found out that Billie and I were not working together. Of course there was the rest of the crew, but Billie was always a lot of fun to be around. It wasn't the same without her. One day, I decided to venture out alone and ended up at my favourite fabric store on Colaba Causeway and waited while this annoying woman sat at the counter, practically harassing the salesman. She was requesting to have something done which the salesman said was virtually impossible, and when someone in India says it is not possible, you know it is really not possible. The more he tried to explain, the more difficult she became."

"That's Priddy," he said smiling.

"After this had gone on for several minutes, I was beginning to lose my patience. Apparently Sabia had been bringing in the latest Italian fashion magazines and having articles made for resale in Sicily and in Rome. This I later found out from her. Anyway the bantering went back and forth until she realized I was listening to the conversation. It all had to do with a special kind of button she wanted to use on a blouse. I remember this beautiful woman with green eyes, olive skin and auburn hair which flowed to her shoulders turning to me and asking my opinion. We finally resolved the question of the buttons and started to talk. We were both staying in the same hotel and she told me she was also a stewardess for an Italian carrier. We left that store on the Colaba Causeway like long lost friends. She was easy to be around and she loved to laugh."

He stared at me, smiled, but said nothing. I felt quite uncomfortable. Was he still showing interest in me after such a long time? Luckily the cricket break came to an end and his team was sent out to field. I sat there alone on the hard wooden bench and watched the rest of the game in the blistering afternoon sun. Soon it was all over, and time to go. The match would resume the following day.

"Did you ever think about me?" he asked as we waited for the traffic light to turn green.

"Of course I thought about you."

"Then why didn't you call me?" he asked tapping his fingers on the steering wheel.

"I don't know."

"You must have had a reason Christine."

"That was such a long time ago, that I really don't remember. Anyway if I had called, it probably would've complicated your life. Have you seen this boy around Bombay?" I asked pulling Ranjit's photo from between the pages of a book I was reading.

"You're changing the subject Christine. However I can't say I have ever seen the child. When was this taken?"

"Back in 1983."

"That means he's a man now between thirty and thirty five. Why are you looking for him?" he asked.

"He was one of the street children I had struck up a friendship with. I liked him."

"And you still remember him after all this time?"

"Yes I do."

"How could you remember a street child and forget all about me?" he asked turning in my direction to hear what my answer would be.

I was having a rather difficult time. I felt as if he were trying to paint me into a corner, even though my heart would flutter if our arms accidentally touched. I cared for him much more than I had imagined, but he was married! Yes, his marriage was a sham but he was not a divorced man. What was I doing to myself?

"He was different," I said. "He never begged for anything. All he ever wanted to do was talk. I think his interest was in learning as much English as he could. Anyway Lila's friend took me to an orphanage where the owner said she knew Ranjit. By the way, that's his name. She said the government removed him from her orphanage and placed him in one of theirs."

"That means that he went back to the streets."

"Most likely," I said. "She was going to get in touch with some government official and get back to me, but she said there's a lot of bureaucracy involved."

"Was it Brian Langley who helped you?"

"Yes. How did you know?"

"I know Lila quite well so obviously I would know Brian. I also know his friend Janice Weatherall who runs the orphanage in Bombay."

"She was very helpful. I hope she finds him."

"And when she does?" he asked, the fourth time I had heard the same question.

"I don't know. Maybe I can help him in some way."

"I'll see what I can do for you," he suddenly said.

"Tell me about Dean."

"Dean! Let's talk about my son another time," he said as if the subject was a sore not only lying on the surface, but festering beneath the skin.

I am called Ranjit

"Sorry if I said something I shouldn't have said."

"I'll tell you what I'll do. When you return to Bombay, have dinner with me and I will tell you everything. How did you find out about him?"

"Your mother showed us his photo and she seemed sad for some unknown reason."

"Like I said, we will talk about Dean when we meet again in Bombay."

9

Back at our hotel, Billie and I were trying to decide what we should wear to dinner the following evening. It was a good idea to dress appropriately, for we had already experienced what it was like to have dinner at someone's home in India and not be properly attired.

"Shouldn't we be taking them something?" Billie asked.

"Damn! I forgot about that. I bought three brooches today and I really hate to give any of them away."

"Well we should think about it. Dinner is less than twenty four hours away and we won't have time to do it tomorrow."

"Must we give something to each of them?" I asked.

"I would take something for the old lady and something for the hosts," said Billie.

"Let's call downstairs and ask. Maybe they can tell us where we can buy a nice box of imported chocolates."

The telephone rang before we had a chance to make the call. It was Brian Langley. He had heard from Janice Weatherall but the news wasn't promising. No one had seen Ranjit for many years. I thanked him and promised we would all get together when we returned to Bombay.

"One more thing Brian, you've lived here for a long time. What would be an appropriate gift to take to an Indian home? We have been invited to dinner tomorrow night at The Mahajans, and we have no idea what we should take. We're concerned because his mother is also there. Should we also take her something?"

"Take Vijay and Sabia a nice box of chocolates; not the Indian stuff, and for his mother perhaps a little token."

"What's a little token? I bought some brooches from an antique store earlier today and I thought of giving her one of them."

"That's a good idea."

"Does Billie have to give her something also?"

"It's up to her. I know his mother is not an easy person, so maybe Billie can get her a nice scarf, but don't break the bank doing it."

"Thanks Brian. How is Hugh?" I asked turning to Billie.

"Hugh's in love."

"It's always nice to be in love," I replied.

"Speaking of love," said Billie after I had hung up the telephone, "how was the cricket game?"

"The game was a lot of fun, but he was asking me a lot of questions."

"What sort of questions?" asked a curious Billie.

"He wanted to know if I had thought about him in all those years, why I never called him; things like that."

"Methinks Vijay is still in love," she said.

"That would be a waste of time. Let's go out and buy what we need."

A mad dash now ensued. We were back on the street where we picked up a box of Godiva chocolates for the hosts and a scarf for Vijay's mother.

Sunday at midday, I accompanied Vijay to the second day of the cricket match, and Billie spent half the day with Sabia. She had seen the home in its entirety and kept telling me about it. My friend Sabia was living in the lap of luxury. I had had no idea that

Vijay was such a wealthy man, and as Billie would always jab, 'see what you've missed?'

When we arrived for dinner that evening, Vijay's mother lay prostrate on a divan with several cushions behind her while Sabia kept an eye on the goings-on in the kitchen. The dining table was laid out it seemed to welcome the Raj to dinner. Baccarat crystal, fine china and sparkling silverware adorned the place settings. A vase filled with red and white roses took centre stage.

"When do we give the gifts?" Billie whispered.

"I'll ask Sabia."

We could distribute the gifts immediately. I handed Bina Mahajan the little box with the porcelain brooch and Billie gave her the neatly wrapped parcel. She opened Billie's gift and smiled.

"Thank you. Nice scarf Bill," she said as she opened the second box. "It's beautiful Screen."

We breathed a collected sigh of relief and then offered our box of Godiva chocolates to the couple who also showed their appreciation, Sabia by kissing us and Vijay by smiling.

"We'll have a great time after tomorrow," Sabia whispered. "She's leaving with Darling Vijay tomorrow morning."

While drinks were being served, two other couples appeared on the veranda. The first couple was quite young, perhaps in the thirties and the other in the early fifties. The older gentleman had a heavy moustache and also a bulging stomach. His wife was petite and quite charming. The younger couple was reserved but smiled a lot.

"Ah Razzia," said Bina Mahajan to the older gentleman. "You are a healthy man. An Indian man must have a belly. You must feed him very well Raisa."

The woman realised that she was being cast into the middle of the fire could only smile sweetly.

"Do you see what I mean?" whispered Sabia in my ear. "I told you she is a witch."

The company laughed uneasily. Whether or not they realised she was taking a jab at her daughter in law, I don't know, but Sabia was stoic and kept a smile on her lips. And Vijay, he just looked at his mother and shook his head. The younger couple seemed to be coming out of their shell and became more talkative.

A woman, the size of a strand of spaghetti, dressed in an orange sari stood at the kitchen door. She would've tripped and fallen over had she come into contact with an ant, so thin was she. She nodded to Sabia. Dinner was about to be served. I was seated next to Billie and for that I was grateful because that way, we could quickly grasp each other's attention. We talked about our lives and I told the invited guests about Ranjit and expressed my desire to see him again.

"But he's a beggar Screen," Bina Mahajan said. "They have their place in this world and we have ours. Some of us are leaders and some followers. God made it that way. We shouldn't disturb the order of things. It's bad enough when races are mixed, but classes are even worse. There will always be trouble when that happens."

I was totally offended by her remarks and so was Sabia. At that point, I should've dropped the subject, but I did recall hearing that very phrase used on a trip to South West Africa. It was like déjà vu. The words made every hair on my body stand on end. I cringed and suddenly realised that all the faces were now looking in my direction. This woman was either heartless or didn't grasp the severity of what she was saying.

"I know that he is a beggar, but isn't a beggar also a human being?" I asked.

I think they all probably expected me to break into a Shakespearean monologue at any minute.

"He was a lovely child, who in spite of his impediment just needed that one small chance. I was raised in a third world country, and understand the hardships that life presents to the poor. Everyone deserves a chance and if I had had the power back then, I would've done something to make his life better. I have thought so much about him over the years, and I thought that if I ever made it back to India, I would try to find him."

"You don't understand Screen. This is India. That is the way things work here," Bina Mahajan retaliated.

"Forgive me for saying this, but don't you think it is time that changes were made here in this country to help the unfortunate?"

"Who would clean our houses? Who would cook our food if that happened?" she went on.

Only the grinding of Billie's shoe on my foot, forced me to bring my conversation to a halt. Mrs. Mahajan continued to spout her ancient ideas, and no one intervened out of respect and because it was obvious that she would never understand, nor try to understand our positions on the subject. Could I have handled the situation with a little more diplomacy? Perhaps! After all I was a guest in her home. After that the conversation moved in different directions, and the subject of Ranjit again reared its ugly head. Some thought it wonderful of me for showing kindness to an unfortunate soul; still no other opinion was quite as harsh as Bina Mahajan's. I pitied Sabia's plight. Had I shown any interest in her son, I too would have shared the same fate as her daughter in law. I think we were all happy when she said goodnight, but not before admonishing me for my western views.

I am called Ranjit

It was late and the other guests left for their homes, and Billie and I for our hotel, not before saying goodbye to Vijay who was leaving early the following morning along with his mother, for the two and a half hour trip back to Mumbai.

"Call me when you get in," he said kissing me on the cheek. "I'm sure Priddy will keep you both busy tomorrow."

**

When I awoke on Monday morning, my mind flashed back to the previous night and to Vijay.

"He and his mother are already on the way back to Bombay," I said glancing at my watch.

"That woman is quite a handful," Billie said with a dirty cackle. "I can understand why Sabia hates her."

"She is much nicer to her than I would be. That woman has respect for no-one."

"I thought World War three would erupt when she said, 'but he's just a beggar Screen.' That's why I kicked you under the table, to prevent it from getting out of hand."

"I think Sabia does the best thing. She just ignores her."

"Why doesn't Vijay say something to her? I guess she's his mother and he doesn't want to offend her."

"But she's very offensive and he is the glue that actually holds everything together. He should do something," I said.

"He has already. He has put distance between the two women, but as you can see the old bat seems to come and go as she pleases. What do you really think of him anyway?"

"I like him. He's still got a wicked sense of humour. We had a great time together at the cricket match."

"You did?" asked Billie.

"I wouldn't have gone the second day if I hadn't enjoyed the first," I replied.

"Sabia thinks he still likes you."

"Of course he likes me. We're friends and have been for a very long time."

"Not that way," said Billie. "She says she knows it by the way he looks at you."

"Well she has nothing to worry about because I am not interested in him. I really like him as a friend and besides he's married to her," I said as the lie fell from my lips.

"Women have a sixth sense Christine or what does Mrs. Mahajan call you? Screen? We have a sixth sense. I'm also sure he's still interested, but can't do anything about it. What do you think?"

"We did spend about eight months together; going out for dinner about twice per week and also sightseeing on a couple of occasions. I know we got royal treatment wherever we went, but I thought that was because he was a man living in a man's world. It was not a committed relationship and then he began making demands on my time, so I introduced him to Sabia."

"Well I don't think he's over you. I think the time together at the cricket match has rekindled the embers and boy, are they burning!" she said laughing.

"What about Sabia?" I asked.

"Between you and me, I don't think there is anything going on between them."

"So what's all this about Darling Vijay?"

"It's a front. My suspicions tell me that there is or was someone else in her life."

"Does he know about it?"

"I don't know."

"Where did you get all this information anyway?"

"I just read between the lines. While you were enjoying your cricket match, we were chatting about life and a couple of little things slipped out. Do you know she returns to Sicily every year for three months?"

"With a mother in law like hers, I would move back to Sicily."

"She will soon be calling, so we'd better get out of bed and get ourselves ready."

**

"Christine, you were not nice to my mother in law last night," Sabia said laughing out loudly. "How I wish I could find a Sicilian to put a contract on her head."

"I wasn't being rude. I was just telling her the truth."

"I loved it when she told you that we all have our place in this world. Now you see what I have to put up with. I think you know how to handle her Screen. I watched Darling Vijay as the two of you went at it. He smiled and then he whispered something in her ear. Ten minutes later she went off to bed."

"Is she always like that?" asked Billie.

"Worse. Thank God she is back in Bombay."

"And by the way," said Billie, "what's this about every Indian man should have a belly?"

"Now you know what I must endure. She's just upset that she couldn't handpick Darling Vijay's wife. Instead he picked me and after twenty three years, she just can't leave it alone."

"How often do you see Dean?" I asked changing the subject.

"I see my son at least once a month. He has taken up with a

bad crowd and I cannot chastise him anymore. I take some responsibility for what has happened to him, but it is not only my fault. He is twenty one years old."

"What about Vijay?"

"What about him?" she asked.

"Does he see him?"

"Of course. In spite of everything, they still have a good relationship. Now the she-devil, that's another story. She speaks badly about me with my son. Anyway she's gone. Why are we spoiling this beautiful day talking about Bina Mahajan?"

I never did have a one to one with Sabia, and now with her mother in law and husband gone, it was like old times again. There were many photos spread across her dressing table. Photos of her and Dean, photos taken with Vijay, Dean alone, Sabia alone and other people whom I did not recognise; probably all family members in Italy. She dragged us into her bedroom and we spent the morning trying on saris and just plain having fun. I noticed that her skin was not as vibrant as it used to be, but I put it all down to aging. When I went to her bathroom, I realised why her skin was so sallow. Spread across the counter, were several brands of skin-lightening creams. How could she do that to herself? At a time when everyone is so conscious of skin diseases and staying out of the sun, my friend is busy bleaching her body. I heard it is a common thing among Indian women, but why would Sabia do something so preposterous? Is she afraid that her skin is considered too dark? I know that wasn't a problem for her husband but I guess she gave into public opinion which judged her by her outward appearance. It did seem like a contradiction, for on one hand, she spent her waking moments lying in the sun, and then she used skin-bleaching creams.

It was a wonderful two days we spent together and soon it was time to go. We would be leaving on the train the following morning at eleven thirty. I felt sad leaving her alone, but she was a survivor and I was convinced she was not at all lonely.

"Christine," she suddenly said turning to me, "what do you think of Vijay?"

"He looks very much the same."

"Are you still in love with him?" she asked.

I felt like a cornered wild animal. I did not claw at her, but I bared my teeth in a smile.

"Why would you think such a thing? I haven't seen or thought about him for a long time."

"And now that you have seen him?" she asked her eyes fastened on me.

"There is nothing between us Sabia."

She seemed relieved and Billie could only look from one face to the next.

The following morning around nine thirty, she called to say that Vijay had forgotten some important papers and a young man would be driving to Bombay to deliver them. We would not be taking the train. She expressed how happy she was to see us again and said we should visit her the next time we came to the city.

And at the appointed time, ten thirty, the Ambassador was there at the hotel. The ride was quite pleasant until we turned onto the highway. I was petrified! Along the route, we saw overturned trucks, their goods spilled on to the street and the drivers standing outside the vehicles arguing with each other. Whose fault was it? The young man was a good driver, and understood the highway, but I screamed each time he overtook another vehicle. He laughed and so did Billie. I didn't want to lose my life on an Indian highway.

After a three ride through hell, we arrived in Bombay. I breathed a sigh of relief. The driver would take us to our hotel and finally deliver the package to Vijay's office. We thanked him, tipped him which we were told not to do, and walked into the lobby which was crowded with lunchtime guests, to pick up our room key.

We were shocked when we reached our room and looked in the mirror. We were both covered with yellow dust, from head to toe. We must have been quite a sight and amusement to the other guests in the lobby. The message light on the telephone was flashing. Maybe it was Vijay I thought, but it was a call for Billie from Hugh Baines inviting us to go out for dinner. I declined the invitation because I had already promised Vijay that I would have dinner with him.

Then I quickly made a call to Sabia to thank her and to let her know that we were safely back in the city.

10

I decided to wear my emerald green dress since I always received compliments when I wore it. It was hip hugging and flared off like a fish tail at the bottom. I waited and waited and still there was no word from Vijay. It was seven pm. and I checked myself once more in the mirror and was pleased with what I saw. Perhaps he had forgotten. I looked out the window at the blackness of the night and the beautiful lights which hugged the shoreline. Billie had already left to meet Hugh and I waited impatiently for the telephone to ring. I imagined Vijay taking me out to dinner and then trying to kiss me. What would I do if he tried? Should I give in or just remind him that he is married man? The thoughts were swirling around in my head when I heard a knock on the door. When I opened it, I came face to face with him. He was wearing a light suit and a white shirt. He must've removed his tie because it wouldn't have been considered proper to turn up for a business meeting not wearing one. He kissed me on the cheek. If he could only hear my heart beat!

"Sorry I'm late. My meeting ran a little longer than I had expected and so I thought I should come straight here and surprise you. You look lovely. Love that colour on you. Where is Billie?" he asked hugging me.

"She has already left to meet her friend."

"I would like to take you to a nice little restaurant, if you don't mind. It's Thai. I'm sure you have had your fill of Indian food."

"As a matter of fact, I would enjoy something different," I said my nerves now fraying around the edges.

"Let's go before it becomes too crowded. I didn't have the chance to make a reservation, but it should be alright," he said with a smile which showed his delectable dimples.

The young and the affluent were on the streets in their expensive cars honking horns and speeding along and just showing off. Still others weaved in and out of the traffic on their motor scooters making the street a very dangerous place to be. We juggled for space beside them and soon were on the outskirts of the city. It was a quaint little restaurant run by a Thai owner, his wife and one Indian helper. We were immediately seated and offered the wine list. He chose a bottle of Australian Shiraz and we chatted and chatted like we had done on that first day when we met. The aroma of lemon grass, garlic, coconut and ginger greeted us as we sat down and our salivary glands longed to taste those delicious morsels that would come from the kitchen. We looked around to see what the other guests were having before we made our choices. Hot and peppery soups, drunken noodles, Pad Thai, Thai curries, and Sticky rice with chicken were some of the tempting items to choose from.

"Did you enjoy your time with Priddy?" he asked while still perusing the menu.

"Yes. It was like old times. We laughed and talked and got dressed up in her saris."

"What do you think of her after not seeing her for such a long time?"

"She is very much the same. Why do you ask?"

"I was just wondering. What about me?"

Our dinner was brought to the table and I waited before replying. It all looked so delectable and appetising.

"You are also very much the same, except that you don't have a healthy Indian belly," I said laughing.

"That's my mother! I think you handled her quite well, so I saw no reason to come to your defence."

"What about Sabia?"

"Priddy's way of handling her is just to ignore her. Luckily they don't see each other very often. My mother as you might have noticed has very strong opinions on everything. I used to challenge her, but now I know it is just a waste of time."

"But some of her remarks were most inappropriate."

"I know. That's why she and Priddy live miles apart. I grew tired of the constant quarrelling and bickering."

"Why didn't you allow Sabia to stay here in Bombay and send your mother to live in Daman?"

"We wanted to get Dean away from the in-crowd, but it didn't work out that way. He found his way back here."

"Does he look like you or Sabia?"

He laughed.

"Did I say something funny?"

"No you didn't. He looks like his mother."

"Will I get to meet him?"

Before he could reply, his cell phone rang.

"What?" he asked looking around nervously. "No I didn't hear anything about it."

He beckoned the waiter and asked for the bill.

"What's wrong?"

"Let's get out of here. The city has been attacked by terrorists."

By this time all the cell phones in the restaurant were ringing.

Everyone knew about it. We left the restaurant and were heading back to the hotel, when he stopped and turned the car around.

"I can't take you back there. The terrorists are targeting places where they are lots of foreigners. That means they could be on their way to your hotel."

"Billie!" I suddenly said.

"Don't panic," he said laying a hand on my shoulder.

He made a call to Lila who had already heard the news. Billie was on her way to Brian's flat with Hugh, and Brian was staying with her.

"You'll have to stay with me. It's not safe out there."

"What would Sabia think?" I asked as my heart almost jumped from my chest.

"She will understand. She must understand," he said gently touching my hand.

"Where are we now?" I asked.

"This is South Bombay. Don't you remember? I've brought you here several times before."

He turned the radio on and the news came in fast and furious. They were close to my hotel but had not yet attacked although they were holding hostages in a nearby building. He brought the car to a stop in front of a beautiful modern building. Perhaps fifteen stories! Then he used his cell phone and opened an outer gate and we drove in, passing three Laburnum trees which were in full bloom. I had no idea such luxury existed in Bombay. Normally one wouldn't see the opulence from the outside, but this was a beautiful complex. He clicked on his telephone, making sure the doors were all closed behind him. We drove into a garage and then walked to the elevator, where he punched in some numbers on a keypad. The elevator opened and we climbed in. When the door opened, it was onto the marble foyer of his home. Two marble columns which looked like a gateway to the Arabian Sea greeted us, and through the glass windows which ran from floor to ceiling I could see the dark body of water which lay at his doorstep. It seemed turbulent like everything else was in the city at that moment. I could see the layout of the living room; the furniture and the paintings which adorned the walls. I stepped out of my shoes and the coolness under my feet made me temporarily forget that we were in a city under siege.

"Great view," I said.

"I just wish there was more time to enjoy it," he replied.

It was a super modern flat where everything was operated by remote control. He pressed a button and slowly the blinds came down making it a very cosy room filled with atmosphere. On a corner table, was the photograph of a young man.

"Sorry but I must close them. Since we are not sure what's going on, we shouldn't expose ourselves to the outside."

He turned on the television set to get the latest news, which came in blow by blow.

"I'm sorry about this," he said with a sigh.

"It isn't your fault. There's nothing you can do but wait."

He excused himself and left the room. I had a closer look at the photo. It was his son Dean. The photo was probably taken when he was about fifteen. He was a very handsome young man with black shoulder length hair. When Vijay returned, he was wearing a jogging outfit, but his mood was no longer jovial like it was at dinner. He seemed to have really become unhinged by the terrorist siege.

"Would you like a drink?" he asked.

I was expecting a glass of champagne or perhaps wine, but

instead a bottle of mineral water appeared on the table.

"Will you join me?" he asked. "I'm going up to the gym. I must burn some of this energy off. There's a television set up there, so we will still be able to see what's going on."

"I have nothing to wear," I replied thinking it the most inappropriate time to be working out. After all, his city was being attacked by terrorists.

"Just a moment," he said returning with a jogging outfit.

"Whose is this?" I asked.

"It belongs to my son Dean."

He showed me the way to the bedroom and I changed.

"Perfect," he said when I returned.

As he had said, we were totally alone in the gym. The beautiful Mumbai skyline stretched as far as the eye could see.

"How long do you think this thing will go on in the city?" I asked.

"I don't know, but you must stay here until it is over," he said as we both tried to run marathons on the treadmills.

No wonder he had remained so lean. It had absolutely nothing to do with anyone's culinary skills. I was drenched in perspiration and when we returned to the flat. He handed me two night shirts and a towel. After we had both showered, we met again in the living room.

The two large paintings which I had noticed on entering the flat, he said they were done by an Indian artist. One could immediately see the likeness since they were positioned facing each other on opposite walls. He told me about the artist and promised to take me to one of his exhibitions when the turmoil was over. I cannot say that I cared for either of them, but I said nothing. I'm sure they were expensive works of art; abstract but a little strangely done with heads of Indian gods and goddesses. A large comfortable couch along with two armchairs barely made a dent in the spacious living area. A circular dining room table and six chairs filled another space.

"Let me show you your bedroom," he said.

It was the same room where I had changed from my dress to the jogging suit. A huge room with a queen-sized bed in the middle and an imposing comfortable chair stood in one corner. On the wall was a television set and a handsome armoire sat below it.

"This is my room," he said opening another door.

A huge king sized bed swallowed up a big part of the room, a small desk with a computer, an armoire with a television set above it filled the space. Then there was the kitchen! It was very modern and up-to-date. There was a big marble island and the latest in stainless steel equipment.

"This is beautiful," I said. "Have you ever used it?"

"About two or three times to make coffee," he said laughing. "But it is there if you would like to move in and use it."

We sat on the couch and this time he brought out a bottle of champagne and two glasses. We stared at the television set and the horror that was taking place in the city. The telephone rang unceasingly. Sabia was on the line. The news had reached Daman and she was worried about us and about her son. He explained that I was staying with him and that Billie was safe. While I focused on the television news, he made several phone calls. He called his mother, his business manager and he tried calling his son. There was no reply from the latter, so he said he would go in search of him. Before leaving, he gave me a cell phone which he called a mobile, and said I shouldn't answer the house phone in case his mother called again, and if he wanted to get in touch with me, he would call me on it.

"You know what she is like," he said. "Do not open the door under any circumstances. I won't be very long."

I wanted to talk to Billie, but remembered I had left Hugh's telephone number back at the hotel, so I sat and watched the drama unfold. The railway station, two top hotels including mine, a hospital, community centre and the port were all occupied by these crazy people. I was worried. Vijay had been gone for more than an hour and I wondered if they, the crazies, might consider buildings like this one. The cell phone rang and I answered. It was Sabia. I told her that Vijay was on the street looking for Dean and she immediately hung up. Then the land line started to ring and I stared at it. I knew I was not allowed to pick it up. Five minutes later, I saw the elevator door open and Vijay entered with a handsome young man with smoky grey eyes, just a tad shorter than he. It was the same face I had seen in the photo in Daman.

"I'm glad you're back," I said. "I was beginning to worry."

"This is my son Dean," he said introducing the young man with shoulder length hair. "That was actually me calling on the land line. I know I told you not to answer it, but I couldn't remember the number of the mobile phone I gave you."

"Sabia called again. Nice to meet you Dean," I said.

"I have already spoken to her," he said getting a drink and handing it to his son. "Excuse me. I must make a few calls."

"You must be really frightened," Dean said to me, rubbing his fingers under his nose.

"Aren't you? Those people are crazy."

"So you know my mom?" he asked still staring at the television set.

"Yes, we met here in Bombay."

"Is that when you both worked as stewardesses?"

"Yes," I said as shots rang out on the set.

"It is really scary," he said, his left leg bobbing up and down.

"It certainly is," I replied. "Are you still in school?"

"I'm actually going to the university," he said very enthusiastically.

"What are you planning as a career?"

"I would like to become a journalist but Dad says I should enter the family business."

He was very articulate, but I noticed that his left leg never stayed still. He had a nervous twitch. Was it because of the drugs? After all he didn't seem shy.

"I met a journalist on the train to Daman, who works for one of the newspapers here in the city. I've got his card and can give it to you. Perhaps he can be of some help to you. His name is Banerjee," I said.

"Anand Banerjee? He's a very well-respected journalist, although Dad doesn't like him."

"What's this about Anand Banerjee?" asked Vijay walking back into the room.

"Dean was telling me that he wanted to be a journalist and I told him about a gentleman I met on the train to Daman."

"You met Anand Banerjee?" asked Vijay with a surprised look.

"Yes. He is very charming. We spoke most of the way to Daman. He said I should get in touch with him if I ever found Ranjit because it would make a great article."

"Who is Ranjit?" Dean asked.

"One of the street children I met here many years ago."

"And why are you looking for him?" he asked looking a bit confused.

"Because I would like to help him," was my reply.

"But he must be an adult now," he replied.

"Around thirty five," I said.

"If I hear anything I will let you know," he said suddenly jumping up. "I'm going to Granny. I know she must be scared with everything that's going on."

"I'll call a taxi," said Vijay. "I don't want you out there on the street tonight. This thing seems very serious, and don't tell your Granny that Christine is staying here."

Under normal conditions, I would've felt insulted, but since I had met and experienced Granny, I understood why he was taking such actions. The bell rang and Vijay checked the monitor and saw that it was the taxi.

The young man hugged and kissed his father.

"It was nice meeting you Christine."

"I'll go down with you," said Vijay.

They both hurried downstairs because it had already taken about forty five minutes since Vijay had called, before the taxi actually arrived. The young man hugged and kissed his father again and they spoke for a few seconds before the taxi drove away.

"I forgot to give him the telephone number," I said.

"What telephone number?" Vijay asked.

"Anand Banerjee's number."

He smiled.

"Just as well," he finally said. "I see he has made quite an impression on you. It was all a show. He means well but he just can't help himself."

"Why do you say that?"

"My son is an addict. He started with marijuana and now he is into cocaine."

"Why don't you send him to a rehab clinic?"

"Don't you think I have already done that? Sometimes he spends only one week and since he is not forced to stay, he checks himself out. He has been in and out of clinics at least four times, but he is my son and I am not ready to give up on him."

"Do you realise that it is just a matter of time before something drastic happens to him?"

"I know, but I must keep on trying. Who do you think he looks like?" he asked.

"More like Sabia than you."

"He is not really my son," he blurted out.

"What do you mean?"

"It's a long story," he said filling the champagne glasses.

"Well with everything that's going on, I seem to have the time. So I am listening."

"When Priddy and I got married, it took a while before she became pregnant, even though we were really trying. No matter how hard we tried, nothing happened. She saw her doctor and everything seemed alright with her, so then I decided to see my doctor. He did all the necessary tests and finally told me that my measurements were not high enough to bear children."

"What measurements?" I asked, surprise showing on my face.

"Not that," he said laughing. "He said my sperm count was much too low to father children. I couldn't believe it was happening to me, so I got a second opinion and it was the same. I could never and would never be a father. Have you any idea what that does to a man's ego?"

"No I don't. I have no children. As a matter of fact, I never wanted any. There was no room in my life for children. But what did Sabia say about your problem?"

"I never told her."

"You never told her you couldn't ever be a father?" I asked in disbelief.

"No I didn't and I was happy that I had kept it to myself because six months after I received that bit of bad news, she called me and said she had some exciting news. I had no idea what she was talking about."

"You are going to be a father," she said to me on the telephone.

"I was happy we were not standing face to face. I would probably have passed out or dropped dead on the spot. I wondered if the two doctors could have made a mistake, and on a trip to London, I made an appointment with a well-known Urologist and the answer was the same as before. The child could not possibly be mine. I never in my wildest dreams suspected that she would be unfaithful to me."

"So after twenty one years, she still doesn't know that you know her secret."

"Neither does Dean. I had nowhere to turn. I couldn't tell my mother because I was ashamed and I knew she would have said, I told you so. I thought about my brother but I couldn't confide in him either. I thought about you and wished at that point I had some way of contacting you. You must understand I had to tell someone I could trust, so I have carried that heavy burden for the last twenty one years. Sometimes I look at Dean and wonder about him and why he has turned out this way. I may not be his biological father, but I love him all the same. He is a lovely child. I wish you could have met him when he was around fourteen years old. A father's pride and joy! I love him and I know that none of this was his fault."

"Thanks for trusting me. It must have been difficult to carry such a heavy burden for so many years. So what is it like between you now? You live here and she lives there."

"Priddy is discreet and for that I am grateful. She has never put me in any other compromising positions, but there is absolutely nothing between us and hasn't been for over twenty years."

The words floated in one ear and out the other. I couldn't believe what he was saying to me.

"I respect Priddy and I care for her, but I know that she was unfaithful to me and I can't ever trust her again. Dean is a nice young man. He just fell into the wrong crowd. My mother must also share the blame. When she continued to make Priddy's life hell, her only escape was with the ex pats living in the city, so I turned a blind eye. I understood what she was going through, but I also expected her to take good care of our son. I can't lay all the blame on her for this mess. I blame myself also. I was too busy making money to look after my wife and son."

"Doesn't she ever ask about your relationship? Why you have no intimacy?"

"I think she has a conscience and knows what she did. It would be stupid of her to start a fight with me, because deep in her heart, she probably thinks I know something," he said sadly. "But please tell me something Christine, why didn't you want me? Why did you leave without saying goodbye? Was it because I am an Indian from this beautiful town called Bombay?" he said in a teasing way, but I knew deep inside he was serious.

"Yes and no."

"What kind of an answer is that?" he asked.

"Our differences would have kept us apart."

"You never even gave our relationship a chance."

"I thought I could never live in this city. Perhaps if we had met elsewhere, perhaps in Canada or some other western country, it would've been an easy decision for me, but knowing the culture of this country, I must admit I couldn't do it to myself. I had heard and read enough about arranged marriages and if I had upset the apple cart, I know my life here wouldn't have been a pleasant one. In addition, when I walk the streets of Bombay, everyone turns to stare at me. Out of admiration? I don't know. I am a different looking woman who doesn't fall into the Indian perception of what is termed 'beautiful.' My skin is not white and I wasn't sure what your motive was. Some people choose to call me exotic, but I say I am different. I sometimes thought it was perhaps just your curiosity."

"What do you mean by my curiosity?"

"Maybe you wanted to find out if the saying was true about exotic looking women."

"Did you really think that about me Christine?"

"Yes I did."

"That was not my motive. I thought you were one of the most interesting women I had ever met, but I realised you had no interest in me when you suddenly brought Priddy into the picture on what was supposed to be a romantic evening. You had allowed me to make love to you just one week before that. Then you left and I never heard anything more from you. I told myself you didn't care for me. Not a phone call or a letter. I tried calling you but the operator said that the number was no longer in service. I got used to Priddy and when I realised you wouldn't be returning, I decided to marry her. She reminded me so much of you. Her spirit was the same and just like you, she didn't stand for nonsense. Tell me something Christine."

"What?"

"Why did you go to Daman? As a matter of fact, why did you

return to India?"

"I told you I wanted to find my little friend. And besides, Sabia invited us to visit her."

"You could've said no. Are you sure it had nothing to do with me?"

"It had absolutely nothing to do with you Vijay. I'm a bit tired."

I could see where the conversation was leading and as tempted as I was, I thought the prudent thing to do would be to go to bed.

"I'll get you some necessities tomorrow," he said handing me a toothbrush and toothpaste. "You can sleep in the other nightshirt."

The story which he had just told me kept spinning around in my head. I realised that in spite of all his wealth, Vijay was not at all a happy man.

11

He was still asleep on the couch when I woke up the following morning and found that the television set was still on. The news was all about the siege. I stood over him and looked at him. He seemed so peaceful. I took a shower and returned to the living room where he still lay exhausted on the couch. The phone was ringing but he didn't hear it.

"Your telephone's ringing," I whispered.

"Good morning," he said looking up at me and holding the receiver to his ear.

Half an hour later, there was someone at the gate. He had ordered breakfast for us the night before. I found out he had also ordered for his mother and Dean, since the police informed the citizens and tourists alike that they should stay off the streets. I put my finger through the slats of the blinds and peeped outside. For the first time since I had been in the city, Bombay was like a ghost town, bare as the dry bones of the desert. Her people it seemed had deserted her out of fear. Where were they? Hidden behind the curtains in their flats and homes and wondering when the madness would end. From the pictures on the television, it seemed that even the beggars had all gone into hiding. Now and then, a brave soul would be seen, because they knew the terrorists had no interest in them. These were mainly the household help who couldn't afford to miss a day's pay or those who catered to the wealthy who couldn't do without them. Vijay's helper, upon his instructions did not show her face in the flat.

"Her biggest job is making up the beds," he said. "I can live without her until this is over."

Bombay lay burning and hostages were taken as the hotels went up in smoke. They had already counted sixty dead. We had just sat down to breakfast when someone rang the door bell. A man arrived carrying a paper bag which he handed to Vijay, who then handed it to me.

"Just a few necessities," he said. "We don't know how long we've got to stay indoors."

Inside I found underwear, deodorant, two sets of cream, toothpaste and a pair of flip flops, too big for me, but it was the thought that counted.

"What size are you?" he asked.

"Indian size? I'm not sure. No one has ever asked me that before. They always just took my measurements."

The man had come equipped. He pulled out his tape and started to take my measurements.

"This really isn't necessary," I said to Vijay.

"You can't wear my nightshirts all the time," he replied.

After the measurements were taken, the man left and we returned to our breakfast, our eyes still fastened to the television set. Things were getting worse; there were more dead bodies and the flames burned brighter.

"You'll get your clothing in a couple hours, and if this is over soon, we can take a break and get out of the city on a day trip."

"You've thought of everything," I said.

"Not really. There's so much more I could do. There's nothing I wouldn't do for you Christine."

The rest of the conversation centred on his relationship with Sabia or lack thereof and what he hoped to do with his business. I listened to him and watched him carefully as he skirted around the issue of his personal life.

"Who is Dean's father?" I asked after we had sat in silence for a few minutes.

"I'm not sure. I don't think he's Indian. Maybe he is Italian. We may never find out," he said.

Once again the door bell rang.

"That could be your clothing," he said.

And it was. A grey haired man arrived with two big bags. He entered the flat and stood in the foyer while I went to the bedroom to try the clothes on. When I returned, their eyes were glued to the television, but they did not speak to each other. The man was still standing in the foyer and Vijay was sitting on the couch.

"I kept three pairs of cotton slacks and four cotton blouses. These I won't keep," I said handing Vijay the bag, who in turn handed it back to the messenger.

I noticed the man's limp when he walked towards the couch. When I turned around and he saw my face, his eyes sparkled and he stared at me. Then a smile crossed his lips. Vijay said something to him in Hindi and he nodded. A bright light suddenly went off in my head.

"I know that face," I whispered.

"What is it they say? All Indians look alike?" he said laughing.

"I'm serious. I know that face. Excuse me," I said calling after the man before he could step into the elevator. He turned around and smiled.

"I'm sorry," I said.

"No problem Madam," he said still smiling.

"I think that was Ranjit."

"You mean your little friend Ranjit? The little street child?"

"Yes, I would know that smile anywhere. Can you get him back here this afternoon?" I asked almost hysterically.

"I can try, but the police are restricting movement on the streets," he said glancing up at me.

"I've got to be sure. Please try. You said you would anything for me."

"How quickly my words are remembered. I'll do it."

I was so happy that I hugged him and kissed him on the cheek. He stared at me but didn't let me go.

"I'm sorry. I didn't mean to do that," I said apologetically.

"You can do it again if you want to," he said, his eyes locking onto mine.

"Aren't you going to call to get him back here?" I asked escaping from his grasp.

It was difficult to get a good night's sleep because the sirens kept blaring throughout the night, and night sky was lit up with the fires which burned all over the city. I got out of bed and gazed out the window. Black plumes of smoke were rising skyward from different areas of the city. Gunfire rang out and return-gunfire could be heard. In the black of night, the trees stood still. Not even a leaf moved. It seemed as if they understood the severity of the situation, and sad that such violence had infiltrated the city. The local residents were numb and biting their nails at the inefficiency of the local police and the security forces. Many lives could have been saved if they had acted more swiftly, but some of them resorted to behaving in a very cowardly fashion.

I went back to bed and when I opened my eyes, the sunlight was filtering through the blinds in my bedroom. I took a shower and went to the living room where Vijay, already up and showered, was sitting on the couch in front of the television set. He hadn't seen me. I was thinking how absolutely divine he looked, when my thoughts were interrupted by the ringing of the door bell.

"Good morning," I said as he made his way to the door.

"Good morning," he said casting me the sweetest of smiles.

The man had returned, bringing with him sleepwear and a morning robe. My heart was pounding. I was going to see Ranjit or the person whom I thought was Ranjit one more time.

"When he comes in, please ask him his name."

"I am called Ranjit Gowdi," the man replied.

"Do you remember me?" I asked him.

"Yes, Madam from hotel," he replied with a smile.

"I knew it. I knew it," I said with excitement ringing in my voice.

"Do you mind if he sits down?" I whispered to Vijay.

And so Ranjit took a seat by the window and gazed around. He seemed rather uncomfortable surrounded by all the wealth. He was probably never asked to sit in any of the homes where he had made deliveries.

"Do you really remember me?" I asked.

In the west his head movements meant no, but in India they meant yes. Vijay kept looking from one face to the other.

"Yes, Madam from hotel by Marine Drive," he said with a smile.

"Why didn't you say something yesterday?"

He glanced at Vijay and then lowered his head. I hurried to my room to get the photo which I had taken so many years ago, and handed it to him.

"Then I was a boy. Now I am a man," he said staring at the photo. "I go back to hotel many times, but you never come back."

"How are you Ranjit?" I asked.

"Life is definitely good. I have very good job and very good boss," he said looking at Vijay who avoided his glance.

He said he had waited by the hotel on several occasions hoping to see me, but I had never returned. I explained that my assignment was over and without notice, I had to leave suddenly. He told me he was married and had a son. I wanted to hug him. I wanted to hug that little dirty street urchin, who was no longer a child. I was happy that he had survived the harshness of the city, and had gotten married and had a son. From the address he gave, Vijay knew he was living in one of the many slums which had sprung up around the city.

"I am very happy to see you. I hope I will see you again before I go home Ranjit."

"Madam not staying at hotel! Hotel is burning," he said. "Very bad people burn Bombay."

I walked with him to the elevator and waited while the elevator doors opened and closed taking away his smile and his wave.

"Will you help him?" I asked Vijay.

"For you Christine, I would do anything. What can I do for your friend?"

"I don't know. I must tell Billie and Jane Weatherall that I found him. I must also tell Brian Langley. He was helping me in the search."

"And now that you've found him?" asked Vijay, a big question mark on his face.

"I'll take him to visit your mother," I said laughing.

He too thought it was funny. I couldn't stop laughing because I imagined Ranjit sitting in one of the chairs in her flat, and Bina Mahajan sterilizing the place after he had left.

He stared at me.

"You are a very good person. I fell in love with you the first day I met you," he said. "I remember how you would ask for the leftovers from our meals at the restaurants to feed the hungry outside. What did you call it?"

"A doggie bag?"

"That's right. A doggie bag! It was a bit embarrassing but your intentions were always good. I just wish things had turned out differently."

"You'll find happiness one day," I said.

"Are you still saying you have no interest in me?"

"No that's not what I'm saying. You are still a married man."

"That can change in the blink of an eye."

"I would never be accepted as your wife. Can you imagine taking me to your mother? I can hear her screaming …. Screen and my son! As if the other one wasn't bad enough, now you bring me an African."

"What my mother and other people think really won't matter. I am the one who matters. Tell me more about you," he said.

"What can I say? You already know everything about me."

"Tell me again. I have forgotten."

"What would you like to know?"

"Anything you want to tell me."

"You already know I was born in England. My mother was British and my father was from the Caribbean. You can see the strength of his genes in me."

He laughed as he ran his fingers gently down my arm.

"I thought you were from one of the French islands. I thought you had the prettiest eyes I had ever seen on a woman with your complexion."

"They call them 'Cat Eyes' in the islands," I said recalling the horror I had experienced as a child in the Caribbean because of my eyes.

"Why cat eyes?"

"Because they are the colour of cats' eyes," I said laughing.

"I knew there was some kind of a mixture in you. I think they call it Creole?"

"Really? And I thought you were Indonesian."

"You never told me that."

"I didn't. We had only just met. Anyway my mother died when I was three years old and my father not knowing what to do with a rambunctious three year old child packed me off to my grandparents in the British Virgin Islands. An island called Virgin Gorda!"

"Were there only virgins on the island?" he asked laughing.

"You're silly," I said.

"I'm just asking. Seems like a strange name for an island. I'm sorry. Please go on."

"I forgot where I was."

"You were saying that your father sent you off to your grandparents."

"Oh yes! At that time we were considered unwanted in the Mother country, and a hard-nosed Brit named Enoch Powell had threatened to send us all back to the West Indies on banana boats. My father probably thought I would get into trouble in a country which did not recognise me as one of its own; at least that was the reason he gave my grandma. She was a dear old lady but was very strict. My father had become absolutely British and the Caribbean no longer appealed to him. Of course he sent money for my education, food and clothing, but that was all."

"You must've been lonely."

"No, my grandpa had taken his place in my life. He used to call me Stinker Sweet."

"Why did he call you that?"

"I was a bit of a tomboy. Because of my English accent, the other children laughed at me and said I spoke funny and therefore the girls didn't want to play with me, so I hung out with the boys and did all the things they did."

"So where does Stinky Sweet come in?"

"Stinker Sweet! By the end of the day, I was really tired from climbing trees and running around with the boys, so I would hop into bed without washing. My grandmother would force me from the bed to have a bath, saying all the while that cleanliness was next to Godliness. Then she would put baby powder all over my body. When I was too tired, I would cover my body with powder and hop into bed without washing. Of course they found out when they realised that the wash basin was as dry as a bone. That's why he called me Stinker Sweet. My grandma would admonish me on a daily basis about playing too long in the sun. 'If you don't stay out of the sun, you will soon look like a tar baby.'"

"That's a funny story," he said recalling similar words his mother used when he would spend the day playing cricket in the sun.

"Today I stay out of the sun, not because I'm afraid it would make my skin darker, but because I know it is unhealthy to spend too much time absorbing the rays. People on the island, especially women, never left the house unless they had the protection of a parasol, never mind they were losing their shoes because they were sticking to the melting asphalt in the street."

"So do you consider Billie stupid for spending so much time lying in the sun?"

"I have spoken to her several times on that subject. She is an adult but I will not judge her."

"We've got more similarities than differences," he said. "Did you ever see your father again?"

"Probably three or four times after he sent me to my grandparents; but they made sure I had a good education. When I was about seventeen, we received the news that he had died and of course we were left on our own. Shortly after that my grandpa passed away. It was now up to my grandmother to take care of me and that she did. It was a struggle, but I finished school with honours, and then went on to Teachers' College where I received a Bachelor of Arts Degree in English Literature. She was so proud of me! At ninety one, she could no longer see very well and lost her desire to live."

He was listening attentively to every word that fell from my lips.

"And what did you do after her death?"

"I wanted to spread my wings. Island life was no longer that attractive. I had gone as far as I could go, and I had no desire to return to England, so I immigrated to Canada where I tried to get into the teaching profession, but that was another struggle. Because I had no Canadian experience and because I was considered different looking, made it quite a challenge, so I gave up any hope of teaching and applied to the country's main carrier to become a stewardess, never believing for one moment that I would be accepted; and the rest is history."

"What happened during those twenty five years when we lost contact with each other?"

"I continued to work and when I had had enough of flying around the world, I found a position on the ground which afforded me the same privileges to go where ever I wanted, and whenever I wanted."

"Tell me about your love life," he said the laughter now gone.

"There's not much to tell. When one is young, one thinks one will remain young forever, so I hung out with my friends and travelled with my friends. I wouldn't have changed a thing. When I decided to take this trip, I asked Billie if she wanted to come with me. Girlfriends are less complicated than boyfriends."

"Do I detect heartbreak?" he asked.

"I wouldn't call it heartbreak."

"Did you ever consider getting in touch with me?"

"To be honest, it never did cross my mind. And if I had thought about it, I wouldn't have called because I would have pictured you with a wife and a few children."

He laughed.

"And now that you know my wife is, shall I say ….. is nonexistent, what do you think?"

"Does she know that we were romantically involved?"

"I never told her."

"Tell me about you," I said steering the conversation away from me.

"You know just about everything. I told you that my brother and I pooled our resources, a bit of money we inherited when our father passed on and opened the company here in Bombay. It was a struggle at the beginning, but we produced more and more quality products and became well-known."

"Was this before or after I met you?"

"As a matter of fact, the company was about five years old when we met. My brother was still in London and was thinking of returning with Rahela, who had just graduated with a degree in Indian Studies."

"Didn't you have a girlfriend when I met you?"

"I would say no. I had friends, but I was so busy building the business that I had no time for a personal life, in spite of the fact that my mother was always trying to push some simple village girl in my direction."

"So what happened when she met Sabia?"

"Is it necessary to ask such a question? She didn't speak to me for almost one year. She didn't attend our wedding, but when Dean came along, she was very excited. This gave her a reason to show up at our flat unannounced, spending two and three days at a time under the pretence of helping out with Dean. She was taking over and Priddy was being pushed more and more into the background. This went on until Dean was around thirteen and I couldn't stand the constant bickering. In addition knowing that I wasn't Dean's father really put a strain on the household. Priddy spent as much time as possible away from the flat, and Dean did whatever he wanted eventually ending up in the situation he's in today. To get him away from bad influences, I sent him and his mother to Daman and I stayed behind. I kept up the façade for much too long. I should have put an end to it from the very beginning."

He paused. There was sorrow, regret and frustration in his voice; a mixture which told me the listener that if he had to do it all over again, there were parts of his life he would change. I decided to change the topic because it seemed too painful rehashing all those bad memories.

"I know you will experience love one day. Life will open its arms and embrace you," I said.

"I keep waiting, but it's not happening for me," he replied.

"I'm sure it will. Just give it time."

"I'm running out of time," he said. "Maybe I should take Mother up on one of her many offers."

My heart sank although I knew those words had come from his mouth and not his heart. I knew he was trying to blackmail me. But suppose he really did start considering Dina Mahajan's offers, what would happen then? I didn't want to think about it.

"You said you are or were a Christian. How did that happen in a predominantly Hindu country?"

"My father! He was impressed by all things British and so he converted to Christianity. My mother decided she wanted no part of it, and so he dragged me along to do his Christianity thing. I was just a little boy and Ravi was just a tiny baby. My father saw only the good of the colonial masters so needless to say he despised Gandhi and his teachings. I'm surprised that he didn't pack us all up and cross the ocean to Great Britain."

"Do you think you could live there?"

"Everything takes getting used to and yes I think if I had to, I could. But you didn't answer my question. Now that you know there is nothing between Sabia and I, do I stand a chance?"

"I really don't know what to say."

"Dear God," I thought. "Billie was right when she said he was still carrying a torch for me. I must call her."

**

"Hello," said a sleepy voice.

"Hello Hugh? This is Christine. May I speak to Billie?"

"Just a moment Christine! How are you coping? Can you believe what's going on? They've all gone stark raving mad. Lucky for us we weren't there when they took over the hotel. Billie's here," he said.

"What's going on over there?" she promptly asked.

"Nothing. What's going on over there?"

"Well I can see and smell smoke; most likely from our hotel. Can't even go outside! As a matter of fact, we can't do anything. I can't believe this is happening."

"Neither can I."

"Anyway I've got some good news. I found Ranjit this morning," I said laughing.

"How did that happen? You didn't go out into the street, did you?"

"No, he came here. He's working as a messenger in Vijay's company."

"What? So you saw him? Did he remember you?"

"He certainly did and when I showed him the photo of himself, he said that he came by the hotel looking for me but I was never there."

Vijay excused himself to take a shower or perhaps to be discreet, since he probably knew that's what women did! They confided in each other.

"He came by yesterday to deliver some clothing for me and I thought his face looked very familiar. When he smiled, I realised it was him, so I asked Vijay to have him come by again. This time he confirmed that he was Ranjit. Married and has a son."

"Well something good has come out of this mess. So what are you going to do now?"

"I'll think of something, but there's more news," I said.

"You didn't!" she exclaimed.

"Of course I didn't but the things he told me make me think that you were right. I think he still loves me."

"So what are you going to do about it?"

"I don't know."

"What about his mother? What about Sabia?"

"His mother, he says is not an important issue. Sabia is another story which I cannot speak about right now," I said dropping my voice to a whisper.

"So we both struck gold," she said.

"Why? What's going on with you?"

"I can't talk right now, but when this blasted thing is over, we will have a very long chat," she replied.

"Is he good?"

"Very! Did you see what they did to our hotel? Can you imagine how lucky we were not to be there at that time?"

"That evening I waited a long time for Vijay to pick me up. It took such a long time that I was thinking of cancelling until the following evening, but fate intervened and got me out of there. Do not repeat anything I've told you to the others," I said.

"My lips are sealed," she replied.

"By the way, if you see Brian, please ask him to call and give me the telephone number for Janice Weatherall. I would like to tell her the good news."

12

I thought of Maxwell Charles Berkeley the third and how he was coping with the goings-on in his beloved city. He was quite a practical person and I knew he would come through it all quite well, even though he would be missing his weekly bowl of Mulligatawny soup and also his chat with whomever was willing to listen. What would he have to say about these circumstances that have thrown his favourite city into such deep dark sadness?

I was hungry. I was scouring the refrigerator and the cupboards for anything we could have for dinner. Wine was in great supply, but since he lived alone, there was hardly anything else there. I soon found out, that dinner had been ordered and would be delivered directly to the flat. Even though most businesses were closed, the restaurant owners, afraid they might be driven into bankruptcy, were willing to take the chance to acquire some much needed income.

"So what's for dinner?" I asked.

Tonight it will be Indian. Not too hot, not too spicy."

His mother called and he was relieved that Dean was still with her. She loved the boy and he loved her. What would she do if she knew the truth? A loud blast interrupted my thoughts and sent us both scurrying to the window. The terrorists had blown the cupola from the roof of another hotel. This we could not see, but he knew exactly where the sound came from because we were still watching the news.

"This is really frightening," I said.

"You're safe here," he said moving closely behind me.

"How long do you think this will go on?" I asked.

"Hopefully not for too long because it's draining the businesses and scaring the daylights out of the people. Even the beggars have gone into hiding. But something good has come out of this madness," he said after a moment's pause.

"What good could come from something like this?" I asked.

"I was able to spend more time with you and you found your long lost friend," he said grinning like a Cheshire cat with dimples.

"Isn't it also dangerous for Ranjit out on the street?" I asked showing concern for the poor man.

"He probably knows Bombay like he knows the back of his hand and will come to no harm."

It was Friday morning and day three of the siege. There was not as much as gunfire as in the previous two days. On the news we heard that there were over one hundred and twenty people killed and also many of the gunmen. It seemed as if the end was in sight. I looked out the window and noticed that most of the fires seemed to have been extinguished. Just one fire was raging and it seemed worse than before. It appeared as if they had intentionally set out to fully destroy the hotel. The doorbell rang the same time as the telephone did. I could answer neither and Vijay seemed to be still asleep. I knocked on the bedroom door but there was no answer, so I opened it to find him fast asleep on his back, completely in the nude. I closed the door again and this time knocked a little harder.

"I'll be there in a moment" he shouted.

"The doorbell is also ringing," I shouted back.

He was out in a flash in a long night shirt. It was breakfast! He then picked up the telephone in the living room, said a few words and then handed it to me.

"You're right," I said. "It is absolute hell. I hope you don't mind my staying here with your husband."

"You are my friend and he was your friend before I met him," Sabia said.

"As soon as this is all over, I want to get out onto the street," I said trying to sound impatient.

"Don't be so hasty," she said. "Who knows what's lurking behind the next corner."

"You're probably right."

"I hope Darling Vijay is keeping you occupied," she said with an expectant pause.

"What else can we do but sit in front of the television set and watch the carnage take place? By the way I found my little friend Ranjit."

"You couldn't go out. Where did you find him?"

"He was right under our noses all this time. He works for Vijay's company as a messenger."

"I don't believe that," she said with surprise in her voice. "We'll talk again tomorrow. I would like to speak to Darling Vijay again."

"I think he is in his room," I said trying to make things clear to her. "Let me knock on the door."

There was no answer but I could hear the sound of running water.

"Sabia, it seems as if he's taking a shower," I said.

"It wasn't important. I'll call him again later," she said and hung up.

**

"Must be Billie," I said when the cell phone rang.

It was Janice Weatherall. Brian had passed the good news on to her.

"Would you come by and see me again?" she asked.

"Yes, Billie and I promised to come by to help you."

"So tell me, where did you find Ranjit?"

"He's working as a messenger in the factory of a friend," I said not naming the friend.

"What's the name of the factory?"

"Mahajan textiles," I replied.

"Oh yes. I know Vijay Mahajan. I'm glad he's helping some of the unfortunate ones. Did you see him?"

I was suddenly afraid because I thought she was referring to Vijay.

"Are you referring to Ranjit?"

"Of course."

"Yes, he looks quite good and no longer walks with a crutch. It looks as if somewhere along the way, he received a prosthetic limb."

"I'm glad to hear that. He probably received it from one of those church organisations. How are you coping with all that's going on?"

"Like everyone else, we must remain indoors until we've been given the all clear."

"I hope you're not in that hotel," she said quickly.

"No luckily for us, we were out to dinner when hell broke loose."

"As long as you stay safe, that's all that matters."

"Thank you very much for calling and if I should see Ranjit again, which I think I will, I'll tell him you would like to see him."

"That was Janice Weatherall," I said to Vijay.

"Did you tell her that you found Ranjit?"

"Yes I did."

"What are we going to do today?" he suddenly asked. "I feel like a caged lion."

"Then I'd better watch out. It's not good being around a wild animal when it is edgy."

He laughed.

"Let's sneak outside and see what's going on?"

I was not about to engage in any suicide missions, so he got into the elevator and went downstairs. I looked out the window and could see him below looking around. He picked up a newspaper, looked up and waved to me, then turned around and I knew he was on his way back because I heard the purring sound of the elevator as it climbed up to the flat.

"I have something for you," he said with a grin.

"What did you find in the driveway?"

"An article about the terrorist plot by Anand Banerjee," he said.

"May I see it?"

"He has lived away from India for too long. He's a good journalist, but sometimes his ideas are not those that pertain to India."

"Why do you say that?"

"One cannot compare India to the United States. India is an old country which has been ruled by Imperialists and we have had to find a way for ourselves, especially after our Independence in nineteen forty seven. I know we have way too much bureaucracy and things are done too slowly, but until a better way is found, we have no choice but to continue on the path we know."

"India is becoming a great nation, and if you want to become a world partner, things have got to move a little faster and a little more smoothly. India is one of the leaders in communications, so there shouldn't be any reason for this slow activity. North Americans praise the work of the computer geniuses in Bangalore. You've got the technology here but seem afraid to use it. No one should be standing in line at a bank for an hour while old men with pencils stuck behind their ears search for ledgers instead of using computers."

"It will all take time Christine. Sometimes the bureaucracy also drives me crazy, but I know that in the very near future, western countries will be knocking on our doors for advice."

"They are already knocking. Use some of this modern technology for yourselves. You are making fuel efficient cars, producing some of the best writers, you've got the biggest film industry there is, the textile industry, fine silks, and heaven knows what else there is."

"You have been doing your homework," he said. "I love talking to you. I don't have to listen to this nonsense about Hollywood and Bollywood. Don't misunderstand me. I love movies, but there is more to life than all these superficial things."

"So what did Anand Banerjee have to say?" I asked.

"Just like all of us, he wants to know who's behind this terrorist activity."

"I'm sure that's on everyone's mind right now."

Our conversations became deeper and more analytical. Here we were cooped up in his flat like two people on a deserted island, and even though the circumstances were not optimal, we were getting to know each other better than we did before, and very often I would catch him staring at me. I had a great mind he said, but the modern age was leaving me behind. He was shocked that I had no idea about texting and so he taught me all there was to know about mobile phones as he called them, and when he wasn't busy on the computer, he helped me to hone my computer skills. I was surprised at the things which I had deemed complicated, and the way he had simplified them for me. Yes I knew how to send emails but what he taught me about this new technology almost blew my mind. He was patient and he laughed a lot at my mistakes. He explained all about the behind-the-scenes operations of the textile industry. We talked about ourselves and everything that went on since we hadn't seen each other in the last twenty five years. He didn't understand why I would retire at the age of fifty, but when I told him that the company had made me an offer I couldn't refuse, he understood. However the biggest question was why I had never married.

He had a collection of wines which were mainly Australian and Italian, and with nothing better to do, we had wine tasting sessions which went into the late afternoon when we both retired to our rooms and slept until the early evening and would awaken in time for dinner. We watched movies from his collection which was extensive. Musicals, love stories! He liked Steve McQueen and the goddess Diana Ross.

Then suddenly it seemed as if the powers that be, thought the city had endured enough, and so on Saturday we felt free again. Such relief! The last terrorist was captured and although the police appealed to the citizens to remain in their homes, they threw caution to the wind and came out in droves onto the streets. They all wanted to see what had happened to their city. Car horns honked and hordes of people came out to witness what had taken place during the holocaust.

"Should we take a chance and go out?" he asked.

"If you think it's safe. I would like nothing better than to get out of here. Not that I didn't appreciate your hospitality, but I'm supposed to be on holiday and have been locked up for too long."

13

There was suddenly movement in the building which had been quiet from the time I had arrived there. Vijay said that he didn't know anyone there since the dwellers all kept to themselves. The occupants now opened their windows and voices could be heard. We too decided to see what was going on, although a strong police presence was still everywhere. Smoke from the remnants of fires, still towered towards the skies and the fire brigade was busy going from one destination to another. At that hour of the night the vendors were thinking ahead and came out with their pushcarts to sell their wares, much to the displeasure of the police. The streets were to be kept clear in case the catastrophe was not fully over, but it didn't matter to them for they had lost four days of revenue, and seemed hell-bent on making it up.

Except for the barricades, burnt-out buildings and the burning smell, the city seemed to be already bouncing back.

"Let's find a restaurant and get something to eat," I said.

We chose an Indian restaurant which was almost empty when we arrived. There was more staff on hand than customers, but as the evening wore on, it was filled to capacity. It became very noisy, since everyone had his or her opinion about the siege. Who had done it? How were they so successful? How had the country been caught so off-guard? Some people blamed the communists, some blamed the hardliners; still others blamed the country of Pakistan for what had befallen their precious city.

We decided to go back to the flat and Vijay thought we should stop by my hotel on the way there. We couldn't get close to the entrance, even though I said that I was a hotel guest. It was still not safe we were told, and we should listen to the news to find out when it would be reopened.

"I guess you're still stuck with me," he said as we climbed back into the Jeep.

"I feel safe in your flat, so I'm really not in a hurry to go back to the hotel if it's still too dangerous to do so."

"That makes me very happy. I will be very sad when you leave," he replied. "You have really recaptured my heart."

"And you, mine," I said.

He stared at me.

"Are you telling me there is hope for us?" he asked excitement dancing in his eyes.

"Maybe!"

"Does that mean I should have a talk with Sabia?"

"Oh don't do that. Not just yet. As a matter of fact, please wait until after I have left."

"Do you really mean it?" he asked staring at me.

"I believe I do."

He sat on the couch and pulled me towards him. I looked at the stain on his shirt where the curry had splashed at dinner.

"Better rinse that out." I said.

"It's not so important right now. Tell me why you've changed your mind."

"I don't have an answer. Maybe it's because I realise how gentle and caring a person you are. The fact that you never told Dean that you are not his father, but treat him like your own flesh and blood I find very admirable. And even though my friend cheated on you, you have treated her with dignity and respect. And the final reason is because you allowed Ranjit to sit on one of your expensive chairs and did not have it cleaned immediately after."

He smiled. He always seemed to do that.

"Those are my qualities. What about love? I know that I love you," he said moving closer to me.

"I think I am almost there. Well let me say this, there is no one else right now that I would rather be with, than with you."

He stared at me then he hugged me; so tight that I felt I would suffocate.

"Christine, I have waited twenty five years to hear those words. Twenty five long years! What are we going to do about it now?"

"I must return home and think about what lies ahead of me."

"You must return to Bombay soon. I don't want you to be so far away from me."

"Oh my Lord," I whispered.

"Don't worry about Sabia," he said thinking he was reading my thoughts. "She will understand. She must understand."

"It's not Sabia. It's your mother."

"Yes that will be quite an undertaking, but I won't allow her take my happiness away just when it's almost within my grasp."

"That's something I'm not looking forward to. She will most likely hate me."

"And I will love you even more."

"Let's go to bed," he suddenly said. "I want you to sleep in my bed tonight. I'll be a gentleman and won't touch you, unless you want me to. I just want to hold you while we sleep."

His telephone started to ring and he looked at it and then he answered. I gathered from the conversation it was Dean. He wanted to know what we had planned for the following day, Sunday, because he wanted to come over.

"I thought we would go to Breach Candy tomorrow," he said when he got off the phone.

"I thought you didn't like the remnants of imperialism," I said laughing.

"It would be a change from the madness around here to be reminded of our colonial days."

"If Mr. Maxwell Charles Berkeley is there, we can invite him to our table."

"Do you know him?"

"I met him when I went there for lunch with Billie and Brian."

"I guess he didn't bring Momar with him."

"You know about Momar?" I asked with a look of surprise.

"This is Bombay. Everyone knows about Maxwell Charles Berkeley the third and his Indian lover."

"But I thought Momar was his man servant."

"Among other things! They have been together since they were young men. What is most annoying is that he treats him like his servant and not an equal, even though they share a bed."

"You think he is a hypocrite, don't you?"

"Of course he is. Aren't all his kind like that?"

"He told us that Momar sleeps outside his entrance door."

"Because he probably put him there," he said nonchalantly. "Imperialists will never change. Well at least Momar doesn't have to sleep on the pavements of the city like the other unfortunate people. That's the least he could do for him, but he should treat him with a little more dignity, after all he is his lover. Let's go to bed."

I showered, put my nightshirt on and cautiously opened his

bedroom door. He was still in the bathroom, so I crawled into his bed and waited. Then the door opened and not expecting to find me there, he stepped out totally naked. When he saw me, he stepped back.

"Sorry! I'll be there in a moment," he said smiling.

He came out again dressed in a nightshirt and climbed into bed. I was afraid. I didn't want to spoil a beautiful thing. He was a man of his word. He pulled me close to him and we lay in bed like two spoons, his arms encircling my body. He then kissed me on the cheek and we fell asleep.

14

The following morning I opened my eyes and found I was still in his arms and he was still sound asleep. However I wish I could say that for the rest of his body. His manhood was pushing itself into my lower back. He had no idea it was happening, so to save any embarrassment for both our sakes, I quietly moved back to the guest room. No sooner had I done that, than the doorbell started to ring. He opened the bedroom door and then I heard voices. It was Dean.

"Don't you sleep Dean?" I heard him ask.

"Well I told you last night I would come around between nine and ten."

"What time is it?" he asked.

"Almost quarter to ten. Where is Christine? You haven't sent her back to the hotel, have you?" he asked looking around.

"No I didn't. She is probably still sleeping."

"Is there something going on between the two of you Dad?"

"Why would you ask such a question?"

"Mom told me you were once in love with her and now that she is here, you probably see the chance to get to know her better."

Vijay looked at his son long and hard.

"Christine has stayed here for four days and we haven't touched each other. She slept in the guest room and I slept in my room."

"You haven't answered my question Dad. I am not a child

anymore. I know that things are not the way they should be between you and Mom. I love my mom and I love you too, and as long as you are happy, I will be happy too."

Vijay's eyes filled up with tears, and they hugged each other tightly.

"You love Christine, don't you?"

"I do. Does it make any difference to you that she's doesn't look like us?"

"You are the one who's involved with her. It's your decision. She seems like a very nice person and if you love her, it is alright with me. Yes she does look different but I know there must be something about her that has attracted you to her. Does Granny know about her?"

"Does she know about Screen?"

"Screen? What is Screen?"

"Mother can't pronounce her name properly, so she calls her Screen."

"Where did they meet?"

"Christine and her friend Billie spent five days in Daman, and that's where she met Mother."

"If she is here with Billy, how can she be with you at the same time?" asked the confused young man.

"Billie is her girl friend."

"Isn't Billy a man's name?" he asked running a finger under his nose and sniffing.

"That's Billy. She spells her name with double l and an e on the end."

They were both laughing as I emerged from the guest room feigning surprise on seeing Dean.

"Well since Christine is awake now, I think I'll take a shower. By the way, why did you come by?" he asked his son.

"I wanted to talk to Christine about Anand Banerjee and you promised you would take me out to lunch," he said with a laugh which really brought out the resemblance to his mother.

His father just shook his head and disappeared behind the closed door. We spoke about Mr. Banerjee and I told him I would be calling him within the next couple of days and would pass his phone number on to him.

"Are you really serious about getting into journalism?" I asked him.

"Yes. Perhaps my Dad has told you about my problems, but I am working on them," he said once again sniffing and rubbing his finger under his nose.

"Are you talking about your addiction?"

"Yes," he said lowering his head.

"You know you can't fight it alone. You will need lots of help and patience."

"I know. I promised Dad I will stick it out the next time I go to rehab, but I don't think he believes me. I have disappointed him too many times already," he said his leg nervously moving up and up down.

"Well you'll just have to make him proud of you. It will be a hard road but you must persevere if you don't want to break his heart by finding you somewhere when it is too late."

"He doesn't know it, but I have made arrangements to go to a 'clean house' in Pune. I chose to go far away from home because I know there won't be anyone to call, should I change my mind."

I couldn't help staring at him. It was Sabia's face but Vijay's strength.

"You are a wise young man and I know you will make it," I said holding his hand.

"Do you think so?" he asked with the expression of a little boy.

"I am sure you will make it," I said emphatically.

"I also know you will help my Dad because I know he loves you, and you love him."

I couldn't find the words to reply to him.

"We are going to Breach Candy today. Would you like to join us?"

"Of course. Dad says I am a free-loader. Of course he was only joking," I said.

"Have you ever been to Italy?"

"When I was younger, Mom took me there for a summer holiday. I met all my cousins and aunts and uncles. I like it there. Have you ever been?" he asked me.

"Many times, but I like northern Italy much better than the south."

"Why is that?"

"I don't know, but I just love Tuscany and the area around the Italian Riviera."

There was silence and then he spoke.

"I understand that you found the little boy."

"Of course he's no longer a little boy but to think that if this Bombay siege had never happened, I probably would never have found him, and he was right there all the time working in your Dad's business."

"What is it they say? Behind every dark cloud, there is a silver lining?"

"I hope that silver lining shines through for you too."

"Will you see him again?"

"I really want to. I would like to see what I can do for him."

He said nothing but studied my face for a few moments.

"You look different and you are different," he said, "but I can understand why my Dad loves you."

"How do you know that he loves me?"

"He told me and my mom also thinks so."

"Doesn't that make you angry?"

"No! Simply because my dad has not been happy for a long time and I know that it has a lot to do with me. He cannot be proud of his son like most other fathers are, but one day I will change all that."

"I think it's only fair when I speak to Anand Banerjee to tell him all about you."

"And if he decides he doesn't want anything to do with an addict?"

"The man I met wouldn't be so judgmental. He knows that mistakes are made. You must prove to him that you are worthy of his trust."

He moved closer to me and then he hugged me.

"What's going on here?" asked Vijay laughing as he returned from his room fully dressed.

Dean smiled with his father and then with me.

"I like her Dad."

"You've got to prove your worth my son. I met her first; even before you were born."

I made a call Billie and allowed the two men to squabble in jest over me.

"Can you guess where I'm going when I get back home?" she asked.

Hugh Baines had invited her to visit him in Australia.

"To tell you the truth Screen, I can't wait to get out of this city. It scares the daylights out of me. What about you?"

"I'm doing alright. What are you doing tomorrow?" I asked.

"Lying out in the sun. I just don't want to go out there."

"Have you been able to get back into the room at the hotel?"

"Not yet and as soon as I can, I'm moving my stuff out of there and I suggest you do the same."

"But where will I go?" I asked laughing.

"I'm sure Vijay won't throw you onto the street."

"Don't you want to go to Breach Candy with us? We are going there for lunch."

"We?"

"We are taking Dean to lunch with us."

"So you have met Dean. I'll pass up on lunch today. Hugh and I are going down to the pool. We are both as white as sheets."

"Why don't you come over here tomorrow and we can go to Janice Weatherall's together?"

"In spite of wanting to get out of Bombay, I will go with you. I feel like a hermit. I have been caged up here for too long."

"Alright, take a taxi and come by tomorrow morning. How is Lila?"

"She's fine. She too is fed up with all this nonsense."

"Did she ask for me?"

"She did."

"Does she know where I am?"

"Yes and she's not stupid."

My conversation with Billie over, we left for Breach Candy. We had a lovely day together and I got to know Dean better. He had a great sense of humour and he laughed a lot. Of course Mr. Berkeley was not there. It was Sunday, but in his place were the affluent Indians with their families and their baby sitters.

The following morning, there was a storm brewing outside. The lightning lit up the sky and the thunder rolled. Then the sky opened wide and wretched, spewing rain down in torrents. Very unusual for this time of the year I believe. The rain seemed to want to wash away all the misery into the gutters and sewers below the city; the misery that had kept Bombay in its grasp for the last five days. In spite of the inclement weather, Vijay thought he should still go into the office. As quickly as it had begun, the dark cover suddenly lifted and the sun poked its way through the clouds.

"It would be better to text me if you want to get in touch with me," he said. "I may be running around the company most of the day. There must be a mountain of work waiting for me. Now the number which I have written here is to open the elevator. Just punch it in on this key pad and it will close automatically."

I looked at what he had written.

300683

"What a strange number! What is its significance?"

"It's a secret," he said with a wink. "Don't leave it hanging around and don't lose it. And don't open the door to anyone except Billie. After the last week only God knows what's out there."

To my eyes, he was the most handsome man and he was going to be mine. Dressed in a white shirt, blue tie and a pair of black trousers made him a very sexy and commanding figure. A figure that I had grown to love in only six days! Was I being silly by not being intimate with him? After all I was an adult. An adult who had crossed the seven seas! What did I have to lose? During the six days we had spent together, I often wondered about his sex life, mainly because he had had no intimacy with Sabia for nearly twenty years. We stared at each other as he picked up his briefcase. There was an uncomfortable pause. Then he hugged me and kissed me on the forehead.

"If you happen to see Ranjit, please ask him when I can see him again."

"I'll see what I can do," he said as the elevator closed blocking him from my view.

I was left alone and shortly after the weather turned stormy again. There wasn't much to do so

I searched the bookshelf for something to read. I came upon a novel by a controversial Indian writer but after several attempts to get into it, I finally gave up. I opened the door to the armoire and saw something which I had never noticed before. When I fully opened the second door, I realised it was some form of a musical instrument. I lifted it out and placed it across the bed. I had seen it once before on television in North America, but had no idea what type of instrument it was. In a way it resembled a guitar, and I proceeded to pluck at the strings which made a horrible noise, so I closed the case and gently placed it back in the armoire. I didn't know that Vijay played a musical instrument. Maybe he will play something for me.

15

"You have hit the jackpot Screen," said Billie as she walked into the flat. "You have been living in grand style over here. This is beautiful. Do tell everything."

"Where should I begin?"

"Let's start here. Is he good?" she asked with a big smile across her face.

"If it's what you're thinking, I must say that I don't know."

"Are you telling me you spent all that time together and nothing happened?"

"Nothing happened. Not because we didn't want it to, but because we didn't want to spoil this good thing we have together."

"There's nothing better than a bit of intimacy when two people who love each other, can show each other how they feel Screen."

"It's a bit more complicated than that. Vijay is a married man."

"Unhappily so, I might add."

"That doesn't make any difference. I told him I thought he was interested in me back then because I was considered an exotic looking woman."

"You didn't."

"Yes I did and he said he felt insulted. Anyway to prove to me that that's not the case, we will wait until we have confirmed that commitment to each other."

"I'm so happy for you Screen."

"Don't call me Screen. I don't even want to think of that woman right now. She makes me very nervous."

"Well if I may so, you are not interested in her, but in her son."

"He's so sweet Billie. Such a nice man! I have indeed hit the jackpot. He allowed Ranjit to come in and sit in the very chair you're sitting in. If only I had realised his worth twenty five years ago, I would've saved myself a lot of heartache."

"Nothing happens before the time Chris. Absolutely nothing!"

"Tell me about you. What's happening between you and Hugh?"

"Like I said, he invited me to visit him in Melbourne, so I will be heading off to Australia with an open ticket as soon as I can rent my house to my some rich person," she said laughing.

"That means you could be there for quite some time."

"That's right my love. Thanks for dragging me here in spite of the fact that I have been behaving like an ungrateful child."

"Who says you can't find love after twenty. Here I am at fifty two and you at fifty one, and what have we found?"

"Love," we both shouted in unison.

**

Janice Weatherall was waiting for us when we arrived.

"I was hoping you hadn't changed your minds. Some of the children are very scared and need special attention."

"Just tell us what to do. We are yours for the whole day," I said.

"I am so happy that you found Ranjit," she said to me. "I hope you told him he should come by and see me. Believe me, I tried and tried but had no success in finding him."

"I hope to see him again and I will pass the message on. Didn't the Government officials know of his whereabouts?"

"My dear, this is India. Bureaucracy and more bureaucracy! When I finally got in touch with someone in the correct office, this is what he said to me. 'Madam, she said lapsing into the way the Indians speak, 'that has been a very, very long time ago, and that will entail a lot of work which will most definitely take me away from my duties.' In other words he was hinting at a bribe. When he realised I wasn't going to open my purse, he started another song and dance. 'Perhaps the young man has left the city or he may be dead.' Do you know the will power it took not to tell him what was on my mind? Everyone in this damned place seems to be corrupt."

A day spent with the children proved to be very therapeutic for them and for us. They were the sweetest and most loving children with whom I had ever come into contact. They took turns in styling Billie's hair for they were amazed at the colour. They had probably only seen one other person with blonde hair and that was Janice, but never had a chance to touch it. Try as they might with my long braids, they couldn't do too much. We read stories to them; not sure how much they understood, but I gather it was our peaceful presence which helped them to settle down once again. At the end of the day there were many tears shed, which prompted us to offer to spend another day with them before we left for home.

I waited impatiently for Vijay as he had promised to pick me up from the orphanage at five o'clock, but five came and went and there was no sign of him. In the meantime, Billie had taken a taxi and returned to Brian's flat.

"It looks as if the children will get their wish," said Janice Weatherall. "Maybe you'll have to spend the night."

"My ride will definitely be here," I replied.

Thirty five minutes later, Vijay showed up, apologising profusely. He and Janice waved to each other.

"What in the name of heaven has happened to your hair?" he asked laughing.

"The children were trying to style it."

"They did a wonderful job," he said laughing.

I peered into the mirror and could only laugh for I looked like Medusa the Gorgon. My braids were standing and pointing in all directions.

"I'm sorry I'm so late. The meeting lingered on and on and I didn't have the chance to call or text you, but I knew you would be safe. I'll make it up to you."

I was happy that the air conditioning in the car was going full blast because the humidity was stifling, and a ride which should have taken half an hour took one and a half hours. The traffic was insane. Pushcarts, taxis, bicycles, cows lying in the middle of the street in addition to the impatient pedestrians, made rush hour in Bombay a living hell.

"Priddy called me today," he said.

"Is there anything unusual about that?" I asked anxious to know what she had to say.

"No but she was trying to interrogate me about you."

"Dear God! I whispered. "What did she want to know?"

"If you were still in the flat, if I still had feelings for you and so on and so on."

"That's what I was afraid of."

"No need to be afraid. I told her I would go to Daman to speak with her."

"Did she ask for details?"

"Yes, but I was much too busy to talk to her."

"Was she angry?"

"She wasn't happy. I have a feeling that she and Dean had some kind of a quarrel. Don't know what it was about, but she will no doubt inform me."

"Maybe we should find out if my hotel has re-opened. I don't want to cause you any trouble."

"Yes we should find out if the hotel has been reopened, so that I can get your belongings out of there. I won't let you go," he said. "It won't make any difference what Priddy says. And if it comes to clearing the air, I will definitely clear it with her."

"Are you referring to Dean?"

"I would never hurt Dean. I'm referring to what she did to me."

We rode the elevator all the way up in silence, and when we stepped out he had a surprise for me.

"I saw Ranjit this morning. I called him to my office and told him you wanted to meet with him again."

"What did he say?"

"He smiled and said he would love to see you too, so I made arrangements for you to visit him on his off day which is on Saturday."

"Thank you. Will you go with me?"

"Of course. I won't let you go alone. I have never been there but I'm sure my driver will know where it is."

It was a bitter-sweet moment. I was happy about Ranjit but also sad that Sabia was beginning to try to lay claim to the man I had fallen in love with. She was living in denial. Although there was nothing between them, she thought she had Vijay under wraps and he would never leave her.

"Smile," he said. "Nothing will come between us. Would you like to go out for dinner?"

"Why don't we get together with the others?" I asked.

"Who are the others? Are you referring to Billie, Brian and Lila?"

"Yes."

"At the moment, it is not a good idea. Don't misunderstand me. If I had already spoken to Priddy, I wouldn't care, but I don't want people talking about her or about me for that matter, behind our backs."

I fully understood his point of view. He didn't want to put her in a position to be spoken of negatively or have others laugh at her. That I found admirable.

"Have you spoken to Anand Banerjee?" he asked.

"I was waiting until I met with Ranjit before I contacted him."

"You'll see Ranjit on Saturday, so why not call him and make an appointment for early next week. There isn't a lot of time left before you go home."

"Maybe I should take Dean with me to meet him."

"Just let him know ahead of time so that he can be prepared."

"Wouldn't you like to go also?"

"No, let's wait until this thing is sorted out and then we can get on with our lives. I am not a social person around town, but everyone knows my name. One can't be too careful in this place called Bombay."

"Did Dean tell you that he is planning a trip?"

"No, where is he going?"

"To a rehab clinic in Pune! I asked him why so far away. He wants to be able to do it all on his own and on his terms as well."

"Priddy never said anything."

"Maybe she doesn't know."

"I'm not surprised he has confided in you. He seems to have found in you, the friend he was looking for."

"So may I take him with me when I go to meet Mr. Banerjee?"

"I see no reason why you shouldn't."

"Would you do something for me?" I asked.

"Anything within reason," he said smiling.

"Give me a moment," I said as I disappeared into the bedroom and returned with the musical instrument which had been hidden away in the armoire.

He jumped up to help me, and brought it into the living room.

"Would you play something for me?"

"I haven't played the sitar for a very long time, and wouldn't do it justice."

"What is it called?"

"It's a sitar. It belonged to my father. It's a very complex Indian musical instrument."

"I'm sure you can remember how to play a few chords."

"I will try if you promise you won't laugh."

I sat on the couch, while he positioned himself behind the instrument. He smiled shyly and then began plucking at the chords. He said that was a warm up. Then he started to play. At first he seemed a little rusty but the more he played, the better the sound became. When the piece was over, I applauded and he bowed in my direction.

"That was beautiful. You should practise more often."

"One day I will introduce you to someone who makes the sitar speak. Would you like to try it?"

"Yes I would."

"Do you play the guitar?" he asked.

"No I don't."

He positioned me in front of the sitar and he sat behind me, gently guiding my fingers. It was hopeless. It sounded like stray cats in agony and I quickly gave up.

"When you hear it played by the master, I know you will enjoy it immensely."

"I'm sure I would,"

"My father's friend is a professional. When you return to Bombay, I will take you to one of his concerts."

**

"Don't forget to make that call to Anand Banerjee," Vijay said.

Anand was very pleased to hear from me and we set an appointment for the following Monday at one o'clock. I told him about Dean and he said he would love to meet him. We spoke about the siege that had taken place in the city, for Bombay with all its problems, was still a peaceful place.

When Dean heard the news, he was very excited, and I could hear Vijay telling him about being on his best behaviour.

"Is there anything else you want to tell me?" he asked his son.

They spoke for a while and I knew that Dean had told him something either about himself or about his mother.

"I'm going to Daman on Sunday," he suddenly said to me. "I'll leave early in the morning and return the same evening."

Why did everything suddenly seem so urgent? I had asked him to wait to speak to Sabia only after I left the country.

"Why are you going there on Sunday?" I asked.

"I will tell you when I return."

In spite of everything hanging over our heads, we made the most of the situation and had a pretty enjoyable week. On Tuesday evening while I was at the hotel picking up my belongings, Mrs. Mahajan went to the flat with Dean, so I escaped having fire and brimstone thrown upon me. My love for her son grew with each passing day and I believe his also grew for me.

**

On Saturday morning we prepared ourselves for the visit to the place Ranjit and his family called home. We were both a little nervous because we knew he lived in a slum, and we had all heard stories about the slums which had sprung up everywhere on the outskirts of the city. We heard about the unsanitary conditions, the vermin, the heat and the disease.

"I told him he shouldn't go to any expense because we weren't staying very long," Vijay suddenly said.

"You just don't want to eat over there," I said laughing.

"Do you?" he asked.

"No I don't, but please don't insult him."

"I'm sure he didn't take it as an insult, just relieved that he didn't have to spend his hard-earned money on the two of us. Only for you Christine Bonnett, would I do something like this. What do you have in those bags anyway?" he asked.

"I bought some clothing and toys for his son, and some foodstuff for the family."

The Ambassador arrived at eleven thirty and we set out for the ride to Ranjit's home. I knew we were close to the area, because I could see numerous shacks in the distance and the wind kept blowing an unbearable stench in our direction. Vijay was more anxious than I and unconsciously kept squeezing my hand. The closer we got, the more overpowering the odours became. From the main road, we could see the homes which were constructed from cardboard and plastic, and for fear of someone pinching something from the car, Vijay decided the driver should wait with the vehicle until we returned. We were totally on unfamiliar territory and just when we decided to move towards the pathway that led to homes, we came across a young man and asked the way to Ranjit Gowdi's house. He said he would show us and we followed closely behind him.

Leaving the well manicured gardens around Malabar Hill and arriving close to Ranjit's home, was like being in two different worlds. What we had seen from the street had hidden the reality of what we were now encountering. A cacophony of sounds greeted us; the squealing of animals and the shrieking of children, the beating of metal and loud music from a radio somewhere in the distance. A lonely rooster strutted ahead of us pecking at the ground beneath its feet and turned to watch us as the comb on its head fell to one side obstructing its view. Feral pigs dug in the mud, their nostrils almost blocked by the cement-like mixture, dogs who had lost their coats through malnutrition or some unkind deed, looked in our direction hoping to snatch a scrap of food. Comatose-like inhabitants stretched out in front of the hovels sleeping off the after-effects of a night of alcohol or drug binging. Our arrival into the slum seemed to have gone out on the wind, for the crowds gathered and followed us step after step. The place was not fit for human habitation, but Vijay said nothing. The young man called out and Ranjit appeared, genuinely pleased to see us. The Gowdi family had put on their best clothing for the occasion and we were offered two wooden benches to sit on, while they crouched on the floor. It was a very small, dark, hot room in which the air stood still. Suffocating! The room seemed to serve as sleeping quarters as well as a living and dining room. It was clean but there was no sign of a bathroom or toilet. Ranjit introduced us to his wife and son, the latter staring at me the entire time.

"What is your wife's name?" I asked him since she didn't seem to understand English.

"Amrit," he said with a broad smile.

"You don't use a crutch anymore," I said.

His face had a questioning look. Vijay translated and he smiled.

"Yes, the church lady measure me and now I have a new leg," he said raising his trousers to show his prosthesis.

"I think you can walk better now," I said staring at the contraption.

"Yes, but sometimes it not so comfortable especially when it hot," he replied.

"I brought something for you," I said and handed him the two bags. "This one is for your son and the other is for both of you."

"Madam you are very kind. I miss you very much Madam. Long ago, I go to hotel everyday and wait but you never come out."

"This is the first time I've come back to India after twenty five years," I said.

One look at Vijay's face and I knew he wanted to leave. He was not a snob, but the odours were not conducive to one's nostrils. The little boy whose name was Sanjay started to search through his bag. When he caught sight of the balloons, he smiled and his mother blew one up for him. Then he came over and touched me but seemed too scared to touch Vijay. He just stared at him. Ranjit said something to his wife, all the while looking at Vijay. She stood up, looked in Vijay's direction, clasped her hands and bowed. I gathered he told her that Vijay was his employer. Thankfully no refreshments were offered and it was time to go. We stood up and Ranjit bowed to Vijay and then held my hands between his.

"Madam, I very happy to see you again. You live in Bombay?"

"No I will return home next week. I can't tell you how happy I am to see you again. I know it won't be the last time."

"When you come back to Bombay Madam?" he asked.

I turned to Vijay and smiled. He too wanted to know the answer to that question. They were all smiling as Ranjit parted the curtain and we stepped out to the crowds still standing in front of his door. A path had to be cleared to let us through. They knew that there were visitors inside Ranjit's house and of course they wanted to know why we were there. We made our way back to Ambassador followed by Ranjit and his family and also a few of the onlookers. We said goodbye and slowly drove away and when I looked back, the Gowdi family surrounded by their entourage were still waving to us.

"Let's get out of here," Vijay said to the driver.

"You must do something to help him. Can't you find him a cheap little flat with running water and a bathroom?"

"What else would you like me to do for him?" he asked smiling.

"Give him a better job. He speaks English."

We returned to the flat where we showered and changed our clothing. We both felt it was necessary to wash away anything unseen which might have attached itself to our skins and our clothing. Then we sat on the veranda and watched the goings-on on The Arabian Sea and along the shoreline. After that we went out for dinner in a city that showed no signs of a week of torture. That was Bombay. She couldn't and wouldn't be kept down. We returned home shortly before midnight and went straight to bed. Suddenly Vijay jumped up as if he had forgotten something. He opened a drawer in the armoire and selected some documents which he immediately put into his briefcase and closed it.

"I'll need those for tomorrow when I meet with Priddy," he said.

16

I was alone and the morning sunlight was filtering into the bedroom, casting shadows across the bed. Vijay had already left for Daman. I opened the blinds and looked out. Two stray dogs, their rib cages clearly showing signs of malnutrition, were running behind each other and sniffing the air, their tails raised high. They were searching for scraps or something thrown from the car of some well-to-do Bombayite. When one found something, it snarled and snapped at the other trying to chase it away from the newly-found tasty morsel. That was survival in its purest form. I suddenly felt afraid and very apprehensive. I didn't want to be alone especially after the happenings of the last week, so I called Billie.

"I was just thinking about you," she said. "What's happening today?"

"That's what I wanted to hear from you."

"Nothing is happening," she said.

"Is something wrong Chris? You don't seem like yourself. Is it Vijay?"

"No I just got up. Vijay isn't here. He went to Daman to speak to Sabia."

"Do tell!"

"Just between you and me, I think he is going to ask her for a divorce."

"How do you feel about it?"

"I am happy but I'm so afraid it will cause complications."

"You said they haven't had intimacy in over twenty years. He's still a young attractive man and deserves more from life, than just a woman on his arm for society's sake."

"I'm still worried about his mother."

"No problem. You can handle her," said Billie full of determination. "Does that mean you will be returning to Bombay?"

"Maybe!"

"You will have a good life here. You won't have to worry about a thing."

"But the poverty is still here. The beggars are still here. Oh by the way, I visited Ranjit's home yesterday morning. Dear God!" I said. "I met his wife and child. Oh the squalor Billie! I just couldn't stand it."

"So what's going to happen now that you've visited him?"

"I don't know. I asked Vijay to find him a cheap apartment with running water. It's mainly for the child. He has also promised to get him a better job. It can't be any fun for him running around on that leg in this heat."

"Will he do it?"

"He didn't respond at that time, but I know he will look after him."

"Should we pick you up for lunch today?"

"That would be nice. I'm so afraid of what's happening in Daman."

"Everything will be alright. Trust him."

"I do."

"Get dressed. We'll be there around one o'clock. We're catching a couple of rays first."

"Do you remember the way here?"

"Brian and Lila are also coming along. We'll find you," she said with her trademark cackle.

It was obvious that none of them, except Billie of course had ever been to the flat. They were surprised, and pleasantly so by the living conditions, and I made it a point to show them the second bedroom which I emphatically said were my sleeping quarters. Not that any of them believed me.

We had a fun-filled day together, but my mind rested on Vijay. He had left early that morning and since then I had heard nothing from him. When we returned, he still wasn't there so Billie stayed with me for a while longer so that we could catch up on the news the others were not privy to hearing.

"What do you think is happening up there?" I asked her.

"The proverbial shit is probably hitting the fan as we speak. Have you seduced him yet?" she asked with a serious face.

"No."

"What the hell are you waiting for? He loves you and he sure as hell isn't expecting a virgin. Go for it."

"I don't know Billie. When he returns and tells me what has happened, I will then make a decision."

"That's him," I said as the cell phone started to ring. "Hello!"

"Christine, it's Sabia."

"Hello Sabia," I said so that Billie could hear.

"I thought we were friends Christine. You didn't want him and you introduced him to me."

"That's true."

"Is it because no one else wants you, that you have now decided you want to snatch him from under my nose. Not only him, but also my son."

"I haven't snatched anyone from under anyone's nose," I protested.

"Whatever you call it, you've done it. My husband has asked me for a divorce and I have decided to give it to him."

"I think he deserves some happiness Sabia."

"And you are more than willing to give it to him, but you will regret it. When his mother turns on you and makes your life hell on earth, you will understand what I've faced over the years."

"You told me the reason you moved to Daman was to get Dean away from Bombay. Dean lives in Bombay. Why didn't you move back to the city?"

"I just wanted to let you know that I know what you've been up to Christine. You will think of me when you are sad and lonely."

With those parting words, she hung up.

"What did she say?" asked Billie.

"Vijay has asked her for a divorce. She's pissed with me. She thinks I took him away from her."

"That's a load of nonsense. She herself told me that he was still in love with you after all these years."

This time I checked the caller display when the phone rang.

"Hello," I said.

"How was your day? I'm back in the city and should be home in about twenty minutes."

"How did it go?"

"Better than I expected. I'll see you shortly."

"That's Vijay. He's back in the city and should be home very soon."

"That's my cue to leave. I know you will have a lot to talk about. You've got an appointment tomorrow, so I guess we'll go to the orphanage on Tuesday."

beautiful."

"Put the earrings on," he said.

I put one earring on while he tried to help me with the other.

"I wish it was an engagement ring. I never thought you would say yes, so I find myself unprepared for this moment."

"This is like a dream. I can't believe that this is happening to me."

"I know you want to tell Billie. Go ahead and tell your friend."

"Not right now," I said, "and I also don't want to go to the gym."

"What would you like to do?"

I did not answer. We just stared at each other. Then he moved closer to me and I did not back away.

"I love you," I said.

He stepped in front of me and kissed me, long and passionately. I could smell the lingering fragrance of his cologne which had almost worn off after a long day in the tropical heat. Fire seemed to be consuming us both and I clung to him.

"Are you sure this is what you want to do?" he asked his voice etched with desire.

"Quite sure," I said snuggling closer to him.

"Every day there's a new surprise from you."

"Are you disappointed?"

"Never! I'm going to take a shower," he said.

My heart was now turning somersaults and my body was pulsing like a heartbeat. Was I doing the right thing? The devil sat on one shoulder and egged me on. An angel sat on the other.

"Don't do it," the angel said.

"What do you have to lose?" the devil asked, encouraging me to go on. "He loves you."

"He could leave you if you jumped into bed with him," said the angel.

I finally decided that I had nothing to lose. He loved me and had done so for a very long time. We were both consenting adult. I quickly undressed and crawled into his bed covering myself with the sheet.

"Are you sure about this?" he asked getting into bed.

I smiled, raised my head and kissed him. He returned my kiss and soon he was covering my body with kisses. My body felt like a volcano bubbling ferociously beneath the surface and it was just a matter of time before it erupted. The subterranean swell continued as he continued to assault my senses and my body floated like a cloud across the sky. The man, with whom I had fallen in love, was now passionately making love to me. First there were small eruptions and after what seemed like a lifetime, the rumblings turned to thunder and lightning into fire that lit up the sky. This was followed by a mighty explosion and the volcano spewed ash and lava down the mountainside taking with it everything that lay in the way. Another explosion! Then his body broke into convulsions and he whispered words in my ears; words of seduction, decent and indecent, and the aftershocks made our bodies tremble.

"I love you Christine. I truly love you. I wish we could stay like this forever."

"I love you too," I said snuggling closer to him.

We lay side by side hugging and kissing and then he whispered in my ear.

"Tell me something Christine, you haven't been with anyone in a while."

"Why do you say that?"

"It was just like the last time."

"What do you mean by the last time?"

"So many years ago," he said laughing and showing his delicious dimples. "You really haven't been with anyone recently?" he asked again.

"No I haven't."

"I like that. It's like you are ……

"Untouched?" I asked laughing.

"That's something my mother would say," he said with a smile. "I remember that first time when I made love to you. You had just returned from a Cuban holiday and I took you out to that little restaurant at the edge of the forest."

"You remember all that?" I asked.

"I remember everything about Christine Bonnet," he said kissing me in the neck. "I was so afraid that night."

"Afraid of what?"

"That I would disappoint you! Afraid that my libido would let me down that night. After all I had waited for more than six months to hold you in my arms."

"You didn't disappoint me."

"I had the impression that stewardesses had a great life. One night here, another night there! Beautiful hotels and boyfriends all over the place!"

"That's just a myth. My friends back home were always jealous of me. They thought I had a wonderful life, while theirs were so humdrum. After doing that job for more than ten years, I had had enough. At home my telephone hardly ever rang, no-one invited me to their parties, and at Christmastime when they were all getting ready to celebrate, I was boarding an aircraft to take other families to their destinations."

"That must have been difficult."

"Of course it was. The passengers upon disembarking with their gifts would wish us a merry Christmas. No one knew that some of us would be spending Christmas day in a hotel room or sitting alone in a restaurant which would be open to have pity on people like us. Of course there were good times, but it can be a lonely life."

He propped himself on one elbow and stared at me as I told my story.

"It was only after I took a position on the ground that I realised what had been missing from my life. My telephone started ringing again. Old friendships were re-discovered and when that aircraft door closed taking the crew and passengers away, there wasn't a pang of jealousy and most importantly, I was going to the bathroom on a daily basis."

He smiled.

"I had done my share of it all. Now it was someone else's turn."

"Does that mean you no longer liked the job?"

"I wouldn't say I didn't like it. I had had enough and wanted a change."

"So what did you do in Bombay?"

"Before I met you?"

"Yes."

"This was a new route for us, so there was a lot to discover. The shopping was great and Billie and I travelled around together."

"Were there any boyfriends?"

"There was no time to build friendships. It was here today, and somewhere else tomorrow. How many men were willing to put up with something like that?"

17

"I've decided to work from home today," he said.

"Don't forget I've got that one o'clock appointment with Anand Banerjee. Please tell Dean not to be late," I said, my arms encircling his neck.

"Are you meeting him there or is he coming here?"

"I didn't ask him."

"I think you should. I'll call him."

It was a stroke of bad luck at that tender hour of the morning that his mother should answer the telephone.

"Is it true?" Bina Mahajan asked her son.

"What are you talking about Mother?"

"Is it true that you have asked Priddy for a divorce?"

"How did you find out about it so quickly?"

"Your wife called me to let me know. I don't know what she wanted to hear from me," she said without an ounce of compassion.

"Was that all she told you?"

"Yes, was there something else to tell?" she asked.

"No Mother. Is Dean there?"

"I think he's still asleep."

"Please ask him to call me. Remind him that he's got an appointment at one o'clock today."

"Vijay," his mother continued, "I know you will be happy now. I know just the right girl for you. I will make arrangements for you to meet."

"Goodbye Mother. Please do not make any plans for me. You will only embarrass yourself," and with that the conversation ended.

Ten minutes later Dean returned his father's call. His grandmother it seems had awakened him.

"Hello Dad. You called."

"I wanted to remind you of the appointment today and would like to know if you will go directly there or come here first."

"It would be better if I came there. What happened between you and Granny?" he whispered. "She seems upset."

"She should be. She wants to bring some young girl over here to meet me."

"Don't take her too seriously Dad. You should know what to expect from her by now."

"That doesn't change anything. I just want her to stay out of my personal life."

"Well I'll see you around twelve thirty," he said.

That settled, we snuggled together on the couch and Vijay turned on the television to watch the news on CNN. The moderator was interviewing several black women, so of course I wanted to hear what the discussion was all about. He was not as interested as I was and immediately his hand came to rest on my thigh and he whispered in my ear.

"Last night was beautiful for me. Was it also beautiful for you?"

Before I could answer, the moderator started her monologue. It was a story on prostitution and seven out of the ten women interviewed were women of colour.

"Please turn it off," I asked him.

"This kind of thing happens everywhere Christine. Anyone with a brain knows that this happens in every race."

"Not everyone thinks the way you do," I protested. "The average person here probably thinks we are all like that, and will start making indecent proposals to me when I walk down the street."

"No one could possibly think of you that way," he said squeezing me. "Let's forget about what's going on outside. Come on. Smile for me."

"Don't bring Dean back with you," he said as I was leaving for my appointment with Anand Banerjee.

"Suppose he wants to come back with me?"

"You'll find a way to get rid of him. I took the day off to be with you."

"I wish you would come with me. Mr. Banerjee is a very nice person."

"I'll get the chance to meet him some other time," he said. "Send me a text and let me know how it's going."

The doorbell buzzed for the second time. Dean was becoming impatient probably because the taxi meter was running. He was very conservatively dressed. No tie, but should one have to wear a tie in this weather?

"Hello Christine," he said kissing me on the cheek.

I looked up and his father was looking down. We waved to each other until the taxi drove away.

"Are you nervous?" I asked Dean.

"A little, but you said he's nice and I believe you," he said playing with his nose, a habit common with cocaine users.

Anand Banerjee was waiting when we arrived at the restaurant, and he jumped up to meet us.

"Hello Christine," he said. "It's so nice to see you again. This must be Dean."

"Good afternoon sir," Dean said shaking Anand's hand.

"You look different today," I said.

"The moustache's gone," he said running his fingers above his upper lip. "Where is your other friend?"

"Billie couldn't make it today."

The waiter came over and we ordered drinks. I noticed that Dean's left leg was shaking and I reached over and held his hand.

"Are you a Mahajan from Mahajan Industries?" he asked Dean.

"Yes."

"Does that make a difference?" I asked.

"Not at all! Mahajan is a very unusual name, so of course when I saw the name I thought you could be related. So you are in your last year of university?"

"It will be over at the end of next spring," Dean said nervously.

"So how will you make up for the lost time you will be spending in Pune?"

"I will do extra classes and go to school at night."

Did Anand believe him? I had to. I must. Any doubts I have should remain beneath the surface. He is depending on me and he trusts me.

"Very commendable!" said Anand Banerjee.

"I told my wife about you Christine and she said she wanted to meet you. I told her to give us an hour and then she can join us."

We ate our lunch while Anand concentrated on Dean and the prospects of his employment. The young man was a little nervous, but made a favourable impression upon Anand. He promised to get in touch with him immediately upon his arrival back in Bombay. Then we discussed Ranjit's story. I noticed that Dean kept looking at his watch. Maybe he had an appointment. He was about to leave when a slim, blonde lady entered the restaurant and walked towards us.

"My wife," said Anand excusing himself and walking in her direction. "Angela, I want you to meet Christine and Dean. Billie couldn't be here."

"Are you American?" she asked.

"Canadian," I said. "Somehow I thought you ……"

"Were Indian? Everyone seems shocked when I put in an appearance. They always expect Anand's wife to be Indian."

"It was really nice meeting you, but I must go" said Dean as he shook hands with them and quickly left the restaurant.

"I'm really pleased to meet you," I said to Angela. "How do you find life in Bombay?"

"Well, what can I say?" she asked looking at her husband. "I followed Anand here, so I'm trying to make the best of it. Sometimes it is very difficult but I intend to win this battle."

Anand smiled and squeezed her hand.

"I must go," he said. "I'm sure you two ladies can carry on without me."

He hugged his wife and left. We sat and talked for another hour or so. She was a very lovely and interesting person. She talked about her struggles in the city and the loneliness she felt when Anand was away from home. She thought the Indians looked down on her and had branded her a blonde floozy. Had we been in California, would Angela have been so friendly, I asked myself? Maybe! She had married Anand. She must be a nice person. It shouldn't matter. But then Anand was a great catch. With everything that was going on, I had completely forgotten to send Vijay a message.

"Excuse me," I said while I escaped outside and sent him a text.

All went well. Returning w/o Dean.

"Sorry about that," I said upon my return.

"Anand tells me you are leaving at the end of next week. I wish that you lived here in Bombay. It is difficult to find people I can really talk to."

"What about the ex-pat association?"

"I did attend a couple meetings, but they concentrate only on the negative aspects of the country and if I want my marriage to work, it would be better to focus on the positive things. After all, my husband is Indian."

They were words of wisdom and I thought of myself and the position I would be in if I decided to return to Bombay to be with Vijay.

"I'll give you my email address and we can keep in touch," I told her.

"It was such a pleasure Christine," she said. "I must be getting home. Anand worries about me when I'm on the street."

"I've got your husband's email address. I'll be in touch."

"And Christine," said Angela, "if you ever get back to Bombay, please let us know and you can stay with us. Everything my husband said about you is true."

"Thank you. I would like nothing better."

We hugged each other and went our separate ways.

18

No sooner had I entered the door than the telephone started to ring.

"Anand Banerjee," said Vijay handing the phone to me.

"Is something wrong?" I asked.

"Everything is just fine," he said laughing.

"Good. So what did you think of Dean?" I promptly asked.

"I think there is great promise there. He seems like a level-headed young man and once he gets over this addiction thing, I will be more than willing to help him. But I do have one question. Why isn't he going into the family business?"

"Perhaps he isn't interested. I really don't know the answer."

"There's another question that's on my mind Christine, and since you are a very straight forward person, I thought I would ask you."

"What is it?"

"You can say that it's none of my business."

"What is it Anand?"

"Are you and Dean's father in some way involved?"

I was shocked by his question and didn't know what to say to him.

"Your silence has answered my question," he said. "And by the way, my wife thinks you are terrific."

"Thank you," I said. "Why did you jump to such a conclusion?"

"It was not a conclusion. You must remember that I am a journalist and I have put two and two together."

"Did you reach the sum of four?" I asked with nervous laughter.

"I certainly did."

"I guess that changes things, doesn't it?"

"Why should it? I just hope that if you decide to stay in Bombay, we can all become friends."

"I would like nothing better," I said.

"What was that all about?" asked Vijay as I hung up the telephone. "Do you know you're missing an earring?"

My hand flew to my ear. It was missing. It was the sapphire earrings he had given me.

"The driver took me to the front entrance although I asked him to take me to the back, and I know I was wearing both of them when I stepped out of the taxi"

"How can you be so sure?"

"I saw myself in the mirror and if it had been missing, I would've known then. I'll run back down and see if I can find it."

The elevator descended and then quickly ascended.

"Mother what are you doing here?" Vijay asked as she Bina stepped out of the elevator.

"I called the office and your secretary told me you were working from home today."

The elevator was not there when I returned from searching for my earring, so I rang the bell and he sent it down for me. I thought he had an unannounced visitor. I was holding the earring up to show him, when I noticed the look on his face. He put his finger to his lips and invited me in. I soon realised who the visitor was. His mother! She was paying her son a surprise visit.

"Screen," she said her voice full of surprise.

"How are you Mrs. Mahajan?"

"I am well. I came by to see my son. They told me he was at home, so I came by to see if he was alright."

I didn't know what to do, so I sat on a chair and observed them.

"Did you hear that his wife is leaving?" Bina Mahajan asked fully knowing that Sabia and I knew each other well.

"No I didn't. Where is she going?"

"Mother, Christine is really not interested in my personal affairs. Can we talk about this another time? Christine and I have some business to discuss."

"What I came to say won't take long," she said as my heart almost jumped from my chest.

"You are my son's friend Screen. My son is lonely and needs a wife," she said in a pleading voice.

"Mother, can't all this wait for another time?" Vijay asked impatiently.

"Screen is a smart young woman and she will agree with me, won't you Screen?"

"I don't want to get involved in family matters," I said, nervously playing with the earring in my hand.

"All I want to tell my son is that I have found him a beautiful girl. Not yet sixteen, untouched and of child-bearing age! She's young and from a good family. The moment I heard the sad news about Priddy, I immediately thought about her. Her sister is beautiful too and I thought I would introduce Dean to her. After all, it seems as if my grandson is getting his life back together."

"Mother I am old enough to choose a wife for myself. Just leave Dean out of this. Give him a chance to make up for the time he's lost. I have nothing against these young, simple women you are trying to push on me, but they are not what I'm looking for in a partner."

I couldn't believe what was happening before my very eyes. This I had been afraid of.

"When can I bring her over? You will like her. Give her a chance."

"I am not interested Mother," he said with defiance in his voice. "I'm old enough to be her father. Only uneducated men marry little girls. I'm sure she is a very nice girl, but definitely not for me."

"How do you know you're not interested? You haven't even met her," the old woman said staring at Vijay.

"Mother, you haven't been listening to anything I said. Stay away and keep your friends away from me," he said the anger evident in his voice.

"How could you speak to your Mother this way?" she shouted hysterically.

"Mother, in western countries, this would be considered paedophilia. I would be arrested for what you are trying to push me into."

"This is India my son. Things have been done this way long before I was born. These are our customs."

"Well Mother, it is time for change in this country. This kind of thing ought to be against the law."

"How could you say a thing like that to me?" she asked on the point of tears.

"Because mother, you are interfering in my life! Stay out of my life," he shouted.

"Talk to him Screen. He's no longer a teenager. He needs someone to look after him. See how thin he is!"

"Mother," he said calmly, "I'm going to marry Christine as soon as I get a divorce from Priddy."

She promptly sat down.

"You?" she said glaring at me. "You and my son? I would like a cup of tea. This is too much for my heart."

"You know where the kitchen is Mother," he said as dots of perspiration appeared above his upper lip.

"Let her do it. You want to marry her. Can she cook?" she asked glancing in my direction.

"Mother I want a wife. Not a servant, nor a cook, nor a slave. I want someone who will stimulate me mentally. Christine and I are compatible in every way."

"I see," she said breathing heavily.

"I'll make the tea," I said longing to be away from them both.

Vijay said nothing as I trotted off to the kitchen, and I could still hear them bantering back and forth.

"What do you know about this girl?" she asked.

"Enough to want her for a wife," was his curt response.

"As if the other one wasn't bad enough, now you've brought your mother …….. a Dalit," she said fighting to get the word out. "People will laugh Vijay. Think about what you're doing before it is too late."

"You'd better leave before I lose my patience Mother. Christine is a well educated woman who has travelled the world and broadened her horizons. She has more class than all of your friends and their daughters, so please do not insult her. I should've stepped in when you were making Priddy's life a living hell, but not this time Mother. Not this time."

"You are no longer my son," she said with bitterness in her voice.

"Alright Mother. I guess you've found someone to look after you. To pay your rent and buy your food! Someone you can call on when you need help."

I came out with the tea and set it beside her. She glared at me and

I quickly made my escape back to the kitchen.

"My grandson is a good young man. He wouldn't allow his Granny to suffer. He has seen the light and everyday he is getting better."

"Mother, Christine is that person who has shown him the light. Do you know he is leaving for a clinic in Pune? All because of Christine! Do you know there is a job waiting for him when he returns? It is because of Christine Mother. Christine has done all that for my son and she has made me a very happy man."

The old woman stood up and stared at the tea which she hadn't touched. Apparently she took her tea with only sugar, but I hadn't asked and had added both milk and sugar.

"I'm leaving Vijay. It will take time for all this to settle in my brain and for you to come to your senses."

"Would you like me to call you a taxi?"

"Yes."

"Whew!" I said.

"I'm sorry Christine. I didn't know she was coming. She just showed up without calling."

"If I hadn't met her before and not known what to expect, I would've been a bag of nerves. That was Sabia's prediction for me."

"What?"

"She said I would remember her when the old lady starts to make my life a living hell."

"I am to blame for that. I should've stood up a bit more for Priddy, but I didn't realise that it had gotten so out of hand."

"Vijay, she's your mother, but I won't take it from her."

"Of course you shouldn't. My mother needs someone to put her in her place."

"What is a Dalit?" I asked remembering the word the older woman had used.

He paused before he spoke.

"They are the lowest caste in Indian society. Most of them are menial labourers and their skins are dark and weather beaten because of the long hours in the sun. Don't let my mother get to you Christine."

"She called me an untouchable?"

"Yes."

I smiled. I had expected worse. Somehow it didn't matter what she thought about me. Perhaps if she had called me a prostitute, then that would've hurt, because it would've been an attack on my character."

"Let's change the subject. Tell me what happened today," he said.

"You should've joined us. Everything went well with Dean, and I think Anand was impressed by him."

"Where is he anyway?"

"I don't know. He left the restaurant in a hurry."

"I hope he is sensible enough to stay away from that no-good crowd. He has a chance and I want him to make the most of it. Tell me what else happened."

"His wife joined us after the first hour. She is an American; a white American. We got along quite well. She even invited me to stay with them the next time I visit Bombay."

"What did you say?"

"I said I would be delighted."

"You said what?" his long eyelashes fluttering like a moth attracted to the light.

"I told her I would be delighted," I said with a smirk. "He also asked Dean if he was related to the owners of Mahajan Industries.

Dean said yes and I asked him if that would make a difference. He said that Mahajan was an uncommon name and thought that all Mahajans were related."

"What about the article on Ranjit?"

"He recorded the entire story and said he would work on it for a weekend article."

"So would you say today was a success?"

"Yes I would! You said I shouldn't bring Dean back with me and I didn't."

"Are you still in the mood after my mother's interference?"

I couldn't seem to get enough of him now that we had crossed over the threshold of uncertainty. Each time I looked at him, I realised how much I really loved him.

The telephone was forever ringing that afternoon. We were a little concerned since we hadn't heard anything from Dean and each time Vijay looked at the number of the caller, a frown registered across his brow.

"You're really worried about him?"

"Of course I'm worried about him. What time did he leave you?"

"It was around two thirty. Why don't you call him on his cell phone?"

"I have done that several times, but it goes directly to his voice mail."

"Call your mother. Maybe she knows where he is."

"She's the last person I want to speak to right now."

This time he looked at the number and wondered if he should answer. It was Sabia's cell number.

"He might be there. Answer," I whispered.

"Hi Dad, it's Dean."

"Where are you Dean?"

"I'm in Daman. I wanted to call earlier but I forgot to charge my phone. I came to see Mom because she is leaving on the weekend for Sicily. I just wanted to let you know that I am fine. Please thank Christine for me. Tell her I will see her on Wednesday."

"So what did you think of Mr. Banerjee?" Vijay asked him.

"Just like Christine said, he's a very nice man and his wife is very pretty."

"I'm glad you liked him. Where is your mother? May I speak to her?"

He returned to the telephone and said his mother was busy.

"I can speak to her another time. What time will you be back?"

"I'm taking the eleven thirty train tomorrow morning and should be there around two o'clock."

"Come to the office and see me," he said with a wide smile as if his son could see him. "And Dean, your grandmother has found you a potential wife, so be careful."

The young man laughed.

"She's probably doing the same thing for your Dad."

"She has already, so I sent her back to the flat, not before she threatened to disown me."

"Don't worry about Granny. That's just the way she is. Bye Dad."

"You're happy with his progress, aren't you?"

"Thank you," he said squeezing me tightly, his manly smell creeping into my nostrils. "You have made my life so much easier in these past eight days and I hope that someday I will be able to do the same for you."

"You've already done it. Your love will sustain me for the rest of my life."

"And yours will do the same for me."

Later that evening I called Billie. I had so much to tell her.

"Why don't we all get together tomorrow night?" she asked. "There isn't a lot of time left and Lila is growing suspicious. She keeps asking me about you."

"What does she want to know? Has she heard anything about Sabia?"

"I don't think she knows anything but what she does know is that you are still staying with Vijay."

"I'm not sure if he wants to get together so soon. He's afraid of gossip."

"Well tomorrow morning at nine I'll be there. We promised Janice we would help out at the orphanage."

Vijay stood on the terrace looking out across the Arabian Sea. He was smoking one of those aromatic Gauloises cigarettes. I had never seen him smoke before.

"Just trying to get rid of the frustrations," he said laughing.

"Beautiful aroma," I said as I stood next to him.

"Would you like to try it?" he asked.

"I've never smoked and I will not start now to pollute my lungs."

"It pollutes the lungs, but it calms the brain," he said putting it out. "Let's sit out here for a while. It's going to be a pleasant evening."

He opened one of the chairs which had been neatly folded against the glass panel and we sat close to each other. He instinctively reached for my hand and held it on his knee.

"The only thing missing is a nice cold glass of champagne," he said.

"Then let's do it."

On the water, there were a few sailboats riding the waves; the owners, enjoying the end of a hot and busy day in Bombay. Water birds flew to and fro taking food to their young and we watched as the ravenous babies in their nests in the trees, attack the parents as they arrived with a crop overloaded with fish. Lovers strolled hand in hand along the shoreline stopping occasionally to buy something from the many vendors who were still patiently waiting to empty their wagons. The big red ball of fire lingered on the horizon. It said, 'I dare you to take your eyes off me.' And so we watched and watched as it slowly inched its way deeper to brighten another day for another people far away. In one fell swoop, it disappeared. Dusk was upon us and the bats came out in great numbers. We watched as they crept from under the eaves troughs and into the night. We could also hear the sounds of the waves washing up on the rocks somewhere along the shore. Splash! Splash! They seemed like cries for mercy.

"Have you any friends?" I suddenly asked.

"Of course I have friends."

"Are they all here in Bombay?"

"Not all of them. There are those with whom I play cricket; my university friends and then there are my dinner friends. Why do you ask?"

"Because I've never met or seen any of them, except those in Daman."

"I know it seems longer, but we have only become closer within the last eight days, and don't forget we weren't allowed to leave the flat during that time."

"It does seem longer," I replied. "I have this feeling like I have been with you forever."

"Are you happy Christine?"

"I am," I said resting my head on his shoulder.

"When you return, I will introduce you to all of my friends."

"And if they don't like me?"

"They will like you, and if they don't, then we will just part company."

The sun had taken the long shadows of the trees with it. In their places, what seemed like tall dark bushes stood peaceful and still. We sat in silence for a while, as if afraid to break to disturb the peace of the evening. In the darkness I envisaged what was taking place on the Arabian Sea. In the distance there was light on the water; small spotlights that kept bobbing along on the surface. The telephone rang and he answered immediately without checking to see who the caller was.

"What time is it over there?" he asked.

"My brother," he mouthed to me.

"Oh yes, you know how she is," he said.

It was a one-sided conversation and I couldn't gather too much from his replies. Then he called my name.

"Of course you remember her. We had dinner together one night. Do you remember my brother Christine?"

"Of course I remember Ravi."

"He's coming to Bombay in two weeks," he said covering the mouthpiece. "You won't see her because she will be back in Canada," he said returning to his brother.

I believed they were talking about Sabia, or were they talking about their mother?

"I guess she is alright. Dean is spending two days with her."

A little more chatter and he hung up the telephone.

"My mother has complained about me, but my brother understands her as well or better than I do because she tried to do the same thing to him. She and Ravi's wife Rahela don't see eye to eye, so she keeps her distance. Let's go inside," he said brushing his hand across his face at the pesky little mosquito that was trying to get at his blood.

19

The days were flying by faster than ever and soon it would be time for me to go. We were both drunk with love. Each morning we would awake exhausted! Every little opportunity was spent grabbing little nuggets of love; the longer periods were left for the evenings when it seemed as if we just set out to just to demolish each other.

We couldn't seem to stay away from each other and when he was away from me, the yearning was so strong that I could still smell him and feel him; his body melting into mine. I had never before experienced anything like it. How was I going to leave him? I would miss his clean shaven body, devoid of any trace of human hair. I would miss his lean brown, muscular arms which were never adorned with a single piece of jewellery. He was all mine! Appetizing! Magical! Delicious! Coming home to me wearing only the night shirt he had worn the night before seemed to arouse the fire in him. It reminded me of his smell and made me feel closer to him. There were no partitions between us. No embarrassment and no feeling of shame; just that indomitable love between us.

"I would like an honest answer," I said to him one evening.

"Am I not always honest with you?" he said smiling, the dimples in his cheeks seemingly deeper than before.

"How did you suppress your desires? You said you were without female company for almost twenty years."

He blushed before answering.

"I have my ways," he said laughing. "And I never said I was celibate."

"So what did you do?"

"What do other men do? They find girls who are willing. No commitment involved."

"I was under the impression that all the young ladies here waited for marriage."

"That's what their parents would like to think, but this is two thousand and eight and India has moved ahead just like all the other great powerful countries. The modern woman in Bombay is no different from the woman in big cities in Canada."

"But do the men here still look for an untouched woman when they are ready to settle down?"

"I can only speak for myself," he said, "and you know how I feel about that."

There were only five days left of our vacation. Billie and I spent two more days at the orphanage and we were discussing whether or not we should give our donation in Canadian dollars or in rupees. When I told Vijay about it, he wrote a personal cheque for fifteen thousand rupees and Billie offered three hundred Canadian dollars. Janice was undoubtedly happy for the contribution and said she wanted to personally thank Vijay. The children were sad when we said goodbye that afternoon and we promised we would return to visit them whenever we were back in Bombay.

Vijay would be late that evening and Hugh was tying up his business before returning home, so Billie and I went out to dinner.

"So what is he like?" she asked with a smirk on her face.

"He's surpassed anything I could ever imagine. Sometimes I feel as if we could be joined together and neither of us would know."

"He's that good huh? See how much time you've wasted?"

"I can't believe that I have lived without him for so many years," I said the thought of leaving him springing to mind.

"Does Screen know about you?" she asked laughing loudly.

"She said I was a Dalit."

"Why would she call you a lentil?"

I could not help but laugh.

"You're thinking of dahl," I said as she too burst out laughing.

"Dalit! That's the lowest Indian caste, the untouchables I believe."

"What? And what did Vijay have to say?"

"He threw her out."

"A man after my own heart! The woman is crazy. I will never forget her saying, 'but he's a beggar Screen.' Well at least you know where you stand with her. She could've called you a prostitute my dear."

We both laughed.

"That's what I said too. Anyway Vijay has promised to find a little flat for Ranjit and his family. Something with running water and a bathroom and he promised me he would find him an easier position in the company. Something that would be easier on his leg!"

"Don't lose him Screen. He sounds delicious."

"He is! I have been kind to Dean and I know that Dean likes and trusts me. I guess Vijay has taken that into consideration. Anand Banerjee also thinks he is a lovely young man."

"Did you tell him about his problem?"

"Yes, I thought it better to be honest and forthright, especially since he figured out that Dean is part of the wealthy Mahajan clan."

"That didn't make a difference?"

"No, but he wanted to know why Dean wasn't stepping into the family business."

"Why isn't he?"

"I don't know. Maybe he has no desire to dabble in textiles. His interest is journalism. And speaking of journalism, I met Anand's wife."

"Where did you meet her?"

"She joined us for lunch and we got along like old friends. She was sorry that you weren't there. Anyway we promised to keep in touch and she has invited me to stay with them the next time I come to Bombay."

"Did you accept the invitation or did you tell her that you've got an exquisite home in South Bombay?"

"I did no such thing. I graciously accepted the invitation."

"Is she pretty? Was she born in India or in America?"

"She's not Indian. She looks just like you. Only prettier," I said squeezing back the laughter.

"I thought she was Indian."

"Everyone seems to think that she said."

"So where do things go from here with you and Vijay?"

"It looks as if I will be moving to Bombay."

"And how do you feel about it?"

"About Bombay?"

"The whole thing. Bombay, Vijay."

"I won't allow him to slip through my fingers a second time. I love him and I want to be close to him."

"Lila seems to know something, but I refuse to confirm her suspicions."

"How did she find out?"

"No idea. I guess that's the way they operate here in this city."

"It's like Peyton Place. Even Vijay knows about Maxwell Charles Berkeley the third. He told me that Momar is Mr. Berkeley's lover and has been since they were young men."

"Get out of here," Billie shouted. "Momar and Mr. Berkeley? I got the impression Momar was only his man servant."

"It's a small world. Got to watch everything you say around here."

20

Vijay was tired when he reached home that evening. He had dinner with a friend whom he said I would get to meet on my return from Toronto. He also said that he had had a conversation earlier that day with Sabia, but he did not elaborate on the discussion. When I persisted, he said she hated me.

"Did she tell you that?"

"No, Dean did. I think he realised she was feeling down and went to Daman to see her."

"I'm sorry about the position I've put you in."

In spite of not having a good relationship, she was still dependent upon Vijay. I had put an end to her comfortable way of life, but didn't Vijay deserve some happiness?

"No need to be sorry," he said. "It would have eventually happened. If it hadn't been you, it would've probably been someone else; and I'm happy it is you Christine. While I'm still reasonably young; I want to be kissed, really kissed by life. I want to be loved and to give love in return," he said hugging me.

"Will I see Dean before he leaves?"

"I wanted to take you both out for dinner tomorrow night, but he said he would rather come by and we can spend the time together. Just the three of us!"

"Is he angry with me?"

"No, but he loves his mother and doesn't want to see her hurt.

She'll be alright. She'll go the Sicily and have a blast with her lover like she always does. When she has had enough, she'll return here."

"How do you know she has a lover?"

"I'm not stupid Christine. She is still taking birth control pills."

"Maybe it's for another reason. Birth control pills aren't only to prevent pregnancy."

"I know she has a lover Christine, and so does Dean."

The conversation was going where I didn't expect and I decided to change the subject.

"Have you seen Ranjit?"

"How could I forget to tell you this? I called him to my office this morning, because the foreman has a position for him at the security desk at the workers' entrance. He will be there to make sure that they clock in and out, and also make sure that no unauthorised persons enter the building. There's not a lot of running around involved. When he came in, that trademark smile was plastered all over his face. Maybe he thought you would be there. Anyway I asked him to sit, but he said he preferred to stand. After I persisted, he sat down. Do you know what he asked me?"

"What?"

"How is your wife sir? How is Madam this morning?"

I started to laugh. Vijay could find nothing amusing about it.

"How did he know that you and I are together?"

"He's a clever man. I guess it showed by the way we looked at each other. Now you understand why I couldn't forget about him. He was different," I replied. "Is there a job for his wife also?"

"Christine, let's take this one step at a time. He now has a better position with better pay and the foreman is still trying to find him better living accommodation."

"I'm sorry. I didn't mean to be ungrateful."

"I'm the one who should be sorry. I'm just so tired. It's all these long nights without sleep," he said putting his arm around me and guiding me to the bedroom.

"And whose fault is that?" I asked laughing.

"Yours," he said pushing me onto the bed.

"Thank you for being kind to Ranjit. All he needed was a helping hand."

"He also wants to know when Madam is returning to Bombay."

"It's not Ranjit who wants to know. It's you," I said sitting up on the edge of the bed. "I've got to pay my bills and think about renting my condo. I must return home."

"I can't live without you Christine. Sell everything and hurry back," he said nuzzling me on the neck

"It's not as simple as that," I said. "I don't want to sell my condo. I have put a lot of work into it."

"Why can't you pay your bills from here then?"

"I don't trust internet banking," I said sounding very much like the old fashioned woman.

"Why not? Let's shower and I will show you how it's done."

I put one of his nightshirts on and watched him as he sat in front of the computer.

"You shouldn't be a slave to this kind of thing when modern technology has made everything so much easier. He pulled me onto his lap and explained it to me.

"It's as easy as that," he said slowly running his hand along my exposed leg. "My brother does most of the accounting in the company, and he does it all the way from London on the computer. Every five weeks or so, he comes to Bombay to have a firsthand look at things. I'm the hands on guy who looks after the day to day to day operation of the company. So you see it can be done.

Let's go to bed."

"Why doesn't he live here?" I asked.

"Who?"

"Your brother Ravi."

"His wife hates it here in Bombay, and after living in London for such a long time, she finds daily life here a real struggle. Ravi loves her and so he does everything to make her happy."

"He seems like a very nice man."

"I would do the same for you, if it came to that."

"Would you?"

"You know I would."

He was really exhausted so we talked for a little while and soon fell asleep.

21

It was two thirty on Wednesday afternoon and I was busy packing my suitcase for my return home. Vijay called and said he would be home early, because we were going to drive Dean to Pune on Friday morning. When the doorbell rang, I instinctively opened the door and went back to my packing. The elevator opened and I realised the error I had made. There stood Sabia. I was embarrassed because I was wearing one of Vijay's long night shirts. She stared at me.

"You've really made yourself at home," she said.

"I was expecting Vijay."

"I notice that. Do you realise Christine that our marriage didn't stand a chance because of you?"

"Because of me? I had no contact with your husband since I left here twenty five years ago."

"That may be so, but your constant presence lingered in the background throughout our marriage."

"Come now Sabia. Let's not exaggerate. You've given him a son. A handsome young man!"

"That you have also managed to take away from me! Since he met you, it's always Christine this and Christine that. What is this power you hold over these two men? What has Vijay told you about me? What has he said about Dean?"

"Should he have told me something?" I asked in a naive way.

I heard the purr of the elevator and I knew Vijay was on his way up. Thankfully!

"What are you doing here?" he asked stepping out of the elevator with a box of Alphonso mangoes under his arm.

"I just wanted to have a word with Christine before I left. Anyway I must run. My flight leaves in just under four hours and I've got to get to the airport before the horrendous traffic jam starts."

"I wish you a happy holiday," I said as Vijay looked from one face to the other.

"I will always have a good time in Italy. Home will always be home."

"I bet you will," Vijay replied as the elevator closed taking her away. "Why did you let her in?"

"I thought it was you."

"Remember I said you should always check to see who you are letting in. Even if you are expecting me, you should still check. There are too many crackpots out there on the street."

"You're right. I'll be more careful."

"These are for you," he said taking the box of mangoes to the kitchen.

"Thank you. You remembered."

"I would like to take the credit, but unfortunately I can't. Someone else knows that you like mangoes."

"Ranjit!"

"Yes, your friend Ranjit brought them to my office, and along with them he sends a thousand blessings. He said that Madam likes mangoes and he brought them for her. It looks as if I will have some competition."

"I hope you told him he shouldn't spend his money buying things for me. These mangoes must have cost him quite a bit."

"I couldn't insult him. Accept the gift as he gave it to you. Graciously."

"I didn't mean to insult him. I just thought he shouldn't be spending his hard earned money on me."

"He would feel hurt if you said that to him."

"Then may I have one now?"

"Help yourself. They are all yours. I can't for the life of me understand why anyone would like mangoes."

"I forgot how strange you are," I said laughing. "You are the only human being in this world who doesn't like mangoes. The most tasty and exotic fruit there is."

My favourite way to eat a mango is to make it really soft, then pinch a hole in the top and suck the juice out. Then tear the skin away and eat what's left of the lovely yellow fruit, until there is nothing left but the hard seed. In order to do this, I had to take a seat out of sight on the terrace.

"I brought you a wet towel," Vijay said looking at the condition of my hands and face.

"I thought I would have another one," I said laughing.

"By the way, he wants to see Madam again, but I must warn you, I won't be going back to his home."

"Don't be such a snob. Next time he will have refreshments waiting for us," I said teasing him.

"I've got good news! I think we've found a home for him. It is only a small flat with one bedroom, water and electricity. It's just big enough for the three of them."

"Have you told him?"

"Why do you think he is sending one thousand blessings? He thinks you've done it all for him."

"What did he say?"

"He cried. Then he fell to his knees and thanked me. I was glad there was no one else in my office because it was very embarrassing."

"He was always grateful for every little thing."

"Why didn't you tell me about him back then?"

"It didn't seem so important."

"Well tomorrow is the only day left to see him, so I suggest you come to my office and you can talk to him there."

"Finally I will see your office," I said teasing him.

"You never did show any interest and besides with things the way they were, it was better that you stayed away. What about Billie? I haven't heard much about her in the past few days."

"Hugh is leaving on Monday and they are spending as much time as possible together."

"Maybe we should all get together and go out on Saturday night. You can arrange it."

I accompanied Vijay to his office the following morning. It was not what I had expected of a textile factory. The foyer was crisp and clean with granite floors and modern art on the walls all accentuated by a black marble counter with two computers. There was no one at the counter, so we went straight into his office. He picked up a file and said he would be back in a moment. I sat and waited and then someone opened the door.

"How did you get in here?" a female voice asked. "This is Mr. Mahajan's office. You shouldn't be here."

"He knows I'm here," I said turning around and coming face to face with the woman who had been sitting next to Anand Banerjee on the train to Daman, "but if you would rather that I wait outside, I will do that."

As I was about to leave, Vijay walked back into the office.

"You've met," he said looking at us.

"I'm very sorry," the woman said. "I didn't know Mr. Mahajan had let you in."

He then introduced us. Her name was Mrs. Kapoor and she was his secretary.

"I saw Miss Bonnett on the train to Daman a few weeks ago," she said.

"That's right. You sat next to Mr. Banerjee," I replied.

"I was on my way home to Daman for the weekend."

"Mrs. Kapoor, could you ask Ranjit Gowdi to come and see me please?" he said apologising for the interruption.

"Of course sir. So nice to meet you," she said with a smile and closed the door.

"Did she try to throw you from my office?"

"She was only doing what was expected of her. Such a small world," I said.

"That's what I say to you always. Bombay is a big city but it is also very small. Anyway don't let her gentle demeanour fool you, Mrs. Kapoor can be like a pit bull."

"I didn't think she liked us. Of course we were discussing politics and about the state of affairs in India," I said.

Another knock on the door and Ranjit came in.

"I've got something to attend to. I'll leave you two to talk. Not for too long. The foreman will be angry with me," Vijay said before he closed the door.

"Madam, it is very, very nice to see you again."

"Thank you for the mangoes Ranjit. Sit down."

"And my wife say thank you very much for the clothes for the boy. She also say thank you for the flat. It will be very good for our boy."

"No need … the pleasure was all mine," I said remembering Vijay's words about insulting him.

"Madam I am not so tired now when I go home in the evening. The new work is easier and my wife is happy."

"Have you seen the flat?"

"Not yet Madam. The boss say it will definitely be ready in four weeks. Then I can move in with my family."

"I am very happy for you. Say hello to Amrit and Sanjay."

"You remember the names of my family Madam," he said with a wide smile.

"Of course I remember their names."

"Madam you stay in Bombay now?"

"I am going home on Tuesday."

"Back to Canada?" he asked.

"How did you remember that?" I asked.

"Yes. I remember everything about Madam. She is very nice."

"When you come again?"

"Probably in about three months," I replied.

"Madam you make me very, very happy. I will say it to my wife."

Vijay opened the door and entered the room, whereupon Ranjit sprang from his chair.

"You've spent enough time with my wife," he said to Ranjit.

The man looked as though he had seen a ghost. He stared at Vijay, then at me, and with a smile he limped to the door.

"Aren't you going to say goodbye to me?"

"Yes Madam. Goodbye until you come back again," he said shaking my hand. "Thank you sir."

"He really loves you," said Vijay.

"Of course he does. I think you scared him."

"Of course that's what I meant to do. If I didn't, I would come home one day and find him in the flat having tea with Madam. What do you have planned for the rest of the day?"

"You are crazy," I said laughing. "I have nothing planned."

"Why don't you call Billie? Maybe you can do some last minute shopping."

22

Dean came over on Thursday evening bringing his backpack and ready to spend the night. That meant we could be on the highway at daybreak. He seemed a little nervous, but he had walked that road before. We had dinner which we ordered in and sat around discussing the day's events.

"Does your grandmother know you're leaving tomorrow morning?" Vijay asked.

"She does. She was a bit sad but she knows it's something I must do if I want to get on with my life."

"Have you spoken to your mother?" he asked.

"Not since she left."

"I'm going to bed," I said. "I'll leave you two to talk."

It seemed as if my head had only just hit the pillow when the alarm went off. Five o'clock! Vijay rolled over and turned it off. I got out of bed and headed for the shower and when I returned he was fast asleep again. I knocked on Dean's door and I could hear his sleepy voice mumbling something and then there was a thud. He had fallen out of bed. It was difficult to imagine anyone falling from such a big bed, but maybe he had been dreaming. Vijay thought that this time around, his visit to the rehab clinic seemed to be affecting him more than before. Could it be the promise of a job waiting for him? Had he found some form of self worth which hadn't been there before? Soon everyone was stirring. We would have breakfast somewhere along the way. At five forty five we had all bundled into the jeep and started out. Never had I seen a highway in India that was devoid of traffic. Except for a few trucks, the highway belonged to us. It was a warm misty morning and Dean snuggled up in the back seat, his head resting on his backpack. He slept most of the way. We were starving and one hour outside of Pune, we stopped and had a quick breakfast, then drove on in silence. It was obvious that Dean's situation was resting heavily on our minds. As we drove into Pune, we passed a market on Laxmi Road which was extremely busy for that time of the morning. The sign read at the entrance read, "You will find it here." We travelled a little farther passing the Jain Temple and a little further along we saw The Panshet Dam. Pune looked like an interesting town, a town that was often mentioned in the British colonial movies, but we were not there on a sightseeing mission. A few minutes later, we were outside the Rehab clinic. Dean seemed apprehensive and Vijay was nervous. I reached back and held Dean's clammy hand.

"It will be alright. You will be just fine," I said as he smiled.

The non-descript building partially hidden by trees bore the name of the clinic. We looked around, then slowly stepped out of the jeep and Vijay rang the bell. It took about five minutes before someone came to the entrance. I hugged Dean and held him tightly, then returned to the vehicle. I gave the father and son a little time to be alone and soon Vijay signalled me to accompany them. A corpulent woman in a green sari opened the gate and beckoned us to follow. We settled down in the sitting area and waited. Dean's left leg was doing overtime. It just wouldn't stay still. He was a basket of nerves, so I sat next to him and held his band.

The lady returned with a young man dressed in a blue doctor's uniform with a stethoscope around his neck. He greeted us and we all sat around a table where water, tea and juice had been provided.

"You've had a long drive, and so we thought you might be thirsty," he said.

I had a cup of tea and so did Vijay, but Dean was much too nervous to consider drinking anything.

Dr. Paxil then went through the protocol and rules of the clinic. He said that outside contact with the patients was not prohibited, but stressed that it was not encouraged. He explained the treatment which the patient would receive and then asked Dean if he had any questions, to which he replied no. Vijay also had no questions.

"Suppose he has some sort of adverse reaction to the treatment, what happens then?" I asked.

"There is always a backup system. What we use here is what we have been using for the past eight years. Of course it is a rough road, but we take good care of our patients and in twelve weeks they should be ready to return home, their bodies detoxified. He asked Dean if he had a mobile phone, which he immediately confiscated.

"When you want to make a call, which will be monitored, we will allow you to use it. Now we can all go to see the room where you will be staying for the next twelve weeks."

We followed him and were surprised to see the room. All the amenities of a beautiful four star hotel room with wrought iron bars on the window! It was a comfortable room but there was no telephone. We left him to settle down and returned to the waiting area where Dr. Paxil handed us a calling card with the number of the clinic.

"This card is just for you. Do not encourage anyone to call him, especially any of his friends. You may call him when you wish to offer him words of encouragement, which he will no doubt need. You may also call me if you have any questions or to see how he is progressing. Now I would like you to say goodbye to him. This makes it easier for him to settle in."

"I will see you in a few months," I said hugging him.

"Thank you Christine. I will miss you."

He hugged his Dad and with tears in our eyes we said goodbye and hurried out to the jeep. We sat in the vehicle in silence for about ten minutes, with Vijay's head resting on the steering wheel. Without a word, he turned on the ignition and we started on our journey back to Bombay. I wanted to visit the market at Laxmi Road, but I knew that he was not in the mood for crowds and traffic and so we sailed by and were on the highway back to Bombay.

"Thank you," he finally said. "You have made this much easier for me and for my son."

"No need to thank me," I replied.

Most of the three hour journey was done in silence. Occasionally he would reach over and hold my hand. I too felt the pain that he was experiencing. On the outskirts of Bombay the rush hour traffic into the city was bumper to bumper. It took one and a half hours to reach the flat; a journey which would normally have taken twenty minutes.

"I haven't the strength to go to the office," he said. "You haven't left and already I feel so alone."

"I will be back," I said putting my head on his chest. "I will be back."

"Thank you. I just don't know what I would've done without you."

Each time the telephone rang, we expected it to be Dean, but it was always someone from the office with a question. We spent the day just as we had after the siege; feeling lost and watching television. Occasionally Vijay would ask the same question.

"Do you think he is alright?"

"Of course he is. Three months from now you will be happy that he made the decision to do this."

"My greatest fear is that he will not stay the entire twelve weeks."

"Trust him. He will. He promised me that he wouldn't let me down."

I would then receive a tight squeeze and a hug.

As evening approached, I suggested getting out of the flat, because being cooped up didn't help either one of us, so we drove out to the beach and watched the waves play against the shore. We laughed as we watched other couples in the throes of ecstasy and being constantly disturbed by the vendors selling their goods along the beach. It was a good idea to get away from the flat because the fresh air seemed to help us forget a bit of our troubles. Later that evening, there was a call from the clinic. Vijay was afraid that Dean was already asking to come home, but it was the night doctor on duty informing him that Dean had had a pretty good day and was resting. He called Bina Mahajan to let her know that Dean was doing alright. Then we called Billie, but she and Hugh were out. We left a message that we would like to get together with them, along with Brian and Lila on Saturday evening for a farewell dinner. Later that evening, they called to accept our invitation.

**

After Hugh left for Melbourne, Billie moved in with us for the remaining two days of our holiday. Although she was sad because of Hugh's departure, her presence was still a reprieve from the reality we were facing. We had an unannounced visitor. Vijay introduced him as his best friend Chico.

"I have heard so much about Christine that I just had to come around to meet her before she left," he said shaking Billie's hand.

"Wrong," she said laughing.

"But you said she was Canadian so I automatically thought that this lady was Christine."

"Sorry to disappoint you," Billie said.

Vijay then introduced him to me and he still seemed a little confused.

"Nice to meet you Chico," I said.

"And who is this beautiful lady Jay?" he asked totally concentrating on Billie.

"Meet Billie," said Vijay. "She is Christine's friend. Billie also lived here back in the eighties when Christine was here."

"Now I see the connection. Have you got anything planned Jay? Why don't we go out for something to eat? I'm a little hungry."

"If the ladies don't mind, I won't mind."

Together we set out in Chico's open Jeep through the crowded streets of the city, Billie and I in the back seat laughing our heads off and the two men discussing where we should have dinner.

"It's been quite a while since I had Chinese food," said Chico. "I know the owner of a Chinese restaurant on Marine Drive. How about it?" he shouted with the wind whistling in our ears.

"Sounds good to me," said Vijay putting his hand back and searching for mine.

Without a reservation, we were still given one of the best seats in the restaurant. Billie was at her best. We were all in stitches by the time the dinner arrived at the table. Other patrons were looking our way and probably wishing they could've been in our dinner party. When the owner walked over to the table we were totally surprised. This was a restaurant we had frequented way back then. He remembered Billie and I and sat for a short while with us.

"Where did you meet Chico?" I asked once we were back at home.

"We were in university together."

"Is his name really Chico?" I asked.

"No his real name is Simon."

"So where does Chico come in?"

"Back in the seventies, we used to get these pirated American videos and there was one called Chico and the man which Simon loved. He actually thought he was Chico; so the name stuck."

"Why didn't you introduce him to us earlier?" asked Billie. "He is handsome."

"Your hands are already full," he said laughing. "Besides he already has a wife."

"Damn!" she said with a smile across her face.

"So when are you leaving for Australia?" Vijay asked.

"As soon as I have paid my bills and rented my house," she replied.

Since we were not ready for bed, Vijay brought out a bottle of champagne, and we sat on the couch and looked out onto the Arabian Sea, while Billie entertained us with her unbridled wit.

"I will miss Bombay," she suddenly said.

"What did you say?" I asked not believing my ears.

"I had a really great time. I forgot how wonderful life could be here."

"I think something's gone wrong with my hearing," I said.

"You heard right darling. I have a new lease on life."
"And you Christine?" Vijay asked
"What about me?"
"Do you also have a new lease on life?"
"She has," piped in Billie. "She has found the man of her dreams."
"Thank you Billie," he said hugging her.
"Don't get too close to him," I said to her. "He is all mine."
A beautiful smile crossed his lips which brought out his lovely dimples.

**

It was the worst of times. Tuesday was upon us and we were leaving that evening for the trip back to Canada. Billie and I had a last minute training session on the computer with Skyping. Vijay was online with his brother in London and pointed out all the pitfalls that could arise if we didn't do it properly. At least we could all see each other while we spoke. All that I carried in my suitcase were gifts for friends; my clothing was all left behind in the bedroom closet.

There were still no calls from Dean and as much as I wanted to say goodbye, I thought it best to leave him alone.

At that hour of the evening, there was still a traffic jam on the highway to the airport, and it seemed as if we were in a funeral procession. No one spoke. Vijay just held my hand all the way there.

"Call me if you need me," I whispered in his ear when I stepped out of the car. "I'll be on the next flight."

"I don't understand why you must go."

"You know why," I said kissing him on the cheek.

Billie hugged and squeezed him.

"Drive carefully," she said noticing the state he was in.

"I'll call as soon as I get in," I whispered.

"It doesn't matter what time it is, please call me immediately."

"I promise."

He showed a piece of identification to the guard at the door and then ushered us to the business class counter and we believed that since he was well known, he could take us there, but he had our tickets changed to Business Class tickets. The aircraft was full and he couldn't envisage us sitting in the back between the crowds.

"You shouldn't have done that," said Billie, "but thank you for your generosity."

He smiled.

There were more hugs and soon we made our way through the immigration checkpoint. I turned to look for him. He was still standing there among the crowds. I waved to him, but he didn't return the wave. He had lost sight of us.

23

My heart is heavy. After a frustrating two hours going through customs and immigration formalities and security, the latter which by all standards was the worst, we finally settled into our seats on board the aircraft. As I dug into my purse for a tissue, I realised I had forgotten to give him the cell phone back. I checked and there was a message. 'I love you. Hurry back,' it said.

"I love you too," I replied.

I could not stop the tears that had started to flow. This almost threw Billie into hysterics and she too burst into tears. Frustration along with my leaving Vijay tore at my heart. I turned my head and gazed out the window so that no one else could see my anguish, but the stewardess had noticed. We therefore had to explain that there were tears of joy. She smiled each time she walked by. I guess she realised exactly what 'tears of joy' meant.

"Then I should expect to see you on the way back sometime soon," she said sometime later.

I smiled. It was a tortuous journey over London and we were indeed glad we were not sitting in economy class.

**

After fifteen hours of being held prisoner on the aircraft, we were finally back in Toronto, and were both absolutely exhausted.

Billie spent the night with me since she had missed her connecting flight home. We spoke of our good fortune while enjoying a light snack which we had picked up on the way, and soon our weary bodies gave way to fatigue.

I reached over and picked up the telephone on the second ring. I had absolutely no idea where I was.

"You're home," he said as I picked up the telephone. "I was waiting to hear from you."

"I was going to call, but I was extremely tired. I cannot remember the last time I was this tired."

"I wanted to hear your voice and to know that you were safely at home."

"Billie is staying with me overnight. She missed her connecting flight. Thank you very much for that surprise at the airport. We really appreciated it."

"I will do anything in my power to make you happy Christine."

"That's very sweet Vijay. Have you heard anything from Dean?"

"No but I received a letter from Priddy's lawyer. She is not contesting the divorce, so it will be a matter of months before the whole thing is wrapped up."

"That makes me very happy. I miss you already," I said the excitement in my voice betraying me.

"I miss you too. Don't forget to buy the camera so that we can see and speak to each other."

"I'll check it out tomorrow and see if I can do it from here."

"It is relatively new here but there shouldn't be a problem. I'm dying to see you. The photo which we took at Juhu beach is now on the bedside table."

"Then you can still see me."

"Chico thinks you are pretty."

"Does he now? I felt so invisible. He had eyes only for Billie."

"That's the way he is. He loves blonde women. His wife is a little old fashioned but still nice. Anyway, we'll chat again tomorrow. What time is it there right now?"

"I'm not sure," I said switching on the bedside light. "It's fifteen minutes after midnight."

"I guess I should let you sleep."

"Call me tomorrow. I don't want to call your cell phone number. It would be too expensive."

**

The following morning I got up and walked to the computer store around the corner from my home. The young salesman informed me that skyping was not a popular thing in Canada but he knew how to do it. Desperation suddenly enveloped me. I needed to see Vijay's face.

"Do I need anything else?"

He explained what I needed and I bought it all.

"Do you know how to assemble it?" he asked.

"I'm not very sure. Perhaps you can help me."

"It takes about twenty minutes to put it together, if you know what you're doing."

"Why don't you come to my condo and assemble it for me. There's one hundred dollars in it for you."

"Are you serious?" he asked.

"Of course I'm serious."

On the way back, I stopped at the supermarket and picked up some items for breakfast. When I returned home, Billie was still asleep. I made breakfast and woke her from her slumber.

"I should be getting home," she said.

"Wait a little while and you can talk to Hugh."

"How am I going to do that?" she asked staring at me.

"I paid the young man in the computer store to come here and put the Skype thing together for me. Said he'd be here during his lunch hour. Around twelve thirty! Are you going to wait?"

"To see my sweetie? I guess I can do that."

At twelve thirty five, the door bell rang and I let him in. It took a little longer than he had anticipated and at one fifteen, we were skyping to Melbourne, Australia. Hugh was pleased to see and hear from Billie. Satisfied that we knew what to do, the young man left with one hundred dollars in his pocket, telling me that if I ran into difficulty, he was just a phone call away.

Then we tried to skype Vijay. His computer was not turned on, but I left mine on as the young man had advised. Billie left for home and I kept watching the computer until finally Vijay was on.

"See it wasn't that difficult," he said.

"I paid a young man at the computer store to put it together. You look good," I said.

"So do you."

His curiosity got the better of him and he wanted know about everything he could see via the camera. He thought it a well designed condominium and advised that I should remove my furniture before renting it. He had heard from Dr. Paxil and Dean was doing fine in spite of withdrawal pains. He had sent the divorce settlement to Priddy's lawyer and everything was sailing ahead full steam, but she wanted to keep the house in Daman in addition to the hefty settlement he had offered her. The house in Daman was the family home and he had always paid for the upkeep, so handing it over to her was out of the question. He informed me that she had decided to leave India and return to Italy, and when she leaves, he would encourage his mother to return to the peaceful town of Daman and her rental flat in Bombay would be passed on to Dean. He would however keep Dean by his side temporarily until he thought he was well enough to live alone. Lastly he said he had seen Ranjit on one of his rounds and he had asked about me.

"So are you starting your search today?" he finally asked.

"I decided to find a real estate agent who would also keep an eye on the condo in my absence, and make sure that the rent money is being deposited to my account."

"Very good idea," he said. "And how long will all this take?"

"I'm not sure. Hopefully not too long!"

"I have a great idea," he suddenly said. "Why don't I fly over to Toronto and we can get married there. Since neither of us is very religious, we can go the Justice of the Peace, spend a short honeymoon at Niagara Falls and then return here together. Besides it would be a great opportunity for me to see The Falls which I have heard so much about and have only seen on television."

He was moving way too quickly. Yes he loved me and wanted me there with him, but I needed time to sort my life out. After all, this was going to be a big change moving halfway around the world to a country with a completely different set of rules.

"You don't like my idea," he said.

"It's a great idea, but I have a lot of things to do which will take time."

"Alright, only when you are ready, I will come over."

**

Six weeks after our return, Billie called to say she would be stopping by to spend the night with me on her way to Melbourne. I was very happy for her and silently chastised myself for prolonging my return to Bombay and to Vijay.

I had three requests to rent my condo. The first was a young lady who had been transferred to the city to work in the head office of one of the major banks. I was impressed by her and asked why she wasn't interested in buying her own place. She did not intend making Toronto home and would hopefully one day be sent back to her hometown where she had already purchased an apartment. She was also interested in renting the condo fully furnished. The second was a young married couple whom I had absolutely no interest in because he was untidy and slopped across my floors in his wet running shoes. The third was an older lady, a young retiree who had sold her home in one of the city's prestigious neighbourhoods and wanted the freedom that a condominium would offer, but she had no interest in the furniture because she already had so much of her own that she needed to get rid of.

Finally I settled for the third lady; simply because she showed stability and there was income from her previous home. In addition, there wouldn't be any wild parties to destroy my retirement nest egg.

Vijay was happy with the news and promised that as soon as my business was finalised, he would be in Toronto to take me back to India.

My friends were horrified at the step I was about to take. Negativity poured in from every corner. I was annoyed, but I knew that they all had my best interest at heart.

"You take a four week trip to India, and return with the news that you will be packing up and moving there because of a holiday fling?"

"It isn't a holiday fling," I protested. "I have known him for more than twenty five years."

"We've never heard anything about him before."

"That's because we had lost contact with each other."

"And he has no wife? No children?"

I lied.

"Yes, he has a son from a previous marriage."

"So he's divorced."

"Yes."

"Don't you have to bring a dowry to the marriage in India?" asked another friend.

"Vijay is a modern man. He expects nothing from me."

"He doesn't, but his parents probably do. Are they alive? Have you met them?"

"His father is dead and yes I've met his mother."

"And what does she think of you?"

"Well…

"That's what I mean. She's probably looking for a fourteen year old virgin for her son."

I couldn't tell my friend how right he was. I couldn't tell him that she had referred to me as a Dalit, the lowest caste in Indian society.

"Well he's one in a million if he's going to marry you."

"Why not? You make it sound as if I have a disease," I said.

"I'm sorry Christine. It is not my intention to rain on your parade, but think carefully about what I'm going to say. Have you ever seen one of those men with a woman who looks like you? And even when they choose one of their own, their parents still try to force them into marriage with someone with whom they have absolutely nothing in common. Are you sure he isn't looking for someone to do the cooking and the washing and be his sex slave? Remember you have no backup over there. When they look at you, they will perhaps see a Black American or an African, although to me you don't represent either of these cultures; they won't see the proud and sophisticated black woman I see standing in front of me."

"You're going in the wrong direction honey," another said. "Everyone in Bombay is headed for Toronto."

Lying in bed that night, I asked myself the same questions. Was I making a mistake? Was it really love which he professed to me? Maybe I was rushing things. I should wait a little longer before I make that move to the other side of the world.

When the telephone rang, I knew instinctively it was him. What would I say to him? Should I tell him of my fears? Should I say I was getting cold feet? The sound of his voice wiped every doubt from my mind and I was once again ready and eager to make that important step.

**

In two days I will be moving in with two of my friends for a short stay. Vijay has also been invited to stay with them. After the cross examination from other friends, I knew I was safe with these two. They were more broadminded and would understand.

Vijay continued to call or to skype me every day. The news about Dean was reassuring. He had gone through his twelve week rehab and was now staying in the flat with his father, so that he could keep an eye on him and pour words of reassurance into his ears. It was also mandatory that he return to the clinic once a month for a full day. That way the doctors could keep check on his progress.

"I'm proud of you Dean. You haven't let me down," I said.

"I made that promise to you, and to Dad, but most of all to myself."

I noticed that his face was a little lean. He had lost a bit of weight during the program, but that I assume was only normal.

"When are you returning Christine? I miss you," he said.

"As soon as your father comes to get me," I replied. "There is still a lot to be done. The movers will be here the day after tomorrow and there are still some papers to sign which the real estate agent says she will be bringing around."

"Goodnight Christine," said Dean. "I'm tired and I'm going to bed."

"Goodnight Dean. Love you," I said.

"Love you too," he said with a smile and a wave.

"Does that mean you're almost ready to leave?" Vijay asked. "Are you still going to your friends' flat?"

"Yes. I'm going to Zack Neumann's and Josh Levy's condo in the city. They have asked me to stay with them and they are looking forward to meeting you."

"But Zack and Josh are both men's names," he said after a short pause.

"Of course. I told you about them. Josh is Jewish and Zack, well his background is all mixed up. He and I used to fly together."

"Oh yes! They are the two homosexual men," he said.

"Gay!"

"What about gay?" he innocently asked.

"In Canada, we don't talk about homosexuals. We say gay."

"I'm sorry Christine. I meant no offence. I don't know too much about these things. Here they never speak about it, and when they do, it is only in a negative manner."

"What do you mean?" I asked feeling a little annoyed.

"They consider it an unnatural act."

"Who are they? And what gives them the right to be so judgmental?"

"You know how some people are Christine."

"They should be ashamed because they are also guilty of many wrong doings. When a fourteen year old girl is forced into a marriage with a sixty year old man, and made to bear his children when her body is not yet mature enough for the trauma of childbirth; that's an unnatural act. When she leaks urine continuously and can't stand her own body odour because of that trauma that was imposed upon her; that too is an unnatural act. When smashing a child's head at birth because it happens to be born female, tolerating a man's right to beat his wife or distorting children's bodies for the sake of money! That's what they should be concentrating on and trying to change. Those I consider unnatural acts. What two consenting adults do is no one's business but their own. Where are the laws that protect women?"

"These are not my opinions Christine. I was just expressing to you the general opinion regarding that kind of lifestyle here in India."

"What gives them the right to be so self righteous?"

"I know that my country is not perfect and that we still have a long way to go. Luckily the younger generation don't think the same way. "

"I'm sorry Vijay. This is not meant to be directed at you. I just hate hypocrisy and narrow minded thinkers. My friends' relationship has lasted more than thirty years. As a matter of fact, it has lasted much longer than many traditional marriages and I consider them both my very dear friends, gay or not."

"Let's start again Christine. We've just started on the wrong foot today. I love you."

"I love you too. Josh and Zack can't wait to meet you."

"I can't wait to meet them. Your friends are also my friends."

"That's the attitude," I replied.

24

The contents of my condominium have been placed in storage and I, along with my two suitcases, have moved into my friends' swanky condo. A backdrop of the CN Tower and the Rogers Centre light up the night sky, as I stare out of their living room penthouse window which runs from floor to ceiling. Such a condo I couldn't afford, but Josh is a stock broker and is very successful at what he does. Zack had also worked and flown with me and had experienced all that Bombay had to offer. He introduced me to Josh and we have been friends for more than twenty eight years. However Zack was not happy with the changes which were coming into my life, and that surprised me. Everything he said, was moving much too quickly. He had seen the good side and the bad side of Bombay for he was usually the first one up in the morning taking photos and exploring the city with his camera around his neck. He knew their way of thinking especially when it came to foreign women, and although I had never had a rude word spoken to me nor an insult thrown my way, my friend was still sceptical about what I was about to do.

"You have no-one over there. If something happens to you, there is no one to call," he said.

"Is he worth it?" Josh asked. "We don't know too much about them."

"You were smart. You didn't sell your condo."

"Is he good in bed?"

"He certainly is!"

"Well I can't wait to meet him to see if he's good enough for our sister," said Zack.

I assured them that all would be well and there was no need to panic on my account. They could all come over and visit when I made the move. However their main worry was the way I may be treated as a black woman living in India. They had heard stories about wife burnings and young women turned into slaves for the husband's family and this worried them. Vijay was a modern man, a wealthy man with his own business which he and his brother founded when they left the university. After my many reassurances, they seemed to relax.

They were out for the evening with friends. They had gone to the theatre and then out for dinner, so there was enough time for me to reflect on my life and also get on the computer to skype to India. Vijay insisted I turn the camera in all directions so that he could see the condo and I pointed out the CN Tower and the Rogers Centre in the background. He told me his ticket had been booked for the following Tuesday and he would be arriving on the Emirates flight from Dubai. I became extremely excited for it was now almost six months since I had seen him and I missed him terribly.

"There is only one setback," he said. "I haven't got the divorce papers in my hands, so we can't be married in Toronto."

"I can wait," I said. "I have already waited twenty five years."

He laughed.

"By the way, Anand Banerjee called Dean into the office. He has now been working for two days."

"Does he like it?"

"He hasn't said very much, but I'm sure he's does because he has been whistling up a storm. I think I'll get him a car for his birthday, so that he can be on time for work."

"I know he would love that."

**

I am extremely nervous. It's Tuesday and Vijay will be arriving in Toronto today. Zack and I took the airport bus and went to meet him. My heart missed a thousand beats while I waited. Suppose he doesn't show up! Suppose he missed the flight! Relief washed over me when he appeared looking even more handsome than I remembered and when I pointed him out to Zack, he too was impressed by his good looks. I saw Vijay's eyes searching the crowds and finally he saw me, when Zack started bouncing up and down and waving his arms like if he was on a pogo stick. Vijay's eyes lit up when he finally saw me.

"We must take a limo back home," said Zack. "We can't put him on the airport bus."

"Don't be silly," I said. "Anyway, what did you expect? A handcart operator?"

"You've got good taste darling. First impressions count. We are taking a limo back home. We can't let him think that we can't afford this little bit of luxury," Zack replied.

He made his way through the crowds and came to us, smiling all the while.

"He is handsome," said Zack. "Watch out."

We hugged and this brought stares from the onlookers, especially the Indians in the crowd who were waiting for their relatives to come through the customs exit.

"Welcome to Canada. So you are Vijay," said Zack. "You are the one who's taking our sister away from us!"

"You may visit her whenever you like. I also expected to see Josh. Where is he?" asked Vijay.

"Someone has to earn a living. He's still at work," said Zack.

"I can't believe that you remembered Josh's name," I whispered.

"I wanted to make a good impression," he said smiling.

"You certainly have."

All the way back to Toronto, we giggled and laughed like three teenagers until the limo driver stopped in front of the building and took his case from the trunk. Vijay looked around at the financial district with its imposing bank towers, all the while holding my hand and smiling. Zack paid the limo driver, picked up the case and we climbed into the elevator where the door opened onto their beautiful condo.

"This is beautiful," said Vijay as Zack opened the blinds and the CN Tower came into view.

"This condo offers several views," said a proud Zack guiding him from one window to another where he could now see the Rogers Centre with a closed roof. "If there is a game on tonight, they will open the roof. It is quite spectacular. You'll get to see it before you leave I'm sure."

Vijay seemed thrilled with what he had already seen. He kept staring out the window pulling me to his side each time, and just like in his flat, he noticed everything was operated by remote control.

"You must be tired," said Zack. "Christine, will show you to the bathroom and bedroom. You may want to freshen up or take a quick nap after such a long flight."

I left him to unpack his case, while I returned to the family room where Zack sat cross legged on the sofa drinking a beer.

"He is really cute."

"And he's all mine," I replied.

"I'm home," a voice called out from the direction of the hallway. It was Josh "I swear this blasted job is going to kill me. Where is he?"

"Please don't let it kill you," said Zack in a playful manner. "Who would pay for all this? Anyhow be careful with your language, Vijay is a gentleman."

I couldn't help but laugh at Zack's quick wit.

"Where is the ring? When will we celebrate?" asked Josh.

"One question after the other," said Zack. "What are we doing later?"

"Let's go out for dinner. Let's show Vijay what our city looks like."

Suddenly Josh's exchange with Zack came to an end when Vijay walked into the living room. Josh's mouth dropped open and he stared at Vijay.

"You must be Josh," said Vijay extending his hand.

"I want a hug," said Josh. "You are even better looking than Christine described you."

"He's gorgeous, isn't he?" I said feeling rather pleased.

It was the first time I saw him blush. There was way too much attention being focused on him. Josh brought out a bottle of champagne and four glasses.

"This really calls for a celebration. Let's go out for dinner and show Vijay a little of what life is like in Toronto. It doesn't make any sense sleeping right now," he said. "You'll never sleep later if you sleep now; not that you will do any kind of sleeping anyway."

"Josh!" shouted Zack. "He's always like that Vijay. Just ignore him."

It was difficult making a decision what we should eat because the city offered so much in the way of restaurants. Finally we settled on a quaint Japanese restaurant because Vijay loved Sushi, something which was not readily available in Bombay. The Sake flowed and we laughed. We talked and talked, then we ate more and drank more until Vijay's eyes began to close.

"It has been a rather long journey so I am afraid my bed is calling," he said apologetically.

With that, he signalled to the waiter and the fight started over who would pay the bill.

"I am staying in your beautiful flat, so please allow me to pay for dinner."

"Yes please let him pay," I intervened.

That settled we started on the ten minute trek home, encountering throngs of theatre goers and late night revellers. Vijay kept stepping to the side whenever a crowd came in our direction or when someone seemed to be headed straight towards us.

"Is something wrong?" Zack asked.

"Old habits," he replied.

"What habits?" Zack asked looking at me.

"Have you forgotten? In Bombay when someone or a group is headed your way, they could be beggars."

"We don't have that here," said Josh. "The Government would have them off the streets in no time. If you see a beggar here, he is usually someone who is a little ga-ga in the head. They won't bother you."

"At this time of the night in Bombay, you must take your life into your hands and must walk directly in the street, because every square inch of the pavement has been turned into someone's bedroom," I said.

"Is that where you are going to live?" asked Josh. "Zack told me a lot about Bombay but I didn't realise it was that bad."

"It just takes getting used to," Zack said.

"And where is the government? Don't they look after their people?" Josh asked looking at Vijay.

"These things are deeply ingrained in our society so it will take time to change them. There are changes, but it is all very slow. There is a lot of corruption. You pay for every little thing under the table. Every man, woman and child has an outstretched hand. Take this evening for example. We had no reservation for the restaurant. In Bombay you first give the maitre'd a bribe and then you will get the best table in the house."

"But it is their job. If someone is kind to us, we may slip him a few dollars but it is not compulsory. Doesn't it bother you?" asked Josh.

"Of course it does, but I am only one person and as Zack said, you get used to it."

Back in the foyer of the building Vijay looked around at the beautiful lobby as if he were seeing it for the very first time. Everything was in its place, nice and shiny and new; and they greeted the security guard like a long lost friend.

"Everything quiet tonight Pierre?" asked Zack.

"More or less! There's a party in the penthouse on the other side, but that wouldn't affect you. You've got guests," the man finally said.

"Yes, you remember Christine! This is her friend who came all the way from India."

"Do you like Toronto sir?"

"It's beautiful," Vijay replied.

"Goodnight Pierre," the two men said.

"Goodnight sir. Have a nice night, and have a great holiday in our city," he said to Vijay."

Vijay was impressed. The main entrance door he noticed was not locked, but one still had to get past the security guard. In Bombay, an open door would be paradise for a beggar. You would probably wake up one morning and find him stretched out on the couch. Nothing like that happened in this fair city. He had been to London, Dubai and a few more big cities, but Toronto was special.

"I'm trying to read your mind," said Josh. "You are planning to uproot everything and move to our beautiful city."

We all burst out laughing and I knew that something like that had been playing around in his head.

"Goodnight children," said Zack.

"By the way, close the blinds when you are changing. If you don't, you will most likely end up on that big screen down on the field," said Josh.

Vijay was way too tired for any shenanigans, for no sooner had our heads hit the pillows, than we both fell asleep. Blame it on the Sake. When we awoke the following morning, we could hear voices. Josh was still at home.

"I'm sorry about last night," Vijay said.

"Why?" I asked pretending I didn't know what he meant.

"After not seeing you for almost six months, I have been negligent in my duties."

"You were tired."

"What would Ranjit say? One thousand pardons Madam."

We laughed and I asked about Ranjit. He said that when he

heard he was coming to Canada, he wanted to know if he would take a box of mangoes for me to which he emphatically said no. He said that Ranjit had also moved into the little flat which the foremen had found and he, Ranjit was busy making repairs to it. He had apparently learnt some carpentry skills when he was in the Government orphanage and was now putting them to use.

There was laughter coming from the direction of the kitchen, so I went out to see what was going on. Josh and Zack were both were sitting at the island in the kitchen, and Josh's head was wrapped in a tourniquet.

"What's the matter with you?" I asked.

Zack laughed until the tears rolled down his cheeks.

"He had way too much Sake last night and now he has a monster of a headache."

"And what's with the cloth around his head?"

"He said the women in his family usually wrapped a cool cloth around their heads when they had a headache."

"And does it help?" I asked rubbing his shoulders, trying to hold back my laughter.

"Get away from me. You are no better than Zack."

"Did you put Epsom salts inside it?" I asked.

"Was I supposed to do that?" he asked.

At this point we were both rolling on the floor which brought Vijay from the bedroom, and we had to repeat the story all over again.

"Vijay, you and I are going to see a bit of Toronto today," said Josh. "I'm going to take you up to the CN Tower, but I won't go if those two are going."

"He's just joking," I said when I noticed Vijay staring at me.

It was all just cultural.

The heat was suffocating as we stepped outside for the short walk to the Tower. There were long lines for the ride to the top, but we finally made it past security and we knew we would be at the pinnacle in just a matter of minutes.

"Everything is so clean," Vijay whispered to me. "I love London, but that too is a little bit filthy. How do they manage to keep everything so clean and sanitary-looking?"

"Hordes of workers I believe, and proud citizens."

There was not a cloud in the sky to impede the view from above. We pointed out places of interest that could only be seen from that vantage point. Queen's Quay, Toronto Island, The Go Train! He had a thousand questions regarding the Tower, no longer the tallest free-standing structure in the world, since Dubai had outdone us. We spent almost one hour going from one vantage point to the next.

"Something smells good," Vijay said.

"Overpriced food," said Josh. "I'll take you to one of our favourite lunch spots. "It's a haven for junk food."

"At this time?" asked Zack.

The two men knew each other well and could read each other's minds.

"It's already two thirty. They're all back at their desks," Josh replied.

Since Josh had called in sick that morning, it wouldn't have been wise for him to be seen by his co-workers enjoying lunch in a restaurant. We took the elevator to the ground floor where Vijay bought some souvenirs for Dean. A T shirt with a photo of the Tower, two baseball caps and two bottles of maple syrup! I also bought two baseball caps.

The junk food turned out to be the juiciest double hamburgers with sauerkraut, onions and bacon. This was accompanied by some exotic type of French fried potatoes and we ordered beer to wash it all down.

"I think we should get the waiter back here," said Zack. "There is bacon on the hamburger."

"So?" asked a surprised Josh.

"I'm sorry. We forgot to ask you," said Zack turning to Vijay.

"It's not a problem. I eat everything."

Relief registered across Zack's face. After our heavy lunch, we walked through the underground mall, stopping and shopping for all the goodies we intended taking back with us.

"This must be perfect during the winter months," said Vijay.

"It is perfect. You don't have to wear a coat because it is sometimes way too warm down here."

"Fantastic!" was all he could say.

In four hours, we were back at the condo. Although it was hot, I noticed Vijay didn't seem as agitated as he usually was when we were out and about in Bombay. One always had the desire to have a good wash after being in the city because it always seemed as if the grime, the dirt and the stench had possessed your body. Toronto it was different. When Zack opened the door, we could hear movement inside the condo.

"Isabel," shouted Josh. "Is that you?"

"Yes Josh," said the woman coming from the area of our bedroom.

"Hello Christine, did you have a good time in India?" she asked affectionately rubbing my shoulder.

"This is my girlfriend," said Josh hugging and kissing the woman. "This is Christine's friend Vijay."

"He's good looking," she replied. "Did you also bring me one?"

"One of what?" whispered Vijay.

"A good looking man," said Zack.

The woman disappeared back down the hall and Vijay smiled.

"Who is she?" he whispered in my ear.

"The cleaning lady," I whispered back.

He thought of Pula, the woman who had cleaned his flat and his mother's flat for over seven years. He had never had a real conversation with her, furthermore to touch her. He had no idea where she lived. She showed up at his home three times per week, and he had always left her pay on the kitchen table. Did she have a family? He didn't know. Was she married? He also didn't know.

25

Day five of Vijay's visit and he had seen more of Toronto than I who had lived here most of my life. Josh took a couple days off from work and we went on a city tour on the Hop on, Hop Off double-decker bus. We drove to Queens Quay, Eaton Centre, through Yorkville, The Rom Museum, Casa Loma, a big old castle on a hill and finally to China Town where we disembarked.

"Time for lunch," said Josh. "Do you like Dim Sum?"

"I don't know what that is," Vijay replied.

"You will like it. At least, let's give it a try," I said.

We were led to our table and our salivary glands started to overflow.

"So what do you think?" asked Zack.

"It's different, but quite tasty."

We kept looking around at what the other Chinese diners were ordering and we ordered the same. Soon it was time to go, and with bloated bellies, we dragged ourselves out the door.

"Are we walking home?" I asked.

"It's only a ten minute walk from here. It will help with our digestion," said Zack laughing.

We kept walking and Vijay kept looking at all the foods hanging in the windows of the Chinese restaurants. He kept staring at the delicious, brown Peking ducks hanging by their necks in the restaurant windows.

"They look good, don't they?" I said.
"We'll have to try some of it sometime," he replied.
"Trust me. They are delicious," I said.

The following morning, we bundled into their little Toyota, which was not at all representative of their lifestyle and set out for Niagara Falls.

"Don't worry Vijay," Josh said lovingly patting the steering wheel. "She only looks fragile, but she isn't. She will get us there and back. We don't see the necessity in buying a new car because as you can see, we walk just about everywhere."

"That makes sense. In Bombay everyone has a car whether or not he needs it. If you think that the traffic jams are bad here, you should see Bombay at five o'clock in the evening."

It was a beautiful ride with Josh at the wheel, driving over the Skyway Bridge, with the industrial town of Hamilton on the right and the turbulent Lake Ontario with its shipwrecks on the left; then through the fruit region, passing the vineyards on the way to Niagara Falls.

"There they are," said Zack as The Falls came into view.

"We will get a little closer," said Josh. "Let's get Betsy parked and we can do a little exploring."

After waiting approximately ten minutes in line to park, we finally reached the cashier.

"That's twenty two dollars sir," said the parking attendant holding out her hand.

"Twenty two dollars?" shouted Josh. "Is lunch included in that? I only want to park here for a few hours, not buy the whole parking lot."

Vijay handed her twenty five dollars and without a smile, she handed him the change back.

"They certainly know how to rob the poor. Imagine asking for twenty two dollars just for parking!" Josh continued.

We followed the sign which read 'Maid of the Mist,' and were surprised at the length of the queue. We thought we would be there forever. However the wait was relatively short and we received our raincoats and suited ourselves up for the ride to the foot of The Falls. It was a beautiful day, but quite windy and our eyes devoured everything along the way. We leaned against the rails and listened to the hum of the motor as the boat slowly made its way towards the cascading waterfall. Soon we were there. Right at the foot of Niagara Falls! It was magical. From afar, it looked like a quiet cascading waterfall, but close up, it roared like thunder as thousands of gallons of water gushed into the chasm below, spraying our hands and faces with the cool mist. Our raincoats offered little protection for the onslaught, but it didn't matter, for we were having the time of our lives. Our clothes were partially saturated and we could hear the water sloshing around in our shoes. The boat made a U turn and soon we were back where we started.

"I am soaked," said Josh as we disposed of our raincoats in the recycling bin, and then removed our shoes to get rid of the water.

"That was beautiful," said Vijay laughing like a kid in a candy store. "How often do you do this?"

"This was the first time for me, and I think for Josh also," Zack said.

"How about you Christine?"

"First time," I said laughing.

"All this beauty and you don't enjoy it?"

"We have this here just for the tourists," said Josh laughing out loudly.

Our next stop was the gallery above The Falls, where we witnessed the water meandering from the Niagara River and then gushing over the Horse Shoe Falls. We could see the American Falls in the distance, but they were not as impressive as those on the Canadian side. We all wished we had kept our rain coats because the spray was so heavy, that we were all soaked again.

"You'll dry pretty quickly," I said.

It was imperative that we pay a visit to the souvenir shops where we bought more gifts for Dean and a few items for the Gowdi family. Then it was off to Lundy's Lane because we were parked close by. No one seemed interested in the casinos or the shopping, so we set out for the quaint little town of Niagara on the Lake with its horse-drawn carriages and exclusive shops. The town was beautifully decorated with colourful flower baskets hanging from each lamp post. The median which divided the street was also a flower lover's paradise. Tourists and locals alike perched on the benches in the park or just lay in the sun as the squirrels happily gathered chestnuts which had fallen from the trees. When Vijay spotted the Christmas store, he said it was a must. We left the store with three bags filled with Christmas decorations.

"What are you going to do with all this stuff?" Zack asked.

"Our first Christmas together," he said smiling at me.

He was absolutely impressed with Niagara on the Lake.

"Why can't they do something like this in Bombay?" he said out loud.

"I guess it's not that important to them."

"Everything is so clean and so beautifully laid out," he said his eyes darting around.

We set out again, this time for the Niagara Region. There we would have a late lunch and explore the vineyards that are famous for the wines of the region. We followed the curve of the river and then turned off into the fruit growing region. Fruit and vegetable stalls lined the sides of the streets and the homes in the area were spectacular. Our first sighting of the vineyards came into view, and we knew the restaurants were also close by. We eventually found one run by one of the region's famous chefs, and since it was late afternoon, we had no trouble getting a good table. We settled for a bottle of Chardonnay and chose from the day's menu which was mainly Italian. I could smell the aroma of garlic coming from the kitchen. It was our Bruschetta. After a delicious meal, and with the afternoon sun moving towards the west, we started our journey home, stopping only to purchase wine for which the region was famous.

Vijay had grown used to Josh's quick wit and no longer took anything he said seriously. He knew that under that quick exterior, Josh was a very sensible person, who worked hard and was good at what he did. The men discussed property values and compared prices in Bombay and Toronto, and the discussions went from one topic to the other.

"Do you mind if I call my son?" Vijay asked.

"Why don't you skype him?" asked Josh. "We want to say hello to him too."

We all crowded around the computer and waited.

"Hello Dean, how are things with you?" his father asked.

"Hi Dad, everything's fine. I can see Christine, but who are all those people behind you?"

"They are Christine's friends, our friends," he said correcting himself. "How are things going with Anand Banerjee?"

"Everything's going just fine," he said.

"Back up a little," said Josh. "I want to see that painting on the left wall."

"That's by an Indian artist called Ray. At least he signs everything with Ray."

"Gorgeous apartment," said Zack. "Ask him to give us a tour."

They were pleased that I was moving into such a prestigious residence. The décor they found very tasteful until Dean finally moved the camera to the second bedroom.

"Sorry about the mess Dad. I haven't had time to hang my things up."

"Just make sure you do it before we return."

"Does that mean that Christine is really coming back with you?"

"She most certainly will be back with me next week."

"I can't wait to see her," he said with the broadest of smiles.

They finished the conversation and we all retired to the living area where more discussions regarding life in the big cities continued. Suddenly Zack grew quiet and withdrawn.

"Is something wrong?" asked Vijay. "You seem rather quiet."

"Don't ask," said Josh. "He is losing his bosom buddy."

"Who is his bosom buddy?"

"Who do you think? Christine of course!"

"Our doors will be wide open and you can come at anytime. As a matter of fact, we expect you to be there for the wedding. My fiancé," he said tightening his arms around my shoulders, "doesn't want anything grand. So it will be a small gathering for just a few selected friends."

"We'll be there," said Josh. "But can you get rid of the beggars before we arrive?"

"I'll do my best," he replied with a smile.

Two days before our departure, the two men said they had a surprise for us. We were going to Casino Rama to see Vijay's favourite singer, The Goddess herself, Diana Ross. Vijay was elated because he was a great fan of that special lady. We would be travelling by limo so that we could all have a drink and not worry about who would do the driving.

She was beyond beautiful when she appeared on the stage in a full length red dress. The crowd went wild. Someone shouted out, "Sing Baby Love." She put her hand over her eyes and stared into the audience.

"Who said that?" she asked peering into the crowd.

The fellow whose name was Joe was the culprit and was now everyone's focus.

"I will sing it for you Joe, but a little later in the program."

The man blew her a kiss and she returned one. Her first song was 'I hear a symphony.' I looked at Vijay's face. His eyes didn't blink. He was staring at the goddess on the stage. After each number, there was a costume change and the crowd just couldn't get enough of her.

"This is my final number," she said in that soft gentle voice. "Turn up the lights. I'm looking for Joe."

The spotlight scanned the audience and Joe waved to her.

"Come on up here," she said. "I want you to sing 'Baby Love' with me."

Without hesitating, Joe sprang from his seat and appeared on the stage beside her. As if he suddenly realised what had happened to him, he stepped away from her.

"Don't be afraid of me," she said to the roar of the audience.

They sang together, Joe totally out of tune, but a good time was had by all. There were two encores and she finally left the stage.

I am called Ranjit

"So what did you think?" asked Zack.
"I've never seen anything quite like it. She is beautiful."

Toronto had left its imprint on Vijay's mind. We stared out the window at the beauty that is Toronto by night. It looked like the city of lights with its imposing well-lit office buildings; Lake Ontario which now seemed tranquil, railway tracks which ran below and carried commuters from the suburbs back and forth into the city with the throbbing pulse.

I know he liked the uncomplicated ways of the city; the ease with which one could go about one's daily life. There wasn't the rigid class system and people did not stand on ceremony. His favourite expression was, 'Have a nice day.' It was difficult for him to comprehend how well so many people of different ethnic origins got along together. Toronto had also swallowed up a large part of the Indian population, but those people seemed miles away from the streets of Bombay and other cities on the Indian subcontinent. They laughed together. They savoured the cuisines from China, The Caribbean, Thailand, Japan and Sri Lanka. Many of these immigrants, his fellow Indians, had fit right into this swelling metropolis. He was not naïve to think that everything worked one hundred per cent, but at least ninety nine per cent.

"Did you enjoy your stay?" Josh asked Vijay the night before our departure.
"Every minute of it! You were the perfect hosts."
"Was there anything you wanted to do that you didn't have a chance to do?"
"I'm sure there was, but what I did see and what I did, I enjoyed tremendously. Thank you for being so hospitable to me and my

fiancé."

"Love it!" shouted Zack.

"Vijay, I must tell you something," said Josh.

"What is it?" asked an anxious Vijay.

"When Christine told us that she was going to marry someone from Bombay, I thought she had gone totally mad. How could she give up everything which she worked for to move to India? We hear horror stories here on a weekly basis about the way women are treated by the husband's family and we were very afraid for her."

"We know better now," said Zack interrupting him.

"I've still got to tell Vijay what I thought. As I was saying, we were extremely afraid for our sister. Here she was leaving her safety net and flying off to a city where she knew no-one. Believe me, I tried to talk her out of it, but then I met you and I changed my mind. You are a decent human being and not only that, a damned good looking one too."

Vijay smiled.

"Anyway, I know that Christine will be in safe hands, and we have seen where she will be laying her head at night. So we approve of the marriage."

"Thank you for being so honest with me. You have nothing to worry about as far as Christine is concerned. I love her dearly and I have waited for twenty five years to hear her say yes. And now that she has said the word, I have no intention of letting her escape."

As if on cue, the two men stood up.

"Thank you for being honest with me," said Vijay.

"Who could that be?" asked Josh when the telephone rang.

"Send him up," said Zack.

It was the Chinese delivery!

"Don't let him go before you've checked for the Peking Duck."

"It's there," said Zack.

The table was impeccably laid for our feast. It looked as if they were expecting some very special guest.

"Everything looks wonderful," said Vijay.

"Nothing but the best for our friends," they said almost in unison.

They had ordered Peking duck especially for Vijay. In the bag there was also orange chicken, sweet and sour pork, hot and spicy shrimp, dumplings, noodles, rice and lots and lots of vegetables. We didn't realise how hungry we were.

"And you thought we would send you back to Bombay without tasting Peking duck?" asked Zack.

"Thank you. You think of everything."

We will be leaving the following afternoon for the trip back to India and my heart is filled with sorrow in spite of the handsome man standing beside me. He hugged me as I struggled to hold back the tears.

"Christine, I realise this is your home and how much you love it. I love it too but I have a business that without me would be bankrupt. I would love to have you by my side, to become my wife, but am I asking too much? I see the closeness you have with your friends. I see how uncomplicated life is here."

"There is also something you haven't noticed. Josh and Zack are partners in every way. That is something I too want for myself. Someone in my life to protect me, someone I can call my partner and be there for me when I need him to be there. Don't you want the same things too? Of course the differences between the two cities are miles apart, but I have made the choice to follow you to your home. I know it won't be easy. I know there will be a period of adjustment, but at least I have already looked the dragon in the eye and conquered him."

He buried my head against his chest.

"Thank you Christine. Sometimes I had the feeling I would be leaving alone. Thank you. Let's go to bed. We must be up early to say goodbye to Josh. What can we give them to say thanks for being such great hosts?"

"I don't know," I said as we curled up against each other and fell asleep.

"I know what we can give them," I said upon opening my eyes the next morning.

"What?"

"They love the theatre and classical concerts. Let's give them something like that."

Josh's farewell was an emotional one. He had enjoyed our company for two weeks and said he would really miss us. After he left, I spoke to Zack regarding the tickets, but he was adamant that they needed nothing.

"Vijay will be very insulted if you don't allow him to get the tickets," I said to him.

"Is this an Indian thing? Alright I'll go with you and see what there is and then we can make a decision."

We purchased the tickets and strolled along the street, stopping by one of the street vendors where we bought some very tasty hot dogs, smothered in onions, pickled peppers and sauerkraut.

It was time to go and another tearful farewell awaited us as Zack accompanied us downstairs. Before I stepped into the limo, I waved my ticket in his face.

"Business class?" he asked with wide eyes. "You are really now our little princess."

We kept waving to him as the limousine made a right turn onto Yonge Street obstructing him completely from our view. We stared at the beautiful buildings until the limo sped onto the highway that would take us to the airport.

26

Nestled comfortably on the Emirates flight six months after my return from India, I stare out the window at the last remnants of the city I had called home for as long as I can remember. As the aircraft slowly made its way to the takeoff position, we held hands and smiled at each other. I watched the flight attendants running up and down with their ready smiles, and wondered how I could've done that job for such a long time. They were young and beautiful and nothing seemed to be too much trouble for them. It was a long flight. We will be spending one night in Dubai, a city I hadn't visited since the eighties. Back then, we had ferried workers back and forth, who either worked in construction or the young women who were seeking their fortunes working as maids in the homes of the wealthy. I remember it as a little non-descript fishing village with nothing much to do, but today as the aircraft circled the city, I saw the landmark wonders that had put her on the world map during the last twenty years. Impressive structures like The Burj Al Arab, The Palm Islands and the many beautiful hotels which dominated the Dubai skyline said money, and lots of it. The super rich made it their playground and those who couldn't afford to own a piece of the country, hung around with those who did.

Without Vijay by my side, I wouldn't have seen much of the city. There was nothing that I could afford, but he showered me with expensive perfumes and two designer bags, which I would most likely need in Bombay. It was the look that counted.

We did not stay at The Burj Al Arab, but our hotel was just as spectacular. We awoke early in the morning and did a bit of shopping, taking in the wonders in the most modern shopping mall in the world. I was happy to leave the country. As beautiful as it was, I found it just a little too sterile and way too perfect.

**

We left Dubai behind, and after a four and a half hour flight the city of Bombay came into view. I was looking forward to a long rest and also to see Dean again. At four thirty we landed at Chhatrapati Shivaji International airport. Even though I had travelled in and out of the airport so many times in the past, I had never really seen it by day. The first and business class passengers led the way to Immigration. It was easy and uncomplicated even though I was only entering the country on a holiday visa. During the immigration protocol Vijay provided the answers to all the questions that were asked. Our luggage quickly arrived and after a few questions, we were simply waved through customs. It was quite the opposite of the trip Billie and I had made on the way there. Did they know Vijay or did they know his name? I am truly convinced that money talks, especially in this part of the world. We stepped outside and waited for the Ambassador to pick us up. A couple minutes later, we climbed into the vehicle for the journey home. If only that ride was as easy as going through customs formalities! Rush hour! Traffic was either heading into the city or away from the city. Bollywood music followed the news and this seemed to stimulate my senses and I fell asleep.

I opened my eyes expecting to be in downtown Toronto, but

I was back in Bombay and the gates to the condo complex were slowly opening. My eyes immediately fell upon a man who was standing outside the complex wall and urinating. We stared at him and he stared back, contempt in his eyes. His expression said it all.

Yes I am pissing against your rich white wall and there's nothing you can do about it.

When he was finished, he shook his instrument and placed it back inside his trousers. Then he jiggled his body a bit, shaking it into place, and walked away wiping his hand on the side of his trousers.

"Welcome back to Bombay," Vijay said.

We were expecting to find Dean in the flat, but instead we found a note.

Hello Dad and Christine,

Am going straight to Granny after work. I am longing to see you both, but I know you would like some privacy on your first night back. I'll come around tomorrow before I go home. Work is great. Anand is very nice. I have the article which he wrote on Ranjit Gowdi. You will love it Christine. Hope you brought me lots of gifts.

Dean

P.S. Mom is back in Daman. Says she has a lot of packing to do.

We promised we would call Zack and Josh the following morning, and after a quick shower, we settled into bed. Sleep came easily for both of us as we were absolutely exhausted.

It was still dawn. The sun had not yet put in an appearance when Vijay got out of bed and went to the bathroom and I could hear him grumbling. There was a power failure and we were left in the dark. He stumbled back into the bedroom, found a flashlight and returned to the bathroom. I hoped that he could see where he was aiming.

"Why don't we pack up and move to Canada?" he asked nuzzling on my ear.

"Didn't we just return here from there?" I asked laughing.

"No, let's get out of here. Let's go somewhere where everything works."

"Canada too has its drawbacks," I replied.

"Name one," he said.

We had fallen asleep again when the phone disturbed us. Vijay reached over and answered it.

"Have you any idea what time it is?" he asked glancing at the clock.

My thoughts went straight to Dean, but it was Sabia.

"What can I do for you at this ungodly hour Priddy?"

"I just wanted to let you know that I am back in India and I'm waiting on the cheque to get the ball rolling."

"You should contact your lawyer. He should be aware of everything that's going on. I contact mine when I have a question."

"I'll do that. Dean is doing very well. I didn't know that you knew Anand Banerjee personally."

"I don't."

"Dean said that he knows you."

"He knows my name. Christine introduced Dean to Mr. Bannerjee."

"She certainly hasn't wasted anytime getting to know who's who of Bombay."

"Didn't you do the same?"

"No need to get testy with me Vijay darling. Is she coming back to India?"

"That goes without saying Priddy. As a matter of fact she is already here."

"She returned with you?" she quietly asked.

"Yes she did."

"I can't believe you really did this to me. I've got to go. I'll be in touch with you if I don't hear anything from my lawyer by the weekend. I should let you know that I have decided to return to Italy permanently."

"I have already heard that from Dean."

"You have made me look very little in front of our friends Vijay. I have no choice but to leave."

"You knew that sooner or later, this would happen. It's just that I hadn't met anyone before that I felt comfortable enough with. Now I have found that person, wish me happiness."

"You have no soul Vijay. I hope she sees the way you are treating me."

"Priddy!" he said after hanging up the phone.

"I gathered that much."

It was no use trying to sleep so we got up to have breakfast but there was nothing in the kitchen. Luckily the inverter had kicked in and we had temporary power. Later in the morning, the electrical power had been restored. Dean hadn't thought about groceries and since he hadn't left Pula any money to do the shopping, there was nothing to be had.

"What will you do with your time now that you are here permanently?" he asked.

"What all the other wealthy women do with theirs."

"I'm serious. What will you do?"

"Well I thought of helping out Janice at the orphanage. I will clean and cook your dinner and be here for you when you return home tired in the evening."

"Wealthy women don't clean and cook Christine. They are household servants who do all that."

"I don't need a household servant."

"This is India Christine. That's the way things are done here. Everyone needs household help. It not only helps with the economy, it always helps the less fortunate. Don't go against the grain. People will think that I am stingy, putting my wife to do the housework. I can picture you out there," he said smiling, "trying to buy food. Those vendors will have a wonderful time with you. They will cheat you at every turn."

"Well we can't have that, can we? Maybe we could ask Ranjit if his wife would be willing to work here."

"I knew that was coming. What would we do with Pula? She has been with me for seven years."

"Maybe she would prefer to go to your mother fulltime. Since I'll be here most of the time, the flat will need more cleaning; there will be more laundry to take care of and Amrit can do the shopping for your dinner."

He laughed.

"In addition I don't know if I can trust someone who comes here and then goes to your mother's home. She has known your mother much longer than she has known me and her allegiance I'm sure will be to her."

"I can understand your concerns. You have certainly wiggled your way into this one. What am I going to do with you?" he asked.

"Just keep on loving me and ask Ranjit if his wife would be interested in working here."

"Get dressed. I'm hungry and as the nursery rhyme about Old Mother Hubbard goes, the cupboard is bare."

"I must have a little talk with my mother," he said as we drove along through the bumper to bumper traffic.

"About what?" I asked, my curiosity getting the better of me.

"I'm going to encourage her to move back to Daman."

"Why?"

"It's better for her there. There's less pollution and it's an easier way of life."

"She'll probably think you are trying to get rid of her."

"That too," he said laughing out loudly, which was something he rarely did.

"As long as I have my living quarters and she has hers, she won't bother me," I said.

"You don't know my mother."

"What will you do with the flat she lives in?"

"It is a rental and Dean can take it over. He will need somewhere to live and now that he is getting his act together. He will need his privacy."

"The house in Daman is very big. She will be rambling around like a ghost all alone in such a big house."

"If she complains, I will find her a rental unit somewhere on the coastline."

"She will probably think it was my doing."

"Don't let it bother you. My mother knows me pretty well."

As annoyed as he was with his mother, he treated her with dignity and respect. Even after making his wife's life a living hell, he made sure she was well looked after. Only time will tell what our relationship will be like.

After breakfast, Vijay stopped in the office to see how everything had gone during his absence. We walked into a flurry of activity. The power outage had caused many problems, and engineers were on the floor tending to machines while workers scurried back and forth. Mrs. Kapoor almost walked past Vijay until she saw me. I took a seat in his office where I smelled the aroma of ripe mangoes. The box was lying on the floor next to Vijay's desk.

"Welcome back sir. Did you have a nice holiday? How are you madam?" she asked.

I wondered if she realized that there was something going on between her boss and me. If she did, she never let on. She was cheerful and polite and ordered tea for us both. Vijay asked her to get his office manager. All efforts to find him failed. He finally came running after fifteen minutes, offering his apologies. He had been overseeing a group of mechanics trying desperately to fix a machine which had broken down.

"Have a seat. How is everything?" Vijay asked.

"Welcome back sir. Good morning madam. If you had asked me that yesterday, I would've said everything is in fine working order, but the power failure has set us back a little. Right now everything is almost back to normal," he said mopping his brow.

"What about the generator?"

"This was really a big power failure, so the generator couldn't handle the power the machines needed."

"Well everything's back to normal. Thank you. I knew I could depend on you. Have I introduced you to Miss Bonnett?" Vijay asked him.

"No sir but I have met her here before. Nice to meet you madam," he said. "Would you like to see Ranjit? He left a box of mangoes for you. He said you were returning yesterday."

"I would like to thank him."

"When you find him, please send him here," Vijay said.

A few minutes later, there was a knock on the door and Ranjit entered. The joy in his face was immeasurable.

"You want to see me sir? Good morning madam."

"My wife wants to talk to you," he said escaping through the door.

"How are you Ranjit?"

"I am very, very fine madam. A thousand blessings to you madam! My wife and my son really like the new flat."

"And how about you?"

"I like it too and it is very, very good for my wife and my boy."

"How is Amrit? Is she well?" I asked.

"My wife is very, very happy. This morning she make curtains for the windows."

"What does she do during the day when you are here?"

"She take the boy to school and wait for me to come home."

"We are looking for someone to help with the housework; perhaps five or six hours a day. Do you think she would be interested?"

"The problem Madam is my boy. He must go to school and my wife must take him. I am very sorry."

"She can start at ten in the morning and leave on time to pick him up from school."

"A thousand blessings madam! My Amrit will like that."

"Please speak to her and let me know."

"Tomorrow she will come. I will tell her this evening and she will come. Madam I bring these mangoes for you. Very sweet Bombay mangoes. I know that after long trip you will want to eat beautiful Bombay mangoes."

"I love them as you know and I'm looking forward to eating a couple when I go home."

"Madam," he said shyly, "Everyone in my building see me in the newspaper. Very, very good story madam. No one know me from the photo because I was a very young boy. I went to all the flats to show them. Some of them did not believe me, but when I show them the part that say I work at Mahajan Industries, they believe me."

"I am very happy for you. I brought you something from Canada," I said as I gave him the T shirts and the two baseball caps.

"Thank you very much Madam. You are very kind to my family. I know my boy will like it."

"Have you got it all sorted out?" asked Vijay returning to the room.

"Yes, she is coming around tomorrow to talk to me."

"I will wait for Amrit tomorrow then," I said to Ranjit.

He left the room and Vijay stared at me.

"What on earth did you do to him?"

"I guess I smiled when he was looking for a kind face."

"I'll be ready in a few minutes," he said staring at the computer screen.

On a table behind his desk prominently displayed, was a photo of Dean. He truly loved the young man, even with all his faults.

"Isn't Dean supposed to be coming over this evening?"

"He said he would."

27

Dean arrived later that evening and brought with him the article on Ranjit which we hadn't yet seen. There was that young boy, perhaps eight or nine years old and the picture of innocence, which most probably he wasn't, since it was a struggle for survival on the streets. Anand Banerjee's picture of me was very flattering. He painted me as a kind and compassionate person who helped a homeless boy when his countrymen hardly batted an eyelash. The heading read, 'Canadian returns to Bombay to find homeless boy.'

"Very impressive article," said Vijay.

"I have a confession," said Dean. "He asked me to write it and we went over it together. Do you really like it?"

"I do. You made me sound like Mother Theresa, as Billie once said. I'll call Mr. Banerjee tomorrow and thank him."

"You won't tell him what I said about the article, will you?"

"Of course not," I said reaching out and hugging him.

Vijay looked from one face to the other. I could tell that he was happy that we were getting along so well. I could feel Dean's love for me in the article which he had written. Words were not necessary because it was all said in that newspaper article. I also noticed that the nervous twitch in his left leg seemed to have lessened immensely. Vijay told him about the offer he had made to his grandmother about the house in Daman and he seemed surprised that she had not put up a fight, but he was glad because he would be the recipient of her rental flat. His father left the room and I asked him about his life. Was there someone special? He smiled and said there was, and that we would meet in the very near future but only after his grandmother had made the move to Daman. He too treaded carefully around the old woman.

I called Anand Banerjee the following day and thanked him for being so gracious. He admitted that Dean had written the article and asked what I thought of it.

"You painted a rather beautiful picture of me."

"I think Dean is rather fond of you," he said.

"As I am of him!"

"He is a bright young man with a great future ahead of him. I am very pleased with his work ethics. He shows up early each morning and stays later just to help me when I am falling behind. I think we have a great journalist in the making."

He also said I should get in touch with his wife. She would be happy to hear that I was back in the city.

Angela was still rather lonely and to keep herself busy, she decided to take a language course in Hindi! I told her about the work at the Janice Weatherall's orphanage and she thought it a good idea to also volunteer her time. She said it would give her something to do instead of waiting for Anand's arrival every evening. We talked about her house helper whom she had caught putting a bag of sugar into the garbage, only to retrieve it later on the way home.

"What did you do?" I asked.

"Nothing. The poor soul probably needed it more than I did."

"But she was stealing."

Angela was obviously a very kind person who did not want to

make the woman's life any more difficult than it already was.

"You should still let her know that you know what she did. You don't want her to think she can take advantage of you."

"You're right. I will tell her about it."

I thought the time was right to tell her about my relationship with Vijay Mahajan.

"I knew there was something going on, but I wasn't sure. I was hoping you would tell me about it," she said with a smile.

"How did you find out?"

"You had mentioned something to Anand before you left, but we were still not one hundred per cent sure about the relationship. When Anand brought home Dean's article and showed it to me, I knew for sure that there was something going on between you and his father. My husband said he knew it from the first day we all met."

"Vijay was still married at the time and I didn't want to flaunt the relationship," I said apologetically.

"I'm happy for you," she said kissing me on the cheek. "So is there a wedding in the works?"

"Yes."

"Oh Christine, I hope you will invite us."

"It will be very small and since you are my best friend .... are you my best friend?"

"Yes, yes. Of course I am Christine. You know that."

"You and Anand are number one on the list. Thanks to you both, Dean is back on his feet and ready to face the world."

"Let's go shopping," she suddenly said. "I feel like celebrating."

Our first stop was a sari shop. We wanted to see how we would look in these exquisite garments. The saleswoman smiled but we knew she thought we were both mad and were probably just wasting her time.

"Know what I'm thinking Christine?"

"No I don't know what you're thinking Angela."

"I think you should get married in a beautiful golden sari."

"The thought never crossed my mind. I was thinking of an ivory two piece outfit."

"It would make your husband more confident about the relationship," she said brushing a blonde strand of hair from her eyes.

"That's what I'll do," I said sounding like a teenager.

After trying on a variety of the exquisite garments, we both left the shop giggling, and each in possession of an expensive sari. The saleslady, who was not so thrilled when we entered the shop, gave us a telephone number in case we needed help when we were ready to wear them.

"Madam, madam," said a woman in a cheap green sari and a ring in her nose. "I want to say something."

We both clung to our purses and packages as she blocked our way.

"Your husband, very good looking man and he love his wife very, very much," she said to Angela.

"Of course I know he is good looking. As a matter of fact, he is the most handsome man in all of India, and I know he loves me," she replied laughing.

"Very powerful man! Very powerful with words! He can make the mighty fall. I definitely see great future for you. And there is a man who love you very much," she said turning to me. "He marry you but I see lot of sorrow. Words of a woman bring much sorrow to you and to him, but after a time, you be happy too."

"Sure," I said with sarcasm ringing in my voice.

We each gave her ten rupees and she went on her way in search of her next victims.

"She was speaking about Anand. How would she know that he is a journalist?" said Angela.

"She didn't know that," I replied.

"She said, a man very powerful with words that will make the mighty fall."

"She was just guessing," I said as we continued on our way.

That evening I told Vijay about the woman and he laughed.

"She saw two foreigners together and knowing how gullible they are, decided to make some quick money. By the way, we are going out for dinner tomorrow evening with someone I respect tremendously."

"And who are we meeting?"

"Do you remember the sitar player I told you about?"

"Now I feel very nervous."

"He won't be playing. This is strictly a dinner engagement. No need to be nervous. He's a very nice man. He and my father were very good ....

The door bell rang and he checked to see who it was. A lady in a red sari was standing by the entrance.

"I think that woman has followed you home," he said.

"That's Amrit, Ranjit's wife," I said looking into the monitor.

Vijay let her in and she entered the elevator. When the door opened and I saw her, she seemed even more fragile than before. She looked scared.

"Come in Amrit. Don't leave me Vijay. I want you to translate for me."

The woman looked around at the flat as if she were in another world. Her hair was shiny and black and tied back in a pony tail.

It smelled of coconut oil which reminded me very much of my grandmother. She smiled a lot and then said something which I didn't understand.

"She said her husband said it is a very beautiful flat," said Vijay.

"Thank you," I said.

"Ask her if she can start at ten and be finished by three?"

She nodded.

"Does she know how to operate a vacuum cleaner and a washing machine?"

She said no to both questions."

"Would you show her how the washing machine works," I said to Vijay.

He had no idea where to begin.

"I'll figure it out," I said to them both.

"What about the stove? I'm always a little worried about the gas."

She nodded about the stove.

"Does that mean yes?" I asked Vijay.

She showed me how she would light and turn off the stove. Vijay stressed to her the importance of working with the fuel. Satisfied that she knew what to do, we decided to hire her. The arrangement was perfect. Five hours per day was exactly what she wanted because she would first take her child to school in the morning and pick him up at three thirty. She would start at the beginning of the following month. That would give us both enough time to sort ourselves out.

**

"You look lovely," Vijay said as we climbed into the elevator the following evening.

We were on our way to meet Mahavir Manjari, the sitar player. At six thirty sharp we walked into the restaurant and were immediately seated. It looked like a simple establishment, but Vijay said it was the best vegetarian restaurant in the city, and many of the who's who dined there. Needless to say, I was extremely nervous because artists are known to be temperamental. We ordered drinks and waited for him to arrive. Ten minutes later, a distinguished older gentleman entered and was led to our table. He was quite tall with a medium build and what was left of his white hair was brushed to the back of his head. A cravat was tied loosely around his neck and he wore one earring in his right ear.

"Mahavir-ji," said Vijay standing to greet him.

"My son," he said, "you look more and more like your father every day. This must be the young lady you told me about."

"Yes, this is Christine."

"I'm pleased to meet you sir," I said trying to get to my feet.

"Don't get up," he said reaching over and shaking my hand. "Please call me Mahavir."

"So you are Christine," he said, as he gazed at me with very soft eyes. "I told her that you are one of the greatest sitar players in India and she is looking forward to hearing you play."

"He is prejudiced," he said smiling at Vijay, "but you must attend my next concert. That way you can judge for yourself."

"Thank you," I replied.

"I notice that Dean seems to be getting his life back together," he said clasping his hands, and showing the longest fingers I had ever seen.

Our dinner which was totally vegetarian arrived at the table and he seemed to be inspecting it as he spoke.

"It is something I had been hoping for," said Vijay. "Christine's words of wisdom seem to have put him on the right track. She has done what we hadn't been able to accomplish in the last six years."

"Most commendable Christine! Now I know why this young man seems so happy," he said helping himself to one of the dishes.

"Thank you," I said.

"When I was a young man, Vijay's father and I were best of friends. Of course things were different back then. My parents were Hindu and it was only natural that I too would be a Hindu. I followed the Hindu teachings and even became a vegetarian. Vijay's father on the other hand had a strong mind. His life took another path. He became a Christian, so while I was following Gandhi's teaching, his life took a different turn; but we remained friends, and I think that in our later years, our friendship grew even stronger. Vijay has acquired the strength and ways of his father. I have always been proud of him and looking at you, I realise why I respect him so much. He truly has a mind of his own. Once he has made up his mind, there is nothing that can change that. That is the man you intend to marry. He knows exactly what he is getting into. When he came to me and explained all about you, I had no advice to give because I knew he was sensible and I respect him and what he has done with his life."

The waiter removed some of the dishes from the table and replaced them with new ones. Mahavir then began to speak about his life. His wife had died when his daughter was only fifteen and he had hoped that Amala and Vijay would fall in love and marry.

"I had an arranged marriage, and even though I had hoped for this union with Vijay, I didn't expect my daughter to share my opinion, although the years with my wife were the most beautiful of my life. It is different today. The younger generation see things quite differently from their parents and grandparents. Anyway I love Vijay as if he were my own son. So tell me, what you think of Bombay?" he suddenly asked.

"Of course it's different. Different from what I'm used to, but I have made a commitment to Vijay, and I will stand by it, because I love him."

His placed his long fingers on the table before he spoke.

"Continue to love and cherish him. Don't worry about those who would want to put a damper on your relationship. Enjoy your lives together. We are older people and should allow the younger ones to choose their own paths. Are you following me?"

"Yes I am. Thank you so much for your support."

"She is a lovely young woman Vijay? Cherish her."

"That's what I have been trying to explain to you. She is one in a million."

Vijay didn't say too much. He just listened, tapping his finger on his cheek, something which he always did when he was thinking or listening intently.

"You should eat Mahavir-ji. Everything gets cold very quickly," Vijay said.

"I told you Christine. He does care about me," he said with a chuckle.

Our conversation touched many topics. Music, family, food and happiness! He finally told us that he is no longer such a strict Hindu, although he hasn't changed his eating habits. He is still a vegetarian. I also got the impression that Vijay had confided in him. Was he giving me words of consolation because of Bina Mahajan's thoughts on the subject, and giving him our blessings for our upcoming marriage? At ten thirty, he was ready to go.

"It's almost my bedtime," he said. "I hardly go out anymore at this time of the evening."

Several other patrons bowed their heads to him as we were leaving the restaurant. He was well known and well respected it seemed.

"She's a treasure Vijay," he said taking both my hands. "Unfortunately I will not be able to come to the wedding. I had an earlier commitment which I cannot get out of, but I expect you to be at my next concert."

"Thank you Mahavir-ji. We will be there."

His driver drove up and he climbed in and away he went.

"So what did you think?" Vijay asked as we drove off.

"He thinks very highly of you. I think he is your confidant."

"I trust him implicitly. He is more like a relative than a family friend."

"Did you know he wanted you to marry his daughter?"

"Yes I did. I looked at Amala more like a sister than a love interest."

"Is she pretty?"

"Yes she is. She and her husband are both lawyers. They actually opened a law firm together. She is very good to her father. Both families live in the same building; but not in the same flat."

"I like him."

"I knew you would," he said.

**

Much to our surprise three weeks later, Sabia flew off to Rome with a very attractive settlement cheque in her pocket. I guess we all breathed a sigh of relief now that she had left for good, because we had anticipated much more trouble from her. Of course Dean was a little sad to see his mother go, but he also wanted her to be happy and Italy seemed to be the place where she was happiest.

"I thought that moving back to the family home would be good for you," Vijay said to his mother. "Since Priddy is no longer there, you can have full run of the place."

"You are back!" the older woman exclaimed.

"Of course I'm back. I have been back for over a month."

"You never called your mother to let her know. Is that any way to treat the woman who gave you life?"

"You know why I haven't been calling Mother."

"Are you getting married again?"

"Yes Mother."

"If it brings you happiness, it brings me happiness also. Will Screen be happy in Bombay?"

"I don't see any reason why she shouldn't be. We love each other Mother. Nothing or no-one will spoil our happiness. I have been unhappy for too long and I won't let this opportunity slip through my fingers."

"I am pleased to see that Dean is doing so well," she said.

"I am too Mother. What about the house in Daman?"

"Maybe you are trying to get rid of me Vijay," she said with a calmness he had never heard before.

"Believe me Mother I'm not trying to get rid of you."

"With all the pollution around Bombay, it's really not good for my sinuses. A bit of fresh air from the ocean may do me a lot of good. But that house is really too big for just one person. I'll be stumbling around in it all by myself."

"If you would like something smaller like the flat you have now, I can organise that for you."

"You seem to have all the answers," she said quietly.

"It's all in your hands. Just tell me your decision and I will help you."

**

We are busy planning our wedding. A total of twenty guests! A word of mouth invitation went out to those living out of the country, to be followed by a written one. Zack and Josh were both elated and said they would be there, and of course, they will be staying with us. Billie and Hugh would also be attending all the way from Melbourne, Australia. Vijay's brother Ravi and his wife Rahela, Angela and Anand Banerjee, Brian Langley and Lila Chandra, Vijay's best friend Simon and his wife Lakshmi, Dean, Bina Mahajan, Vijay's secretary Mrs. Kapoor and a couple more business associates were also invited. We were not sure if his mother would attend, but Vijay thought it the respectful thing to do, to invite her. Dean insisted on being my witness and Ravi would be Vijay's.

I was happy with the guest list because many of them were personal friends and should Mother Mahajan decide to grace us with her presence and perhaps throw a tantrum, I needed as many supporters as possible. Vijay pressed me on a daily basis about my wedding dress, which I said would be very simple when I bought it. This constant questioning made me call the sari shop because I had no idea how to wear this outfit and I needed help. The saleslady graciously said she would be at my home to help me, but that I needed another outfit for the reception. I did not want another sari, so she promised she would bring something beautiful for me to try. She also said that brides usually have henna painted on their hands, and recommended that I do the same, but that I decided against.

28

"I have made my decision. I will move back to Daman," said his mother during a phone call one morning. "I am also taking Pula with me. Poor Pula, she has no family."

"Did you ask her mother or did you tell her you were taking her?"

"What are you trying to say Vijay? I asked her if she would like to continue working for me and she accepted. How soon do you think I can make the move?" she asked.

"You seem to be in an awful hurry."

"Yes I decided that since Dean no longer needs me, I should look after myself. So when do you think I can leave?"

"Whenever you would like Mother! I thought you would leave after the wedding."

"I won't be attending the wedding Vijay. The occasion is for young people and I just won't fit in."

"I am your son and if I am getting married, I would like you to be there," he said sounding a tad annoyed.

"It would be too much for me come such a distance for just one day."

"Mother, you are making excuses. You just don't like Christine, do you?"

"It has nothing to do with Screen."

"Then what is it?"

"I don't think she would want me there."

"Christine has nothing against you. I just wish you would open your arms and embrace her into the family."

"Let me think about it," she said after a short pause. "Anyway I would like to go up to Daman this weekend. I want to get myself settled in."

"I'll send the Ambassador around for you and Pula. Would you prefer Saturday or Sunday?"

"Saturday would be better for me."

He turned the phone off and wondered what his mother was up to. Why the big hurry to leave Bombay? He knew she was leaving because she had no intention of attending the wedding, and he immediately felt a sense of relief.

**

A very unpleasant thing happened to me this morning. On his way to the office, Vijay dropped me off at the orphanage. I rang the bell and waited for Janice to open the gate, when I was approached by an older woman. She was not a beggar and I couldn't understand what she was saying to me. I could however see the hatred in her eyes. She screamed and then spat on the ground. Caustic and abrasive! The only word I thought I heard was ' prostitute'. Did she think I was a prostitute? Janice Weatherall came out to open the gate just in time to rescue me and to give her a good tongue lashing.

"What did she say?" I asked.

"The first thing you must do," Janice said sternly, "is to take a language course. That's very important. The next time Mr. Mahajan brings you here, he should wait until you are securely behind the gate before he leaves. She probably saw the two of you together and it was beyond her limited imagination what you could be doing together."

"Do you think I'm making a mistake?" I asked Janice.

"What mistake?" she asked.

"By moving to this country," I asked on the verge of tears.

She laughed.

"The only mistake you will be making is to allow such fools to make you doubt that gentleman's love for you."

"But ......

"There are no buts Christine. I moved to this country many years ago. I too followed my heart. Then my heart followed me back to Brisbane and there he showed his true colours. Today I'm in this country looking after these beautiful children and he is living in my country. He was and still is a very nice man, but what he was seeking was acceptance. When any female in Brisbane smiled at him, he thought they wanted to get into his pants. It all goes back to the colonisation of this country. The Indians here feel that they are never good enough. They seek acceptance and do stupid things like lightening the colour of their hair and bleaching their skins. Damned fools!"

I started to laugh.

"You are feeling better," she said. "Good! Now let's look after the children."

"I am going to bring someone else to the orphanage to help out. That's if you don't mind," I said sheepishly.

"Who? Any help would be most welcome."

"You must've heard of the newspaper journalist Anand Banerjee. I told his wife you needed help and she said she wouldn't mind volunteering."

"An Indian volunteer would be great," she said. "Someone who understands the language!"

"Sorry Janice. She's not Indian. She's a white American."

"I should've known. Another piece of advice I should offer you, is never to live with your mother-in-law," she said as I wondered how the statement fit into what I had said.

"That would never happen. She would never live under the same roof with me."

"Did she say that?"

"Not in so many words. She said that I am a Dalit."

"And what did Mr. Mahajan say?"

"As much as it hurt him to do it, he asked her to leave."

"He's a good man. I know you know what the word means, but take it all with a grain of salt. Some Indian wives have the same problems with their mothers in law."

"Thank you for listening to my tales of woe."

"You are strong Christine. You can handle it. Just get to that language course. It will give you an upper hand. How is Billie? Is she coming to the wedding?"

"You know she is now in Melbourne. Yes she will be here."

"The children would love to see her again."

**

My wedding is just two weeks away and today we met with the chef along with his array of menus. We decided that since we were having international guests, we would try to cater to everyone's palate. The chef suggested certain menu items and we decided to talk it over before we made a decision.

After much going back and forth, we settled on lots of finger foods and beverages while the guests milled around; then a cocktail reception for the twenty guests. We thought they would get to know each other better if they were able to move around and chat with each other. The chef's suggestion was that everything be bite sized. His recommendations included mini surf and turf, a choice which he thought our North American guests might enjoy; smoked salmon, a variety of cheeses, chicken satays, skewered lamb, skewered vegetables, onion Bhaji, lamb samosas, pakoras, and curried shrimp; all bite sized. This would be followed by an assortment of desserts, and a well-stocked wine bar would be located in the room where two bar tenders would be in attendance.

I received a call around eight thirty one morning and found it was the saleslady from the sari shop. She said something beautiful had arrived at the shop that she thought I might like, and offered to bring it over to the flat to show me. She would be there within an hour. When she arrived, she brought with her and enticed me into buying a delicate looking ivory coloured two piece outfit which had been patiently hand beaded by some poor woman for a couple rupees. She seemed totally surprised when she entered the flat. I don't know what she had been expecting, but she was probably surprised to see where I lived. My good sense said I shouldn't buy the outfit, but it was very beautiful, so I gave in to fashion, and this I also hid in the back of the armoire where Vijay would never find it.

**

With all the preparations going on, I had completely forgotten about Amrit. Today would be her first day working with us. She arrived on the dot of ten still looking scared. We had to find a way of communicating with each other, so I decided I would show her how to use the washing machine and the vacuum cleaner. As a matter of fact, I did most of the work with her protesting. I now saw the necessity of a language course. If I were to communicate with the local people, I had to try to speak their language. Anyway Amrit was a hard worker and she had the flat in tip top shape before midday. She motioned to me putting her hand to her mouth.

"Are you hungry?" I asked pointing to her.

She wanted to know when she should start making dinner. That was not necessary I tried to explain because we would first have to do the shopping. On her insistence, we set out in a taxi to the open market. I had never seen anything like it. It was loud and each vendor was vying for our attention. Curious stares followed us as I pointed to whatever I wanted and she bargained with them. Sometimes it became rather heated, but in spite of the arguments, we had purchased enough to make dinner that evening. She was obviously not as timid as she looked. In an hour we were back at the flat and she set about marinating the lamb and skewering the prawns we had bought. The aromas emanating from the kitchen were titillating my nostrils but I had to wait until Vijay arrived home. She vehemently objected to taking some of the food with her but I insisted. She and Ranjit were poor but they had strong moral fibre and pride; something I can't say for many of the people with whom I came into contact. Many of them wanted to cheat me and some were not even willing to acknowledge my presence. I question myself sometimes about being in this part of the world especially if I had had a very trying day, when the heat was unbearable or when the sanitary conditions made me question my being in the city. I have bought seven pairs of slippers for the house; five of them are for visitors, one pair for Amrit and the other for Vijay, much to his annoyance. I have noticed that Angela Banerjee has also done the same.

**

I am feeling very excited. Josh and Zack are already on their way to Bombay. Vijay insisted that we send the Ambassador to collect them, but I wanted to be there to greet my friends the moment they stepped through the customs doors. We hugged and we cried. It was as if we hadn't seen each other in twenty years.

"Welcome to Mumbai," said Vijay hugging each of them.

"It's so nice to be back and for such a special occasion," said Zack as the children hovered around with open palms.

"So this is the famous Bombay," said Josh as we climbed into the Jeep and headed into the city. "Does it always smell like this?"

"You'll get used to it," said Zack kicking him to keep him quiet.

During the day the flat was full of friends. I had never seen Amrit smile as much as when Josh and Zack were around. She now insisted on shopping alone since the prices always seemed to escalate when she took me along. Josh teased her at every turn. They talked to each other constantly but neither understood what the other was saying. He always greeted her with, 'My little Amrit,' and a beautiful smile would cross her lips. There was always something in the kitchen to snack on because she was always making something tasty especially for the two visitors.

I was happy surrounded by friends. I wished it would never end and my Vijay, he was tired when he arrived home in the evening, but with Josh fixing him a drink and Amrit's cooking waiting in the oven, he was a happy man.

Billie and Hugh finally made it in from Melbourne and the greeting between Billie and Zack was worth saving for posterity. They laughed and they cried as they hugged each other. Angela Banerjee said she felt left out and wanted to meet as many guests as possible before the wedding, so she too was a constant in the flat. The last to arrive were Ravi and Rahela from London. I had heard a lot about Rahela, but I had no idea she was such a gorgeous woman. A face and figure from a Bollywood poster. I do remember a lean Ravi from many years ago, but he had gained quite a few pounds which had all settled around his midriff and made him seem rather jolly. I looked at his stomach and smiled. It would be his mother's pride and joy.

Billie looked well. She was perfectly tanned and almost as dark as I am. The accommodation had also worked out well. She and Hugh have taken over Brian's flat forcing him to temporarily move in with Lila, and Ravi and Rahela are with Dean in Mother Mahajan's former flat.

29

"Who's bringing Mother down from Daman?" Ravi asked.

"She's not coming," said his brother.

"Her son is getting married and she's not putting in an appearance?" he asked looking around at the family members.

Rahela's eyes and mine met. Unspoken words!

"Well we shall see about that," he said.

"If she doesn't want to come, you shouldn't force her," said Rahela, happy to hear the last bit of news.

"But it's her son honey. She should be celebrating with us and welcoming Christine into the family with open arms."

"You have lived in London for too long honey. You have forgotten what life is like here."

"Leave it alone," said Vijay somewhat sternly.

"I'll go up to Daman after the wedding to speak with her," Ravi said. "This is nonsense."

"Let's not spoil this happy occasion with things beyond our control," said his wife.

**

We brought all the guests together for a pre-wedding party. The Indian equivalent of a cocktail party! Most of all I wanted Vijay to meet Anand Banerjee and his wife before the wedding; after all they had helped Dean on the road to recovery. The hors d'oeuvres had been ordered and Amrit said she would do the serving. I was not sure it was a good idea, but what did she have to do? Keep them warm and serve them? I showed her how to put them onto the serving dishes and I must say she was quite eager to please. Anand and Angela were the first to arrive, which gave the two men a chance to become acquainted, and slowly the other guests trickled in. The last was to arrive were Simon or Chico as he was affectionately called and his wife Lakshmi. The moment I saw her I thought of Vijay's description of her. She was really a plain Jane. She wore a beautiful sari, no makeup and hair which flowed over her shoulders giving her that Mona Lisa resemblance. Simon seemed a little nervous and as she approached me, I noticed a look of surprise on her face. A look which said, 'who is she?' Vijay introduced us and she smiled; because it would have been impolite not to do so.

"Why didn't you tell me?" she hissed at Simon and walked straight over to Rahela.

The two women hugged and kissed. It was obvious they had known each other for a long time. Her husband headed straight for Angela Banerjee. He seemed bewitched by her blonde hair. The rest of the party was in little groups chatting with each other and becoming acquainted. Amrit walked around with her tray of goodies and napkins supplying their needs.

"What's going on here?" Lakshmi asked Rahela.

"What do you mean?" Rahela asked unaware of what she was referring to.

"How could he do this to us?"

"Do what? What on earth are you talking about?"

"Simon told me that Jay was marrying a Canadian, but I didn't expect this," she said, the steam coming from her ears.

"Forgive me Lakshmi, but I don't understand what you are talking about," said an annoyed Rahela.

"How could he think of marrying her?"

"Are you referring to Christine?"

"Yes I think that's her name."

"Christine is a lovely person. Have you met her?"

"I just did!" she said pouting.

"Sometimes I forget what I left behind here in India. This country needs an infusion of good sense and manners," said Rahela.

"I see I have offended you," she said.

"You certainly have. You have made it even clearer to me why I have no desire to live in this country again. You are upset because Jay hasn't chosen your spinster sister. He has found an educated woman who would stimulate him intellectually. He was looking for someone with whom he could have a one on one conversation, not a trouble maker like you or your sister," Rahela said walking away.

"Huh!" the plain Jane said walking back to her husband.

"Who's the sourpuss?" asked Angela Banerjee.

"You were just talking to her husband," I replied. "Lakshmi and Simon Bhatt.".

"He seems nice enough, but she is a little strange. I think she and Ravi's wife just had a bit of a disagreement."

"A disagreement with Rahela? I think they've know each other for a long time. I wonder what could've brought that about," I asked staring at them both.

"I don't think she likes me," I whispered to Vijay.

"But I love you," he said with a smile and returned to his conversation with Anand Banerjee.

A couple minutes later, Simon and Lakshmi Bhatt were leaving the party. She said she didn't feel well and would be better off at home.

"Why did you let me walk into that without warning me?" Lakshmi shouted at her husband.

"I have no idea what you are talking about."

"You told me she was Canadian. You didn't say she was black or whatever colour she is."

"What difference does it make? Jay loves her and that's the important thing."

"Where did he find her?" she shouted.

"Had we stayed long enough at the party, you would've had the opportunity to ask her yourself."

"I can't believe he has done something like that," she said, the hatred evident in her eyes.

"What? Not married your sister?" her husband asked smiling.

"My sister is happy. She doesn't need Jay Mahajan to make her complete."

"That's not the impression I got."

"Anyway I wonder what Bina Mahajan has to say about all this?"

"Lakshmi, I am warning you. Don't be a trouble maker. If you say you are Jay's friend, then you should respect the decisions he has made concerning his life."

"Well I guess I won't be going to the wedding."

"It will be lonely there without you, because I intend to bless them both with my presence."

"I forbid it Simon."

"Lakshmi, I have been a very patient man for the many years that we were married. Please do not put me in an awkward position."

"You are just like Rahela. What has that woman done to turn

all you into such little robots? Is it the voodoo or her performance in bed that has turned Jay's head? You know the reputation they have?"

"I wish you had the same reputation," he whispered.

"What did you say?"

"Nothing! Lakshmi, I am warning you. Jay has been my friend for many years. We grew up together. Please don't let me have to make a choice."

For the rest of the journey home, the couple drove in silence. When they reached the flat, she stepped out and slammed the door. Not wanting to put up with her bad mood, he sped off leaving her staring after him. The best place to be was back at the party, where of course everyone inquired after his wife's health.

**

"Good morning Mrs. Mahajan. This is Lakshmi Bhatt. I didn't realise you had moved back to Daman."

"How would you know that? We never really talked that much."

"That's true but you know we always kept in touch with Vijay. I guess because we are around the same age. I hope the weather is better there than here in the city."

"The weather here is better for my sinuses. I find it just a little too polluted in Bombay and since the house is empty now.... I guess you heard that Priddy went back to Italy."

"Yes I heard. I knew that things weren't going well but I never expected her to leave on such short notice."

"Well she has left and I'm roaming around this big house, except for Pula of course!"

"Dean seems to be doing very well."

"Yes my grandson is my pride and joy. He has pulled himself together and is now working with the best journalist there is in all of Bombay."

"Bless his father for doing all that for his son," the malicious Lakshmi said.

"Now dear, is there something I can do for you?"

Realising Bina Mahajan was not taking the bait, there was nothing left to do but to get straight to the point.

"I understand there is to be a wedding," she said.

"Yes my son has decided to marry again."

"Have you met her?" she asked.

"Naturally I met her. My son introduced me to her," she said not giving any more information.

"Are you happy about it? Couldn't he find someone else to marry rather than this Christine?"

"I gather you don't like my new daughter in law," said the woman.

"I have nothing against her, but couldn't she find one of her own kind to marry?"

"My son loves her and she loves him. She has done a lot for Dean and for that I am grateful."

"Are you trying to say that you approve of the marriage?"

"If she makes my son happy, then I am happy," said Bina Mahajan.

There was nothing left to do but bring the conversation to an end. She said she had to go and put the telephone down.

Even Mother Mahajan has fallen under her spell, she thought.

**

Who could be calling at such an early hour I wondered? I picked up the telephone so that it wouldn't awaken Vijay. I heard his mother's voice on the other end.

"Just a moment," I said. "I'll get Vijay for you."

"Screen," she said. "I have something to say to you."

My heart started to race. She was going to wreck the blissful atmosphere just a few days before my wedding.

"I was wrong," she said. "I know my son is upset because I won't be coming to the wedding, but please do not be angry. I know my son loves you and from what my grandson says, I know you love my son. You have my blessing to marry him."

"Thank you," I said.

"Is he there?"

"Just a moment please ….. Thank you," I muttered.

It was a one way conversation with his mother. He said yes and no and uh-huh! I couldn't really get the gist of it but I knew she was probably repeating the same things she had said to me. I followed him into the bedroom where he threw himself on the bed.

"What's wrong?" I asked.

"She asked my forgiveness for everything she's done," he said with sadness in his voice.

"Then you should be happy."

"She still won't be attending our wedding. She confuses me Christine."

"Older people are like that," I said.

"There's one more thing I must do," he said picking up the telephone and dialling a number.

"Hello," said the voice on the other end.

"Lakshmi, Vijay here," he said quickly.

"Of course I know it's you Vijay. What can I do for you?"

"I hope you are feeling better. You must've been catching the flu or a cold."

"Yes I am feeling better. I'm sorry that I had to leave in such a hurry."

"Lakshmi, your husband and I grew up together, almost like brothers. I am extremely disappointed in your behaviour. I am going to marry Christine whether you or anyone else thinks I'm crazy. How dare you approach two of my family members to state your disapproval of my fiancé? I would like to tell you that on the seventeenth of July, please do not attempt to attend our wedding. You are no longer welcome."

With those words, he ended the call. He was standing up for me. He had said more than once that if his friends didn't approve of me, that that would be the end of the friendship. He had lived up to his word. Would Simon attend the wedding without his wife?

30

Today is the seventeenth of July and the day I say 'I do' to Vijay Mahajan. There is a mixture of anxiety, joy, fear and happiness in my heart, and luckily I am surrounded by friends. My best friends! Mother Mahajan has lived up to her word and will not grace us with her presence. It has worked out well because I have also invited Janice Weatherall, since she has become my adviser on all things Indian.

The saleslady from the store arrived to help me with my sari and she is very nervous; so nervous that I am beginning to think she is the bride and not I. She fussed and ran around me like a headless chicken. She pulled here and prodded there and then she stepped back and smiled.

I stared at myself in the mirror and the woman looking back at me left me speechless.

"You look absolutely lovely Madam," she said. "Don't forget to take the outfit to change. You won't need me for that."

When I walked from the bedroom, Dean who was patiently waiting couldn't find the words to express himself.

"Oh Christine," was all he could say.

"Thank you," I said laughing.

"It's time to go. Wait until Dad sees you!" he said as we travelled down in the elevator.

When we arrived at the hotel, the guests and the employees alike all stared at us. I could tell from the looks on their faces who were well wishers and those who were not. The doorman opened the door to the temporary chapel and the chatter came to an end. It was a beautiful sight. All the chairs were covered in white satin and placed in a semi circle, with a path in the middle for the bridal party.

When I walked in on Dean's arm, they all stood up and faced us. I could hear the gasps as they saw me. They hadn't expected me to wear a sari; everyone of course except Angela Banerjee. Vijay turned to face me and he was smiling broadly, but somehow seemed nervous. It was a simple, but beautiful ceremony which lasted one hour. I had a moment of panic when the priest asked if anyone knew of a reason why the marriage shouldn't be performed. I knew this was standard, but the pause seemed to last forever. I pictured Sabia Tosi walking in and giving all the reasons to stop the wedding. I breathed a sigh of relief when he finally continued.

That part over, we walked out to the sounds of camera lens clicking away. The doorman swung another pair of doors open, and the beauty that was the reception room came into view. It was handsomely decorated with white flowers of every description, with white ribbons dangling from the chandeliers. Beneath the chandelier at the far end of the room, a four piece string quartet played softly. Vijay and I disappeared. It was time for me to change into my second outfit.

The hotel staff had outdone itself with the food and the decorations. Absent from the guest list were Bina Mahajan and Lakshmi Bhatt. Her husband was there of course making excuses for her absence, but having a good time nevertheless. He was either hanging around Billie or Angela Banerjee; such a pity his wife wasn't there to see it.

The food was delicious and we received compliments on the choices we had made. They loved the music which I later found out was a gift from Dean. Dear Dean!

"Don't forget the box Dean," said his father.

"What box?" I asked.

"The wedding gifts," he replied.

Since we still had house guests, we decided to remain in Bombay and the honeymoon would follow later; but tonight we would spend at the Taj Hotel and return home the tomorrow morning.

"I'll look after Zack and Josh this evening," said Dean with a smile. "Enjoy your honeymoon."

Vijay took a week off from work to show Josh and Zack the sights in and around the city. He had placed a row of seats at the back of the jeep and the two men sat there with Billie and Hugh in the middle seats. We were having the time of our lives. Zack even asked Hugh when he would follow Vijay's example and make an honourable woman out of Billie the Tramp. We all were in hysterics, especially Billie as tears ran down her cheeks.

"You are a bad lot," she said. "I can't ever remember having this much fun in Bombay, except when Christine and I were returning from Daman, and she screamed all the way because we had seen quite a few accidents along the way. The poor driver I'm sure was convinced that Vijay would fire him when he reached the city."

"Was she that bad?" asked Vijay.

"Worse," said Billie.

"Where is my friend Amrit today?" asked Josh.

"It's her day off," said Vijay. "Have you met Ranjit?"

"Who is Ranjit?"

"Amrit's husband! He is also Christine's friend. For him the sun rises and falls upon Christine Mahajan. That sounds good, doesn't it? Christine Mahajan," said my handsome husband.

"It does sound good, but I think someone is jealous," said Billie.

"I must make a quick stop at the office," Vijay said ignoring her comment. "Come in and I'll see if I can find him. It will be the highlight of his life for the next six months."

Mrs. Kapoor congratulated us again and went in search of Ranjit. She returned with him five minutes later and from the look on his face, I knew he was surprised to find so many people in the room, all of them speaking English.

"This is Ranjit," I said to the group.

"I remember him," said Zack. "He was the one with all the curls, but it can't be because that young boy had only one leg."

"That's him," I said. "He's wearing a prosthetic limb."

"I remember you sir. Most definitely" he said looking at Zack. "You stay in same hotel as Madam and always had camera."

He didn't remember Billie, probably because she had spent all her time sunning by the pool, someone said.

"One thousand blessings to you Sir and to you Madam! May you have many children! My wife say that Madam was definitely most beautiful," he said as he clasped his hands and bowed before leaving the room.

We all burst out laughing at the remark about having many children.

"See what I mean," said Vijay. "The sun does rise and set upon Christine."

**

All good things must come to an end and after a week of

frolicking and carousing, our friends were all ready to leave. Zack and Josh were heading home. Recalling the experience we had at the airport on the return trip to Toronto, we left home with ample time for them to board the aircraft with the least frustration possible. Amrit was beside herself with sorrow. They had been very kind to her and she would miss them. I watched her smile as she retrieved something which Josh had put into her pocket.

Our ride to the airport was done mainly in silence.

"Love you," said Josh hugging Vijay. "Come and see us again. I don't think I can handle Bombay although the shopping was the best."

We watched as they made their way through the crowds, turning around often to wave to us. Finally they disappeared from view and we climbed into the Jeep for the journey back home.

"I will miss them," said Vijay.

I did not reply because I was close to tears. That night we made up for all the nights we were forced to refrain from behaving like two people in love. It felt like the first time we had made love. He was gentle but not overly so and we finally fell into each other's arms as the sun began to rise, totally exhausted.

After paying a farewell visit to the orphanage, which the children enjoyed immensely, Billie flew back to Melbourne with Hugh. One week later, Rahela and Ravi also left for London, not before Rahela cornered me in the kitchen with a warning.

"Be careful with the people in this city. Choose your friends well and remember a leopard never changes its spots and make sure Vijay brings you to London to visit us," she said hugging me.

**

The monsoon rains were now upon us, bringing with them howling winds which stripped the trees of their flowers and brought the vermin from their underground burrows scuttling for shelter. The sidewalks were covered in fallen flowers from the jacaranda, cassia and flamboyant trees and the mixture of yellow, violet and red turned into a mass of muck as hundreds of tired feet trod upon them. The rain whipped against the glass in the living room which faces the Arabian Sea. I was glad that Amrit was there for fear gripped my heart. It reminded me of the hurricane season back in the Caribbean, and I watched as people scurried by with plastic bags or umbrellas over their heads going about their everyday lives. The birds it seemed had found safety somewhere other than the trees. Soon the streets had turned into rivers, and the Arabian Sea was angry; she became very turbulent. Amrit had come prepared with an umbrella and a plastic raincoat which had belonged to Bina Mahajan. Soon after the downpour, the sun would peep out again, but that didn't last for a long time, for again the sky yawned and wretched and those found in the open, had to run for cover.

My life is full, and together with my husband, I have started to enjoy the cultural life of Mumbai. Tonight we are attending Mahavir Manjari's concert and I've decided to wear something extra special because Vijay explained that the elite of the city would be in attendance. My husband looked very handsome and I felt like the luckiest woman alive. The Ambassador stopped in front of the music hall, and arm in arm, we climbed the steps into the building. The women were all beautifully dressed in silk saris and I had never seen so many handsome men all in one place. They turned to look as we entered the foyer. There were some disapproving looks, but some of the guests nodded in our direction, while those who knew Vijay greeted us heartily and he introduced me to them.

"I've been looking for you. I'm so glad you've come," said Mahavir as he approached us. "Congratulations to you both. Christine, you look divine. Come with me," he said leading the way.

We walked along a series of narrow corridors until we came to his dressing room. We could hear voices coming from inside.

"Vijay," said the lady hugging him.

"I want you to both meet Christine," said Mahavir. "This is my daughter Amala and her husband Kumar."

"My father has spoken so highly of you that I decided it imperative to meet the lady who has captured Vijay's heart."

"It's really nice meeting you," I said.

"Vijay must bring you over sometime," she said. "We can have dinner together."

Kumar smiled sweetly and engaged Vijay in conversation, while Mahavir poured us glasses of orange juice.

"How is Ravi?" Mahavir suddenly asked.

"He and Rahela are doing very well."

"That's good to hear. Welcome back to India Christine. So Christine, how is Mumbai treating you?"

"I'm as busy as ever. I don't know if Vijay has mentioned that I volunteer at an orphanage and I am also taking a course in Hindi."

"That's wonderful," said Amala. "The next time we meet, we should try to speak in Hindi."

"My son, you have chosen well," said Mahavir

"Thank you sir."

"Not many of my people with such privileged lives would dream of working with the less fortunate," he said to me.

There was a knock on the door and we knew it was time for the concert to begin and time to take our seats. We said goodbye to each other, promising to keep in touch.

"Vijay," he said as we stepped out the door, "it is your duty to make her happy."

We took our seats and soon the lights were dimmed, and the spotlight shone on the stage. Beside Mahavir were three other musicians along with their instruments, none of which I recognised. The master sat with the instrument on his lap and started to play. Goosebumps covered my arms as he gently plucked away at the chords. After two and a half hours, the concert was over, and he returned to the stage three times to applause and standing ovations.

"That's what you call, doing justice to the sitar. He is a true professional," said Vijay.

**

I spend two days per week helping out at the orphanage and two days with Angela and a private tutor, who suggested we learn Hindi since that was the language spoken by most of the Bombayites, but wherever we showed up, people always spoke to us in English. I guess they think that all foreigners speak English. The language is quite difficult, but with gentle nudges from Janice Weatherall, we have no choice but to persevere. At least we now know how to say the important things one needs to know to survive in such a harsh environment.

When I am alone with Amrit, I try to learn as much as I can from her and she has also picked up enough English from me to get by. She now knows how to answer the telephone and how to make a call. She knows all the English names for fruit and vegetables and also for objects around the house. I immediately thought of Mother Mahajan one day when I asked her to say my name.

"Scureen," she said which drove me into fits of laughter.

I was happy for her company especially when Vijay went away on business. Sometimes I accompanied him and other times I stayed at home and Angela Banerjee would come over to keep me company. She is in the same position as I and spends a couple evenings with us when Anand is out of town. She has become my best friend and bosom buddy, something which would probably never would have happened, if we were both still living in North America.

Dean is still a regular visitor to the flat, teasing Amrit and having her cook all his favourite dishes. It is great having him around especially when Vijay is away. He is now twenty two years old and doing very well in his position at the newspaper and happy to be doing what he really wanted to do. His life is on track, and to me he is the son I never had. There hasn't been any word from Sabia since she flew off to Rome; not even her son has been in communication with her. Today he arrived with a photo which he, his father and I had taken together. He removed the old photo of himself and replaced it with the new one. The perfect family photo!

One year has passed and I had grown used to Bombay and she too it seems has gotten used to me. The Banerjees have become our closest friends. Sometimes I wonder if Anand and Vijay really like each other. Their conversations or discussions on occasion are usually very heated but they are grown men and behave like grown men. When these knock-down, dragged out brawls are over, it was as if they had never begun. We have also grown close to Lila and Brian Langley who incidentally have decided to take the plunge and have become husband and wife. I was happy for Lila. She had had enough unhappiness with men. Simon Bhatt visits occasionally but since he cannot bring his wife, his visits are rare. We are constantly on the computer skyping with Billie and Hugh. The latest news was that her visa was about to expire and she would kill two birds with one stone; go on a shopping trip to Singapore as well as have her visa renewed there. I haven't seen Bina Mahajan since we got married. She prefers to remain in Daman and Dean and Vijay drive up to see her once a month.

I'm not sure if it is the strains of the city but recently I have found myself comparing Bombay to Toronto. This was brought to my attention by Janice Weatherall who said I shouldn't forget it was Vijay's home, and although he may not say too much on the subject, I should be careful about making such remarks especially in his presence, so I am genuinely making an effort to take her advice.

"I know what you're going through, but it was a decision you made," she said to me one day. "You've got a good life. Make the most of it."

**

Amrit asked if she could speak to me on a very urgent matter. She seemed very shy and then suddenly blurted it out.

"It is my son Sanjay Madam. I want him to learn English. I want him to speak good English like you and Mr. Mahajan."

And so there was more to keep me busy. Sanjay came by every Friday afternoon after his mother picked him up from school and we sat on the terrace speaking English.

"Can I live here too?" he asked one day.

"Why?" I asked.

"Because this flat is big and beautiful. Our flat is small but much better than the old flat. Pa-Pa says that you helped him to get the new flat," he said staring at me with those huge black eyes.

"Sorry Sanjay, this flat is just for me and my husband."

"And where are your children?" he asked.

He was learning English much too quickly I thought.

31

It was a warm November morning and I awoke to the sound of crows cawing noisily in the tree outside my bedroom window. Vijay was out of town but was returning home later that afternoon. I looked out to see what the commotion was all about and wished I could've shooed them away, but they wouldn't have heard me anyway, so great was the noise they were making.

My thoughts turned to Toronto. It was evening there and most likely bone chilling. Fall in my opinion, was the most pleasant season of the year, but sometimes it could be unmerciful. I pictured the people there scurrying around in their warm jackets or light coats trying to keep the cold out and the last solitary robin hopping across the grass pecking at the insects that had worked their way to the surface. I also pictured the finches and the chickadees flying back and forth from the bird feeder which I had hung from a tree on the terrace, and the menacing squirrels dangling precariously upside down, trying to gorge themselves on as much bird food as they could. How I missed Toronto. I missed my friends and I missed the dinners and the restaurants where we would all gather to celebrate one thing or another.

The telephone rang and I picked it up expecting it to be Vijay.

"A very good morning to you too," I said.

There was a pause and then I heard Dean's voice on the line.

"Christine is my father there?" he asked without greeting me.

"No he won't be back before this afternoon. Why don't you call him on his cell phone?"

"I'll call him later," he said and hung up.

He had never spoken to me that way before. He had always been polite and cheerful. What was wrong with him? I called him back.

"Tell him when he comes home that I want to talk to him," he said sternly.

"Is something wrong Dean?"

"They have all lied to me. Every single one of them! Even my grandmother, who pretends that she loves me, has also lied to me."

"Dean, please tell me what's wrong. We have always talked about everything."

"Perhaps you know about it too Christine," he said coldly.

"Dean," I shouted, "I don't know what you are talking about. Come over so that we ....

He had hung up on me. I tried to call Vijay but his cell phone kept going to voice mail. I left him five messages and finally around eleven o'clock, he called home.

"I'll be home in about two hours. Five phone calls! You must really miss me," he said laughing.

"Have you spoken to Dean?"

"I tried returning his call but it keeps going to voice mail," he said cheerfully.

"He is really upset," I said. "He said that everyone keeps lying to him."

"Did he say what he meant by that?"

"No he didn't. Please hurry. I'm afraid something is really wrong."

"I'm on my way," he said.

While I waited for Vijay to arrive, I called Anand Banerjee's office. It was Dean's day off and he hadn't seen him. I wanted to call Bina Mahajan but I thought it better to leave that to her son. Where could he be? Why wasn't he answering his phone? Amrit came in with a cup of tea. Whenever she suspected that something was amiss, she always brought a cup of tea as if she thought tea would be the answer to solving all problems.

The doorbell rang and I looked to see who it was. Dean, unshaven and wearing the red baseball cap we had brought him from Toronto.

"What's wrong?" I asked hugging him.

He was rather despondent and sat on the sofa and closed his eyes.

"Talk to me," I pleaded. "I am your friend."

"How could she do this to me?" he asked.

I wondered who he was referring to. Maybe it was a girlfriend although he hadn't spoken about any girls since we had met.

"Who is she?"

"It's Priddy. Why did she do this to me?" he asked as the tears streamed down his face.

"What did she do Dean?" I asked nervously.

"She told me last night that Dad was not my biological father."

"Dear God!" I whispered, getting up and closing the kitchen door.

Knowing the problems that her son was dealing with, why did she do such a thing? She couldn't hate the flesh and blood she had brought into the world. But why had she told him that horrible secret which only two other people in India knew? Vijay and I!

"Why would she say such a stupid thing?" I asked not knowing what else to say.

"She said she was getting married again and I told her that you and Dad had gotten married."

"Is that when she told you that?"

"Yes."

"She was just being vindictive," I said. "That was the only way she thought she could hurt your father."

"No Christine. She told me my father's name. She said she knew from the time she was pregnant that Dad was not my father."

Where are you Vijay? I wondered. Please come home.

Like clockwork, Amrit came from the kitchen with a cup of tea and a wet cloth. Dean thanked her and while he drank the tea, I wiped his forehead with the wet cloth. Suddenly he said he had to go. Nothing I said or did could convince him to stay and wait until his father arrived. I was beside myself with fear. Where was he going? What was he going to do? Then I remembered Dr. Paxil. Maybe I should call him.

"Get him to the clinic as fast as possible," the doctor said.

Vijay finally arrived home just after three and in the confines of our bedroom I explained the situation it to him.

"Where did he go?"

"I don't know. He wouldn't tell me."

"That ungrateful woman! After all I did to give her a comfortable life! She knows how fragile he is. Why would she do that to him? Why? Why?"

"Because he told her that we are married," I replied.

"Did he say that?"

"Yes," I said staring at him.

Fire seemed to be shooting from his eyes. I had never seen my husband so angry. He called his son's cell phone, but it was turned off.

"We should go out and look for him," I said.

We called his flat, but there was no answer. He was somewhere in the city but what was he doing was the question? There seemed to be more traffic and lots more obstacles in the way as we worked our way from one street to another. We searched all the places we thought he would frequent but there was no sign of Dean. Our last stop was his flat. He wasn't there, but his car was neatly parked in its spot.

"What am I going to do Christine?" Vijay asked staring at me.

"Call your mother. No, that's not a good idea."

We had no idea what else we should do. His phone was turned off, and still there was no answer at the flat. We did not want to tell Mother Mahajan; at least not yet. We decided to go home and wait for his call. A call that never came! Anand called to find out what was wrong with him, but we didn't have an answer. Then I remembered what Dr. Paxil had said. We should get him to the clinic as soon as possible. This was also echoed by the attending physician since Dr. Paxil was now off duty. He stressed that even if he wasn't using any abusive substances, we should still bring him in.

Three days went by. Three days of absolute hell and still there was no word. Vijay couldn't eat and he couldn't sleep. It was time to tell Mother Mahajan. Perhaps he had gone to Daman to think things over. The old woman hadn't seen or heard from him and was now beside herself with worry.

"Why would he just disappear?" she asked. "He seemed to be getting his life back together."

"I don't know Mother. I just don't know. I think it's time to call in the police."

"Anything that would bring him back to me," she said through tears.

Naturally Amrit was now aware that Dean had disappeared and she said that Ranjit had offered to help to find him. We thought we should give the police a chance to do their job, but night after night we still scoured the streets and back alleys of Bombay, taking our lives into our hands, trying to find him. The newspaper carried the story and a photo of Dean. A reward of one hundred thousand rupees was offered to anyone who could tell of his whereabouts, and they should contact the police. This was to prevent every crackpot in the city from calling the flat or the office.

"I'm going crazy," Vijay said. "I must keep busy."

And so he went to the office even though he was deeply distressed. He isolated himself in that small room, calling home occasionally to find out if Dean had contacted me.

There was a gentle knock on his office door one morning! It was Ranjit.

"I want to help. You most helpful to me and my family sir. Please, I want to help."

"Sit down," said Vijay studying him carefully.

"How well do you know the city?"

"I know Bombay like I know my family sir. I know all the streets. I know where to find the drugs, the brothels and good meat."

In spite of his heavy heart, Vijay broke into a smile. Drugs, brothels and good meat? What a combination!

"Let's go," said Vijay.

Ranjit sat beside him in the front seat and with Dean's photo in hand they scoured every back alley and every slum. Some of the places, Vijay never knew existed.

"You stay," Ranjit would say. "I go and I look."

He would return brow beaten. One day, he encountered a man who said he knew where Dean was, but he needed money for the information. Vijay was sceptical but what did he have to lose? The man insisted on the money up front.

"No," said Vijay. "Show me my son, only then will I pay you."

He led them to a building in the guts of the city, but when they saw the young man, they realised it was not Dean, but another young man whose life had been reduced to a pitiful state.

"Drugs," said Ranjit.

"My son is an addict. Did you know that?" he asked Ranjit.

"I know sir. I am very sorry."

Vijay checked with the police and still they had no information on his son. It was now almost one week and still he couldn't be found. All the usual places were checked and rechecked but Dean had simply vanished.

"Where is my son Christine? What happened to him?" he asked as if I had the answer.

I couldn't bear to see the strong, level-headed Vijay Mahajan in such a state of depression. Dark clouds shrouded his vision which in turn blackened his mood. I called London and spoke to Ravi who said he would be there as soon as he could. Two days went by and Vijay never left his bed. I had to explain the sad news to each caller. Billie was in Singapore so there was no one to pour my heart out to. I couldn't tell it to Angela Banerjee because it was all too deep and too personal. I didn't think that Vijay wanted everyone to know about his deepest, darkest secret.

Ravi arrived two days later and was shocked to see the condition of his brother. He refused to eat. Only Amrit's ginger tea was keeping him hydrated. Day six and finally there was word from the police. They thought they had found Dean. The three of us jumped into the Jeep and headed towards the police station.

"I don't think Madam should be here," said the police chief.

I felt as if my blood had drained entirely from my body. Dear God! The situation must be dire if he said I shouldn't be there. Maybe Dean was dead. I was right. Dean had overdosed and his body was lying in the Bombay morgue alongside the other unclaimed bodies. Never in my life have I heard such a sound. It had come from the back of Vijay's throat. His son was dead and no-one could do anything to bring him back. I sat with him in the back seat of the Jeep and hugged him while the passers-by peered in and the beggars still held out their hands.

"How long has he been in the morgue?" asked Ravi.

"They took his body there this morning."

"Where did they find him?"

"I'm not sure," said the officer.

"I want to see my son," said Vijay.

And so we set off for the morgue. Ravi said I should wait in the car and he would accompany Vijay to see the body. When they returned, I decided it was better not to ask any questions. They had seen the body. Dean was indeed dead. Ravi later revealed to me that the coroner thought he was given a lethal dose of heroin.

Hundreds of condolence messages poured in. The doctor was called and Vijay was given a sedative to help him to rest. He did not allow me to move from his side. His eyes remained closed, but he held onto my hand all the while. Ravi now had to impart the bad news to his mother, because without a doubt, it would be in the newspaper the following day, so it was better to prepare her for the sad event.

"Has Sabia been informed?" Ravi asked.

I put my finger to my lips hoping that Vijay hadn't heard his question.

"What's wrong?" he mouthed to me.

"Give me a moment," I whispered.

"I'll tell him," Vijay said.

The whole sordid story he had related to me on that first night of the siege came pouring out of his tormented soul. Amrit must have heard his voice, because she knocked and brought us three cups of ginger tea.

"Thank you Amrit," he said.

It was the first time he had actually called her by name. She smiled at him and left.

"I am your brother. Why didn't you confide in me?" asked Ravi.

"You were having your problems back then when Rahela had a miscarriage. I couldn't burden you with my troubles."

"So will someone tell Sabia about Dean?"

"She can rot in hell," shouted Vijay. "She has taken my son away from me. She killed him."

32

If this was what hell was like, then we were deep in the middle of hell. Dean was laid to rest in a private cemetery on the outskirts of the city. It was a simple ceremony. Only the Banerjees, Ravi and Rahela, Mahavir, Vijay and I were in attendance. Sabia had not been informed. She had no idea that her words had pushed her son to the edge and at that very moment, his body was being interned in a deep dark hole. Such grief I had never witnessed! I felt a presence behind us and when I turned around, the Gowdi family were all standing there. They all seemed to be weeping. They had turned up uninvited, but we knew that deep in their hearts they cared for and about us. Father and son wore the blue caps I had given to them when I returned from Toronto, as if it were a sign of respect. Behind them was a young man, whom I immediately branded an opportunity seeker. He stood in the distance so I dismissed him from my mind. Mother Mahajan did not attend. She said she wanted to remember Dean just as he was during the last year of his life; a young man whose life seemed full of promise and on the path to a better tomorrow. She could not understand why he would've done such a horrible thing. He had so much to live for.

When the short service was over, we just stood there staring at the mound of earth. It was time to leave, and I realised the Gowdi family and also the young man had already left.

To lose a child in the morning of his years I learned is the worst thing a parent could ever experience. Every day my husband's grief seemed to be overtaking his body more and more. He didn't sleep and he didn't eat. His days were spent in endless nothingness and his nights, treading softly like a weary soul through a maze of unending twists and turns. When he did sleep he would awaken calling out Dean's name. I could only watch helplessly as the man I loved fell deeper and deeper into this abyss of chaos and futility. I was glad to have Ravi's and Rahela's company for I couldn't have managed alone. Ravi left for the office every morning on the dot of eight o'clock to take Vijay's place and worked until five in the afternoon.

Words of consolation came from Mahavir Manjari. He called each morning to speak to Vijay and each time he would ask me if we knew why Dean had committed such an act. Vijay decided to confide in him and tell him the sordid details. Words failed the elderly gentleman, but their daily talks were still a source of inspiration for Vijay.

"Christine, I think Vijay should to talk to a professional," Rahela said as if she didn't want to use the word psychiatrist. "Every day he seems to be getting worse."

"I was thinking the same thing, but I thought he needed a little more time. It has only been three weeks since Dean's death."

"He is so withdrawn. He doesn't eat and he doesn't sleep. I hear him every night walking around the flat. There is just too much grief. He has to let it out."

The following day, Simon called to say he was dropping by to see him, so he did made an effort to shave and shower. He seemed a little less grieved, but there were long periods of silence in their conversation.

"Lakshmi wanted to come over to see you, but I thought it wouldn't be a good idea at this time."

He only smiled. The phone rang and we knew it was an overseas call. It was Josh and Zack.

"How are you two coping over there?" Josh asked.

"Under the conditions, we are holding our own," I said softly.

"And does the bitch know what she has done?" shouted Zack on the extension.

"She hasn't been told."

"He was such a nice young man. I really liked him. He was going to be Mumbai's's first known gay journalist he said to me."

"What?" I asked. "I didn't know that he ….."

"Was gay?"

"No I didn't know."

"You're losing it Christine. You didn't know? Well this isn't a good time to tell Vijay. He took us to a bar in Bombay but we first had to promise not to tell the two of you."

"Was he happy? You know what I mean."

"As happy as he could be under the circumstances."

"I can't believe I didn't even suspect it," I said.

"He told us he had to be careful since it was still a punishable offence in India and was considered unnatural. Boy, are they behind the times over there! He thought the police might have been only too happy to expose his lifestyle; the son of a wealthy businessman. Of course he said he would've paid anything to protect his father's name."

"Dear Dean!" I said loudly which made Simon look in my direction.

"No one understands the hell we go through," Josh said. "Finding out that the man he called Dad was really not his father, added to the fact that he had to hide his sexuality was probably just too much for him."

"Let me look," I said walking towards to the bedroom.

"What?" asked Zack.

"I just wanted to get away from the living room. Simon is here."

"I hope he didn't Mary Jane with him," said Josh.

"No he didn't."

It was the first time in three weeks that I laughed. I could always count on those two to lighten the atmosphere.

"It didn't matter that Dean wasn't his own flesh and blood," I said. "Vijay loved him more than he loved his own soul."

"It's horrible when things like this happen. Was his friend there at the funeral?"

"I didn't know he had a friend. What does he look like?"

"About Josh's height, dark hair naturally, light complexion and skinny."

"There was a young man standing at the gate of the cemetery, but I didn't get close enough to see what he really looked like. What is his name?"

"Shantay or Santay. Something like that. He works on that big street where we used to buy leather and jewellery."

"Colaba Causeway?"

"That's it. We bought some jewellery in the store. If I can find the bag, I'll tell you the name of the store. I'll send it to you in an email. That would be safer."

"Thanks for the information Zack. Send it to me as soon as possible."

"Are you two really feeling a little better?" Josh asked.

"Yes we are. Today Vijay shaved for the first time since the funeral and he also had a long, warm shower."

"Give him our love and if you need a change of scenery, we will always be here. Please say hello to our friend Amrit too."

When I went back to the living room, he was alone. Simon had left promising to return soon.

"That was Zack and Josh," I said.

"How are they?" he said drawing me close to him and laying his head on my shoulder.

"They said if you need a change of scenery, the door is always open."

"That's very nice of them, but I must get back to work."

"Why don't you remain at home a little longer? The rest would do you good."

"I must put my mind to work," he said. "All I think about constantly is my son."

"Dean wouldn't want you to suffer like this."

"I know. He suffered too and it's only a small thing if I can share his suffering."

"Well if you must go in, go for just half a day to start."

"I'll see," he said standing up just as Amrit came in with a teacup and a bowl of soup on a tray.

"Drink. It very good for the nerves," she said to him.

"What is it?" he asked.

"Something my mother drink. She work hard and was always tired because we had no father. When she was .... (the word she said in Hindi) she always drink this and she feel very good again."

"What did she say?" I asked him.

"She said when her mother was depressed, she always drank this."

He put the cup to his lips.

"Amrit, are you trying to kill me?"

"Taste is not good sir, but you feel good tomorrow."

He finished the disgusting brew complaining at each sip, but the next morning, he said he wanted to go for a drive. The brew had done its magic. It was very difficult. Everything he saw reminded him of Dean. Everywhere we went, he said it was Dean's favourite place to go. He was torturing himself.

"You don't know why we called him Dean, do you?" he asked me.

"No I don't know."

"Priddy loved Dean Martin and she hoped that one day he would sing just like him."

"He did better. He wrote beautiful articles in the paper. It was just a matter of time before he was just as well known as Dean Martin."

I could've slapped myself, but the words were out before I could hold them back. He sighed.

"Yes, he'll never be well known. She brought him into the world and she took him out by her careless words."

"Good Lord!" I whispered. "That's what the woman said. The words of a woman will bring sorrow to you, but you will be happy in the end."

"I could never be happy again," he said. "Let's go home."

Every day Amrit made the bitter brew and every day he drank it, complaining about the taste with every sip. I think it really helped to pull him from his depression. I asked her what was in the tea and she promised to bring me some of the bush. Ravi and Rahela were pleased to see the progress he was making and we were sad because we were soon going to lose them again to London.

"How are things at the office?" he asked Ravi one day when he hadn't gone in.

"Everything is going well. I have something to tell you," he said with a bit of hesitation.

"What is it?"

"Rahela and I decided we would move back to Mumbai."

His face lit up like a thousand lights on Diwali.

"But you don't like Bombay," he said to Rahela.

"That's true, but I thought that if Christine can do it, why can't I? I was born here and I speak the language. Besides you both need us now more than ever."

"We've got to find a flat," said Ravi. "We can stay in Mother's old flat for the time being, but Rahela doesn't want to live there. Too many nosy neighbours and no privacy and what makes my wife happy, also makes me happy."

How did someone like Bina Mahajan bring such lovely sons into the world? Was it fate or was it the Gods who brought Vijay and I together? I remembered the words of the woman on the street. He will marry you and you will be happy in the end. It is my destiny. I will stay by his side come what may. It is my duty to make him happy.

"You can stay here until you find a place. Christine loves having you here," Vijay said.

"Of course you can stay here. There are no nosy neighbours and you can have all the privacy you want."

"It depends on how long it takes to find a flat. In the meantime Rahela is going back to London to put our home on the market and make sure the boys are alright in the boarding school."

"It's all settled then. You are a good brother," said Vijay hugging him.

"One more thing," said Rahela. "Since we'll be staying here, that means more work for Amrit. Do you mind if we gave her a little money at the end of the week?"

"She would like nothing better and her husband would think it was all Christine's doing. If he had two legs, I'd swear he was after my wife," said Vijay with some joy in his voice.

We all laughed and Ravi said we should do something to pass the evening. We all settled on a game called Skipbo which someone had left at the flat. We laughed and competed against each other. It was so good to see Vijay laugh again. Rahela and I went to bed, leaving the brothers sitting on the couch watching a game of cricket on the television.

The following morning while Rahela and I made breakfast, Mahavir called to see how things were going with Vijay. They spoke for a little while and I gathered he was asking about Ravi.

He has decided to return to Bombay along with Rahela."

"That does my heart good. This is India and it is his home. Yes we can leave for a while, but then we should return to Mother India. It is our birthright."

"I am very happy to have my brother here again Mahavir-ji."

"As you should my son, as you should."

On the table a real western breakfast awaited the two men! Scrambled eggs, toast, jam and peanut butter and rich hot coffee! She went through the flat, her voice ringing like a bell. It was time for the men to join us. I looked at their faces. There was absolutely no resemblance in the faces of the two brothers. Halfway through our breakfast the telephone rang and I picked it up. It was Billie. She had just returned from Singapore and had heard the news about Dean. I tried to steer the conversation away from his death and told her I would send her an email.

Vijay became very quiet, but we tried as best we could to keep the atmosphere cheerful.

"Let's go for a drive," said Ravi. "I'll be the chauffeur."

We cleaned up the breakfast table while the men showered. There was another phone call. This time Rahela answered the telephone. We knew it was inevitable. We knew she would call, but now that Vijay was crawling from his deep dark hole, we were not happy to hear her voice.

Sabia said she had been trying to get in touch with Dean but his telephone seemed to have been turned off.

"He's dead," Rahela said and hung up.

Five minutes later, it rang again.

"Christine," she shouted. "Was that your idea of a bad joke?"

"It's not Christine," shouted Rahela. "Christine, do you want to speak to Priddy?"

I took the telephone from Rahela.

"Hello Sabia."

"I've been trying to find Dean. Do you know where he is?"

I didn't know what to say.

"Christine, are you still there?"

"Yes Sabia."

"Do you know where Dean is?"

"Dean is dead Sabia."

There was only panic on the other end.

"What happened to my son?" she screamed. "Why didn't anyone get in touch with me?"

There was a moment when neither one of us spoke.

"What happened to him Christine? Was it an accident?"

"No Sabia. Your words brought an end to his life. Why did you tell him that Vijay was not his father? Why did you have to tell him that after twenty one years?"

"I want to speak to Vijay," she said calmly.

"I can't allow you to speak to him. He is just coming out of a deep depression and I don't want him to suffer anymore than he already has."

"Talk to him Christine. Please ask him to call me."

In spite of what she had done, my heart went out to her. After all she was Dean's mother but I couldn't allow her to push my husband back into the chasm just when he had reached the top, by recalling the events of the past months. Knowing Sabia, I knew she would call again, so I kept Vijay's cell phone out of the bedroom under the pretence that it was not allowing him to get enough rest. Before we left the house, I intentionally turned it off and told him there was no need to bring it along since I had mine and Ravi had also brought his along.

33

Three months had gone by since Dean's death and we hadn't heard anything more from Sabia, but Dean's friend Shantay was still on my mind. Ravi and Vijay now went into the office together every morning. There was still one thing left for me to do. I had the name of the jewellery store where Shantay worked and I wanted to meet with him and to speak to him, but it was difficult since Rahela was always around, and when Vijay was there, he hardly ever let me out of his sight.

Early one morning, a call came in from the real estate agent. A flat had become vacant and he was sure it was something they would be interested in. I was going to use this opportunity to visit the young man Shantay. After they left, I took a taxi and went to the jewellery store. I immediately recognised him. He was wearing one of the T shirts which Vijay had bought for Dean with the photo of the CN Tower on the front. He had also seen me, and I could tell from the look in his eyes that he knew who I was. He was just as Zack had described him, medium height, light complexion and a slight build.

"Are you Shantay?" I asked.

He smiled and nodded.

"I know who you are," he said shyly. "You are Dean's mother."

"Why do you say that?"

"Dean always referred to you as his mother."

I almost choked on my tears. The owner of the store realised I was only chatting and showing no interest in jewellery, so he drew closer to hear what the conversation was about.

"Have you had your lunch?" I asked him.

"In ten minutes I will go to have my lunch."

"I will wait outside for you," I said.

I had no idea where we would eat because I never ate from the many roadside stalls that dotted the pavement, so he recommended a nearby cafe that only the tourists frequented. We were soaked in perspiration by the time we got there, but there was a ceiling fan close to where we were seated. The waiters were concentrating strictly on the tourists, because they knew they would receive better tips than from the local population. It was only after I raised my hand that the waiter finally looked in our direction. He came to us and with a half-hearted apology, took our order. I settled for a cup of coffee and Shantay, a cup of tea and a sandwich.

"Do you know what really happened to Dean?" I asked.

"I don't," he said sadly. "I was with him on the Tuesday night when he had just heard the news about his father. He was depressed. I told him it didn't matter who his father was, because the man he called Dad was a good father to him."

"What did he say?"

"He said I wouldn't understand. I say to him that he should talk to you because he trusted you, and he said he would."

"Did you see him again after that Tuesday?"

"Yes. I only met Dean after he had come back from Pune. He had many problems. He was afraid his father would find out that he was gay; then there was the drug problem which was always on his mind. He was very fragile but he was getting better. He was very nice to me," he said as tears rolled down his cheeks.

I handed him a tissue and he dried his face and continued.

"Two nights before he died, I found out where he was."

"How did you find out when no-one else could?"

"Every day after work, I go around looking for him. I show his photo to a group of children playing in the street and they pointed to a house. I went in and I found him. He was a mess. Dirty and hair on his face! I didn't know what to do. How was I going to get him out of there? I didn't have enough money and it looked as if someone had stolen his wallet. I know he wouldn't have wanted his father to see him like that, so I left to borrow enough money for a taxi so I could take him home and then I would call his Dad. When I returned, I couldn't find him. He was gone."

"Did you know there was a reward offered for anyone who could tell his father where he was?"

"Yes, I think I heard it was one hundred thousand Rupees."

"It was a lot of money. Why didn't you take it?"

"I couldn't do that to Dean. I loved him and he loved me. I returned to the house and I saw the same group of children again and asked them if they had seen him. They said he was still inside the house and they would show me. How did I miss him? How did I miss him the second time?" he asked himself over and over again. "Anyway when the children took me inside, I saw him. His eyes were open, but he was cold and his face was blue, no grey. I shake him and I call his name. Dean! Dean, but he did not hear me. I cry so much Madam. I didn't know what else to do, so I called the police and then left the area. That's how they found him."

"Was he still alive when you saw him?"

"I don't know but seeing the condition he was in, that was not possible."

"Where do you think he went when he disappeared?"

"Someone was hiding him I think."

"But why?"

"Maybe they give him bad drugs that killed him or they wanted to get the money from his father."

"Were you at the funeral? Was it you standing at the gate?"

"Yes but it was difficult finding out what his family would do with his body. I know there are not many cemeteries in Mumbai, so I went to the only one I hear about and I saw you and the rest of the family."

By this time, we were both in tears. Finally he pulled his cell phone from his pocket and showed me a photo; the same one Dean had placed on our living room table. Everyone seemed to be looking at us, and I was happy to go. We left the café and walked back to the jewellery store, dodging beggars along the way. It was an extremely hot day and we both again drenched in perspiration. The owner, seeing that I was now showing interest in his jewellery, brought a fan and set it on the counter beside me and also a chair so that I could sit. He even offered me a cold drink which I declined. I bought a golden bracelet much to his delight and realising I was not a poor woman, he tried to seduce me into making more purchases. I looked at several pieces of his inventory and in addition to my bracelet I also bought a pair of earrings for Rahela. This experience took me back to my earlier days in Bombay and I remembered why I had been and still was so enthralled with the city.

I wrote my cell phone number on the back of the receipt and handed it to Shantay. He gave me his in return.

"How is Dean's father?" he asked.

"He's getting better," I replied.

He carried my purchases to the door and we embraced. All the way home, I just kept thinking that if only Shantay had called me, things would've turned out differently. If only he had used better judgment and tried to get in touch with me! But I remembered that he thought Dean wouldn't have wanted us to see him in the condition he was in. Social mores or embarrassment because of appearances had led to such a tragedy. One call is all it would have taken. The difference between life and death! By the time I reached home, I felt emotionally drained. Luckily Amrit was the only one in the flat, so there was no need for any explanations.

34

"Good news," said Rahela as she came through the door. "We've found a flat. Directly on the water! And it's only fifteen minutes away from here. You and Vijay must see it."

I was going to miss them. I was going to miss the no-nonsense Rahela who didn't hold anything back and also Ravi who never took anything seriously. He was always ready for a good laugh.

Shantay and our talk rested heavily on my mind. I wanted to tell someone, but I couldn't tell Vijay about it, at least not yet.

"You're not yourself Christine. Is something wrong with Vijay?" Rahela asked.

"No. I've just got something on my mind."

"Would you like to share it?" she asked.

We went to the terrace and I closed the door behind us.

"Dean was gay," I said. "Vijay must not find out about it."

"How did you find out?"

"I met his friend and lover today. He's a very nice young man and his name is Shantay. I went to the jewellery store where he works."

"What did he say?"

I related the story Zack had told me and also what Shantay had told me earlier that day. For the first time since I had met her, Rahela was speechless. We stared out onto the water, neither one of us saying a word. Finally she broke the silence.

"He could've received the reward. Why didn't he take it?"

"He said he couldn't do that to Dean."

"How would Vijay react to something like this?" she asked.

"I don't know and I have no intention of telling him."

"I'm surprised Dean didn't confide in you."

"Maybe he thought I would tell his father."

"What a bloody shame!" she said standing up and opening the door. "I think you should tell Vijay."

"Dean is dead. What good would it do to tell him now? Maybe it would throw him back into a depression."

"But Vijay seemed to really like your two friends who were at the wedding. Jack and Zosh."

"Zack and Josh," I said laughing.

She too laughed at the way she had mixed up their names.

"Yes they are our friends, but Dean was his son. That's the difference."

"Vijay has always been a very open and honest man. Unfortunately his wife made a mess of their marriage by being dishonest. How long did he keep that secret? Twenty two years! Trust him! Tell him what you found out about Dean's life."

"I should've figured it out. I had never heard him mention anything about a girlfriend and then again, he got along too well with Zack and Josh. Maybe because we were so busy, I didn't give it a second thought."

"Give Vijay the benefit of the doubt. Tell him. Don't keep any secrets from him now that he is so fragile. He may never forgive you."

"I guess you're right. I'll find the right time to tell him. Will you and Ravi come by when I decide to tell him?"

"Just say the word and we'll be here."

"One more thing Rahela. The young man said he always referred to me as his mother."

"He did? He seemed to have found a really good friend in you," she replied.

"Such a pity his life was cut short!"

We stared out onto the Arabian Sea, neither of us saying a word.

"Was your marriage an arranged one?"

She looked at me as if I had just slapped her across the face.

"Ravi and I met in a discotheque in London where we were both studying. We both graduated and when we returned here, we found out that our parents had already had our futures planned out. They had arranged for both of us, separately of course, to meet men and women they had chosen for us. I was not in the least bit interested and returned to London, and Ravi followed shortly after that."

"Is that the reason you have no relationship with your mother in law?"

"Yes. I was the worldly woman who led her son astray. Anyway I found a position in London teaching Indian Studies at the university, and Ravi worked from home on the computer with Vijay. He does most of the housework since he's there most of the time."

"A very liberal family," I said smiling at her.

"I wouldn't say liberal. We share the housework. It's a completely different world from the world I left behind here in India."

"Now that you are returning, what do you hope to accomplish?"

"I would like to continue teaching, but I will take a year off to get used to the ways of India again. After that, who knows?"

"I am very glad you have decided to stay. I could use a good friend."

"Oh Christine! What a lovely thing to say! I knew we would become great friends the moment I laid eyes on you."

"And I thought you were the most beautiful creature I had ever seen. By the way, I have something for you. It's just to say thank you for being such a good friend!"

She loved the earrings.

"Thank you. You shouldn't have gone to so much expense."

"Vijay always says, accept it with grace, the way it was presented."

"That's true. I appreciate them."

"You and Ravi have been our life savers during the past couple of months. I am so grateful for your friendship. I have only one question. What happened between you and Lakshmi Bhatt?"

"It's not worth speaking about," she said. "The mentality of some of the people here is stuck back in the eighteenth century, but I will not stand for any of their nonsense. There's only one thing I can tell you about Lakshmi. She knew that things weren't going well between Vijay and Priddy, and so kept pushing her sister in Vijay's direction, but she was not his type. So you see Christine, it is a case of sour grapes."

"Is she pretty?"

"Who?" Rahela asked with a furrowed brow.

"Lakshmi's sister."

"That? Lakshmi looks like the Mona Lisa and Sandeep, like the Virgin Mary,"

We had a good laugh and were only interrupted by Amrit who came to say she was leaving.

"Oh Christine, life here is very complex. One day when I have enough time, you and I will sit down together and I will explain this complicated society to you. We are both lucky. We have found two very good men; men who have minds of their own."

35

The following morning, Amrit knocked on the bedroom door and said there was a lady on the telephone who wanted to speak to me. It was Sabia. I knew she would call again, but I couldn't help her.

"What can I do for you Sabia?"

"I know you're both upset with me," she said. "Put yourself in my place. I want to know where you've buried my son."

"Why don't you ask Vijay? I am not at liberty to divulge that information. Besides you can find that out quite easily. There are not many cemeteries in Mumbai."

"Vijay won't talk to me," she said.

"Does that surprise you Sabia?"

"We used to be friends Christine. What happened?"

"You killed my husband's son Sabia, and you have almost destroyed my husband's life."

"I'm sorry about that. I told Dean about his father in a very heated moment. I wish I could take those words back."

"It's too late. If Vijay won't talk to you, you can ask Ravi," I said, my heart going out to her.

"Do you mean Ravi Mahajan?"

"Yes, try him at the office."

I immediately called Vijay. He said he knew she was in Mumbai and was trying to find Dean's grave.

"Tell her Vijay. Please tell her. I know her words took Dean to his grave, but that is something she must live with until the day she dies. Let the hatred go and tell her where her son is buried."

"Christine, I can't talk to her. It still hurts too much."

"Then let Ravi tell her. Would you invite him over for dinner? With Rahela in London, I'm sure he could use a good home-cooked meal and some good company. Besides there is something I want to discuss with you."

"I'll ask him," he said. "Christine, I love you. You have made such a difference in my life."

"I love you too. I'll always be your rainbow behind this very dark cloud."

"Why don't you give Amrit the afternoon off?" he suddenly asked. "If you do I'll be at home around three. I've really missed you over the last couple of months."

I heard the gate open and I looked down and saw the jeep. I entered the code and sent the elevator down for him. A smile registered across his face when he saw that I was wearing his nightshirt.

"Is she still here?" he asked as he entered the flat carrying a parcel under his arm.

"Who?" I asked smiling.

"You know that I'm referring to Amrit. Don't tease me," he said reaching for me.

"She went home. You said I should give her the afternoon off. What have you got in the package?"

"Something addressed to you, but it can wait. Ravi says he's looking forward to dinner so there is no time to waste," he said dropping the briefcase and the package at the door.

In less than a minute, I found myself in our bedroom.

"No bra! No underwear. I like that," he said as he too hurriedly undressed.

He was like a starving man on a deserted island who had just had his first taste of food in a week. He was ravenous.

"I missed you so much. I'm so sorry Christine. I'm sorry for not being the husband that I should've been."

"Shhhh," I said putting a finger to his lips.

In a matter of minutes, it was all over, and he wrapped me in his arms.

"I love you Christine. What would I have done without you?"

"I love you too."

"I'm sorry," he said. "I guess I was too anxious. What should we do now?"

"We can carry on after Ravi leaves later this evening."

"That wouldn't be fair," he said as he kissed me.

Time stood still as we again fell into each others' arms. Time was healing all his wounds.

"How are you?" he asked raising his head and smiling.

I could only smile back. Vijay was back! My husband had walked through the valley of the shadows of hell, and was well on his way to a recovery.

"So what did you bring me?" I asked as we lay in bed.

"It is a package from Zack and Josh."

'Happy Birthday' it said on the outside. They had made a subscription in my name to one of the Toronto magazines. They thought I needed something to remind me of home.

"They're such good friends," I said.

"They certainly are. I was afraid ....

He stopped mid sentence.

"What were you afraid of?" I asked.

"Promise me you won't get upset," he said.

"Just tell me," I said.

"Even though you told me all about them, at first I was still hesitant being around them. What would I have done if they had approached me?"

I started to laugh. I just couldn't stop laughing.

"Why do you think it's so funny? Don't you think I'm attractive enough?" he asked

"Of course you're attractive. You're not attractive. You are the most handsome man I know and you belong to me."

He smiled.

"Gay men also have values; at least my friends are like that. The perception of many heterosexual men is that because a man is gay, he is looking to grab any man who passes along. That's really not the case."

"I know that now and I no longer have the fear of being alone with either one of them."

I had to tell him about his son's life later that evening. Maybe this conversation will make it easier for me to broach the subject.

"I am glad that you know you have nothing to fear. Tell me something Mr. Mahajan, what is the significance of the elevator code?"

"You haven't yet figured it out. That's the day we met. June thirtieth, 1983."

I had completely forgotten about that. Could he really have been thinking about me all this time?

Ravi arrived just after six o' clock telling me how hungry he was. I was a little apprehensive to start on the subject of Dean, but I had no choice but to tell Vijay all I knew about his son.

After dinner, we sat around the living room and I tried to muster up enough courage to tell Vijay what I knew about Dean. Instead I found myself relating to them something Amrit had said to me.

"We have a son and you lost your son. Everybody is so sad. You take our son and treat him like your son. We will still be able to see Sanjay. He like you and he like it here. My Ranjit say you make good parents."

I thanked her very much for thinking so highly of us, but I reminded her that Dean had been a grown man, capable of living alone. Sanjay is a child who needs lots of care and attention, and we couldn't possibly take him away from them.

"This goes beyond being grateful," said Vijay. "They want to give us their son because they think it will make us happy?"

"Unbelievable!" said Ravi. "I have heard of this kind of thing, but never really experienced it."

"I told her I would continue to help him with his English but couldn't imagine him here without his parents."

"Is that what you wanted to discuss with me?"

"No there is something else. It has to do with Dean."

The smile vanished from his face. Had I made the right decision to throw fuel on the embers of a dying fire? With Ravi there, I felt a sense of security. How would Vijay take the news?

"What about Dean?" he asked.

I glanced at Ravi and I knew he was aware of the secret I was about to reveal. His look said I should go ahead.

"Last week I went to a jewellery store to meet a young man who knew Dean very well. He was actually Dean's lover," I said with bated breath.

"Go on," he said.

I told the story to Vijay in every little detail as I watched the faces of both men. Both of them poker faced! Why was I getting the impression that Vijay had already known about Dean? There was total silence in the room. I was beginning to feel very uneasy until Vijay spoke.

"I suspected something like that because I had never heard Dean speak of a girlfriend. When we were younger," he said looking at Ravi, "it was not uncommon to see young men and boys holding hands and walking together. That was our way of showing friendship. Today people would be totally shocked if they saw you hold another man's hand. We live in a very homophobic society here in India, and when I noticed how easy it was for my son to be around Zack and Josh, I knew right away. That was my confirmation. However I kept hoping that I was wrong because I couldn't imagine him living in this city as a gay man."

"Vijay is right," said Ravi. "Male teenage friendships are tolerated, but once they reach adulthood, it comes to an abrupt halt."

"There is still something that bothers me," said Vijay. "Why didn't the young man claim the reward? Since he called the police station, he could easily have taken the money and gone on his way. Dean no longer needed his protection."

"I guess there are still some good people out there," said Ravi.

"Thanks for telling me everything you knew about my son. Thank you. Someday when I am over this traumatic turn of events, I would like to meet the young man."

I breathed a sigh of relief.

"There is something else we've got to do," said Ravi. "What are you planning to do with Dean's flat?"

"I'll give it back to the owner. It's just a matter of getting rid of the contents. Is there anything you would like? There are still a couple antique pieces of furniture there."

"I'll wait until Rahela returns and see if she wants anything. It would be a start. Right now I'm still using my bed as a place to sleep and a place to eat."

"When do you expect to get your furniture?" Vijay asked.

"In about six weeks," Ravi replied.

"Do you think the Gowdi family would like the rest of the contents Christine?"

"I'm sure they will be more than happy to have them."

"Excuse me," he said jumping up to answer the telephone.

Ravi and I exchanged glances.

"That was easier than you thought," he said putting his arms around me.

"It certainly was. I was so afraid of how he would've reacted."

"When is Rahela expected back?" asked Vijay when he returned.

"Sometime this week! Well I've got to go. See you tomorrow evening," he said winking at his brother.

Something was afoot and Ravi almost let the cat out of the bag. The two brothers climbed into the elevator and I heard the engine of Ravi's SUV, and then the slow climb of the elevator.

"There's something I didn't tell you," I said.

"What is it?"

"The young man Shantay told me that Dean always referred to me as his mother. He also showed me the photo on his cell phone. The same photo of the three of us which Dean put over there."

"My son!" he said sadly. "He'll never know how much I loved him."

"I'm sure he did."

"Let's go to bed. What time is it?" he suddenly asked.

"Fifteen minutes before midnight."

We talked about Dean for some minutes and the path his life

might have taken, and then at the stroke of midnight, he reached under the pillow and handed me a small package.

"Happy Birthday. Open it," he said smiling at me.

It was beautiful.

"Do you like it?"

"This must cost a fortune," I said staring at the ring with a huge sapphire surrounded by diamonds.

"Remember that engagement ring you never received?" he whispered.

"I love it," I replied.

"Do you really? Give it to me," he said.

I handed him the ring and he slipped it on my finger, above my wedding band.

"You thought I had forgotten your birthday, didn't you?"

"With everything that's been going on; yes, I thought you had forgotten."

"Never," he said.

"You have to get up early for work," I said. "You'll be a wreck tomorrow."

He smiled and gently hugged me.

"I'm staying home tomorrow. I'm spending the whole day with my wife. It's her birthday."

36

The following day, Vijay said he would take me out to dinner to celebrate.

"We're going to a very nice restaurant, so you may want to wear something elegant."

I decided on an emerald green hand-beaded dress I had found in a small store when Angela and I went shopping together.

"You look lovely, as always," he said.

It was indeed a nice restaurant, and every head in the place turned when we walked in. We were seated in a secluded corner away from the entrance. Vijay ordered a bottle of champagne and we toasted. It took ten minutes before the waiter returned. This I found unusual, but I said nothing. He spoke to Vijay, then took the bottle of champagne and our glasses and asked us to follow him. We climbed a flight of stairs and waited outside the door at his request.

"What's going on?" I asked Vijay who seemed a bit annoyed.

Before he could answer, the waiter returned, opened the door and ushered us in.

"Happy Birthday Christine," they all shouted.

All our friends were there. Anand and Angela Banerjee, Lila and Brian Langley, Simon Bhatt, Janice Weatherall and most surprising, was Rahela.

"When did you return to Mumbai?" I asked hugging her.

"Sorry about holding up the festivities," said Ravi. "She was so tired I couldn't wake her up."

There was one other young man standing alone, just observing everything that was going on. It was Shantay. How did he get here? Who invited him? It didn't matter. I was happy to see him. To me it meant that Dean was there with us.

"You are Vijay's relative from another state, if anyone asks," I whispered to him.

He smiled. He fully understood what I meant. Dean was dead. A gruesome death! It was no use having his name dragged through the mud at this point and time.

An evening of festivities came to an end when the guests started to leave. Shantay was the last to go and helped us to carry the many gifts to the jeep.

"Can we take you home?" I asked.

"That's not necessary Madam. Thank you for the invitation."

"Let's take you home," said Vijay. "It's late and most likely you will be working tomorrow."

"Thank you sir," the young man said and climbed into the back seat.

**

Vijay had just settled into work, when there was a knock on his office door. It was Ranjit.

"Sit down Ranjit," he said.

"Not possible sir. I have only one minute. The foreman will be very, very angry with me."

"Is something wrong?" asked Vijay looking up.

"Most definitely not sir! My Amrit say yesterday it is Madam birthday and my family want to welcome you to our house Saturday evening. You know my Amrit is a good cook and we all want to welcome you for .... to our house."

"To dinner?" asked Vijay smiling.

"Yes. Most definitely for dinner."

"Let me speak to my wife and I will let you know."

"If it is not too much trouble sir, I give you my telephone number. He handed a piece of paper to Vijay, smiled and left the room.

"We're invited to dinner on Saturday evening," said Vijay.

"I know. Amrit has already told me."

"Are we going?" he asked.

"I see no reason why we shouldn't. Remember what you always say, 'receive everything gracefully.'"

I thought of his mother Bina Mahajan. She would be beside herself if she knew her son was dining with the Gowdis. I can hear her voice ringing in my ears. 'It's bad enough when races mix but much worse when classes do it,' she had said.

We arrived at the Gowdi home around six thirty in the evening. Lots of the other residents were looking out of their windows, or hanging around the little garden when we got there. It seemed as though they were expecting someone. Their eyes followed us until we were out of sight. The Gowdi family greeted us at the door with their arms wide open in a welcoming gesture. My husband was a bit apprehensive but that was soon put to rest when we saw what Ranjit had done with their home. It was clean and Bina Mahajan's furniture and dishes which we had given to them had been put to good use. Amrit had sewn colourful curtains which billowed in the light evening breeze. With glowing pride, they showed us what they had done to the flat. We also noticed that the dining table was set, but only for two, something which I didn't understand

"My wife and son sleep here," said Ranjit showing us the bedroom which was outfitted with Dean's bed.

"And where do you sleep?" I asked.

"Here Madam," he said pointing to the floor. "My Amrit say that I can't sleep on the sofa, but everything is alright."

The Gowdi family had outdone themselves. The food was delicious but we had to force them to sit. No wonder the table had only been set for two. They had no intention of sitting down with us. They ran around moving this and moving that, and only after we said we wouldn't eat if they didn't sit, did they finally take a seat at the table. After dinner we retired to the sofa, and I asked Ranjit about his mother. Since his English was not good enough to relate the story, Vijay translated everything he said.

"I don't remember too much about her. I know there was a lady who would take me with her when she went out to beg. Then one day she suddenly disappeared and I was left in the home with all the other children. When I was about five years old, a man in a white coat came to the home. He brought lots of sweets with him which made us very happy. Then one by one they called us into a room, and I remember they put something on my face. That was the last thing I remembered. When I woke up there was a lot of pain. My leg hurt so much. I sat up and looked to see why there was so much pain, but there was nothing where my leg used to be."

Vijay gasped before he spoke. I knew immediately that something horrific had happened.

"My leg was gone and several of the other children were missing arms, legs and hands."

No one spoke. It was just too gruesome a tale.

"A few weeks later, they gave me a crutch and sent me onto the streets to beg. Some people were very unkind and slapped us. When we returned to the home with very little or no money, they would beat us or not give us anything to eat. It was a bad time," he said bowing his head.

"One day my friend Nari and I decided we would run away, but where would we go? Then we heard that the government was picking up the beggars from the city and taking them far away, so we decided to stay in the home. At least we would be safe. When the people at the home thought it was all over, they sent us back to the streets again. That's when I met Madam," he said looking at me. "We used to go close to the hotels because the tourists were nice to us. Whenever we said we were hungry, they would give us money. But Madam never gave us money. She would give us food and clothes. She used to talk to us, and she asked us a lot of questions. When I returned to the home, they would take away the clothes and wear them. I remember how unhappy I was once. She had given me a shirt that said 'Toronto' on the front, but I didn't get a chance to wear it because the man at the home took it away, put it on and sent me back to the street He kept it for himself."

"Do you remember that?" asked Vijay.

I nodded. I remembered that T shirt.

"I went back to the hotel, but I never saw Madam again. I kept going back and I waited and waited, but she didn't come back. Whenever I saw anyone who looked like Madam, I tried to get near to them, but I was always disappointed."

I blinked back the tears that had welled up in my eyes. I didn't realise how much our little talks had meant to him.

"My friend Nari and I heard about a lady who would take us in, so we went to the orphanage. She was from Australia and she took us in because we were both hungry. I remained there until I was thirteen years old. It was a good time. She was nice and gave us lots to eat. She also taught us to read and write. Then the government said we were too old to stay there and put us in a government home. It was not as good as Miss Janice's home, but they taught us to use hammers, nails and saws."

"Carpentry skills!" I said.

"Yes, yes. Carpenter."

It seemed as if Sanjay understood that his father's story was a sad one because he climbed onto his lap and threw his arms around his neck. His father looked down at him and rubbed his head.

"When I was sixteen, I had to leave the government orphanage to make space for other children. I worked here and there, getting just enough money to eat."

"Where did you live?" I asked.

"On the street until I met a man who said I could stay at his house. He seemed like a good man, but he did bad things to me. He liked to play with boys, so I moved back to the streets until I was twenty and then I met Amrit. She worked in a restaurant washing dishes and cleaning the floors. She had pity on me and when the restaurant owner wasn't around, she would give me food at the back door. Then one day she gave me an address and said that there were people there from a church who would help me. I went to see them and they were very good to me. They said I had to become a Christian. They also gave me a new leg. Since I could speak a little English, I stayed and worked with them, helping them to recruit new members. They let me sleep on the veranda that had a roof. It was better than sleeping on the street. I kept on visiting Amrit and convinced her she should also become a Christian. She did and we got married and moved to the home you saw when you came to visit us. Then our little Sanjay came along," he said smiling at the child.

No one spoke. Vijay who had been translating the story, put his head between his hands, and I wiped the tears from my eyes. Amrit was stoic. She just watched us, not saying a word.

"Today I am happy. I have a good job, a beautiful flat, my wife Amrit and my boy. So Madam, you see you are my angel guarding me. And sir, I cannot thank you enough for what you have done for my family and for me. We will always be grateful."

"You have also been very good to us especially in the time of our greatest need," said Vijay recalling Ranjit's help when Dean was missing.

"And where is your friend Nari?" I asked.

"He died. He was hungry and stole something to eat from one of the street stalls. They started to chase him and he ran into the path of an oncoming bus. It was horrible. I didn't recognise him anymore. A cart came and picked up his body. Like a dead dog, they took his body away."

Then there was an uncomfortable silence. How does one follow a story like that? We had heard enough and since it was getting late, we decided it was time to go.

"Say bye-bye to Auntie and Uncle," said Ranjit to his son.

The little boy hid behind the hem of his mother's sari and peeped out at us.

"I'll see you on Friday," I said to him.

"Bye Auntie. Bye Uncle," the child said waving to us.

We thanked the Gowdis for dinner and left knowing that we had done something good to improve their lives. Once outside, we sat in the jeep for a while before Vijay turned the ignition on.

"That was quite a story," he finally said.

"I know you did it just for me. Thank you for coming along."

"It really wasn't what I had expected," he said.

"What did you expect?"

"I don't know," he said. "That was quite a revelation! All they needed was a helping hand and I'm glad we helped."

I smiled because my husband was finally grasping the severity of what life was like for the poor of the city.

"I am so glad that I finally found him."

"I'm glad I married you," he said reaching over and holding my hand. "I knew it was tough out there, but never knew such horrible things happened in this city."

"You were much too close to it, so it was difficult for you to see what was going on. All these people need is to be shown a little bit of kindness."

"I suppose you're right, and because you're such a wonderful person, I have a surprise for you."

"What is it?" I asked.

"Wouldn't be a surprise if I told you now." he said smiling. "And you truly deserve it. Since Ravi is now living here, I think I can take you away on that honeymoon which we never had."

"Cochin?" I asked looking at the tickets."

"You always said you wanted to go to Cochin."

He walked away and returned with a map which he spread across the table. I stared at it, but said nothing.

"I thought this would make you happy," he said.

"I am, but after hearing Ranjit's story, it makes me aware of how really lucky we are."

"We are lucky," he said wrapping his arms around me. "We are indeed lucky."

**

Janice Weatherall's advice has put things into perspective for me. Mumbai will never be Toronto, but it is my home along with its eccentricities and complexities, and I am treating it as such. She showed great surprise when I told her that we had had dinner with the Gowdi family. She stared at me in disbelief and then she hugged me.

"This country needs more people like you," she said. "People with heart!"

Had anyone suggested that circumstances beyond my control would force me to spend seven days with a man whom I hadn't seen or thought about for many years, and then disrupted my life to be with him, I would have said that person was absolutely mad, but here I am in India. My negative thoughts I have cast into the murky waters of the Arabian Sea, for when I see the goodness in people like Amrit and Ranjit Gowdi, I know I have a lot to be grateful for. We have not forgotten the poor of the city, and help wherever and whenever we can. There is a man, who in spite of the looks we sometimes receive, loves me as he loves himself. We have faithful friends like the Banerjees and Lila and Brian Langley, and I have met many of his other friends. Then there is Ravi with his dear wife Rahela who have taken me into their hearts and treat me like a sister. I could not ask for a better life. There is not a day that goes by when we do not think of Dean, but we now remember him not with sadness, but with joy, for he was a dear young man. Shantay calls and comes by occasionally. He is all that there is left to remind us of a young vibrant Dean.

One day each month, the two brothers drive to Daman to visit their mother who hasn't set foot in Mumbai since the day she left.

Ranjit Gowdi has taken his family to the orphanage to meet Janice Weatherall and she was pleased to see that he had done so much with his life. He also goes by every Saturday morning to help with the odd jobs there and Amrit also takes Sanjay to visit the children and to help Janice however she can. She is our rock. We couldn't have asked for a better house helper. She is honest and is always willing to help us in whatever way she can.

Earlier this evening, as we took our daily walk along the shoreline of the Arabian Sea, I noticed two elderly gentlemen walking towards one of the benches. They seemed tired. One was Caucasian supported by a cane, the other was Indian. I was not sure if they were together, but they both sat down next to each. Neither of them spoke. They just sat there staring into the dark waters. The Indian gentleman wore a grey Kurta pyjama while the Caucasian gentleman, dressed in a white linen suit and a straw hat, smoked a cigarette. I watched as the wind took the curls of smoke slowly across the water. When we got closer, I realised it was Maxwell Charles Berkeley the third and the other man with a cat on his lap, I assumed was his long time companion Momar. I never knew Momar's surname, but as I watched the old couple, I realised that love could be found in the least expected of places. Charles Berkeley and Momar had evidently come to terms with their lives, and had found lasting peace with each other.

CPSIA information can be obtained at www.ICGtesting.com
Printed in the USA
LVOW13s1300120214

373411LV00029B/1317/P